To Am & Michael.

WINDS THE ROAD NORTH

By
Geraldine O'Connell Cusack

Geraldine.

authorHOUSE™

1663 LIBERTY DRIVE, SUITE 200
BLOOMINGTON, INDIANA 47403
(800) 839-8640
WWW.AUTHORHOUSE.COM

First published by AuthorHouse 11/03/05

ISBN: 1-4208-8797-1 (sc)

Printed in the United States of America
Bloomington, Indiana

This book is printed on acid-free paper.

For: Connell, Tiarnán, and Saoirse

Chapter One
KOROGWE

It takes only ten hours to fly from the sanitized chrome and glass of Amsterdam's Schipol Airport to the parched and dusty runways of Dar es Salaam but it is a continent and a world away. Kaniah and I studied the passengers who were queuing in the crowded departure lounge. Who were they? Where were they all going, and why?

A contingent of khaki clad tourists milled about with a confident air. No doubt *they* were heading off to the safari meccas of the Serengeti Plains. Small clutches of native Africans, perhaps returning from business or study trips abroad, busily tinkered with duty-free mobile phones and Walkman radios. They would be going home. But what about all those white Africans slumbering lazily on padded benches with airs of self-satisfied indifference? Where exactly was home for them? Were they returning from a visit home or were they going home?

A little fraction of a man weaved excitedly in and out of the queue, eager to engage in conversation with anyone who would oblige. He had lived in Zimbabwe when Zimbabwe had been Southern Rhodesia and he was off on a trip down memory lane. He hadn't been back since Harare was Salisbury and life had been good in colonial Africa. He was as excited as a child on Christmas morning. I hoped his memories were not about to be shattered by reality, although I had no idea what that might be. This was our first trip to Africa and we, too, were excited. But we carried no memories. We had no wild expectations. It wouldn't be, 'Out of Africa,' - romantic, mystical, and haunting. That much we knew.

This would be modern Africa and we knew there would be a harsh face to that. But what else could we expect to find?

Dar es Salaam, Swahili for The Haven of Peace, was described as a "dusty colonial town, filled with three or four story structures painted in pastel colors and adorned with shuttered windows, looking much like they did a century ago." This was from one of the best selling guides to East Africa on sale in bookshops throughout the world. But within minutes of arriving at Dar es Salaam airport, Kaniah and I were confronted by the real thing – and we were quickly disabused of any romantic fantasies we might have been harboring.

Towering tenement blocks stretched out along the airport road. The low-lying structures wedged in tightly among the tenement blocks were pitted and crumbling. Their delicate pastel colors could only have been hallucinations in the mind of a fanciful travel agent. Battered and overflowing buses navigated their way through streams of spanking new Land Cruisers. Cars and bicycles mounted broken footpaths and disappeared down back alleys. Luxury four-star hotels squeezed out their fading neighbors and scrawny cows foraged for scraps of grass among the tottering shacks.

Prosperous businessmen met in modern conference rooms while begging cripples crouched on nearby street corners. Ragged children dodged in and out of grid locked traffic and wiped grimy windows for tossed coins. Peddlers lined the main city streets, selling 'genuine' ebony trinkets, batik handprints, bars of soap, packets of boiled sweets, postcards for the tourists, cigarette lighters, second-hand shoes, used clothing, knives, plastic dishes, pots and pans, hair lighteners, hair straighteners, hair oil, and new and used books. All of these – and more - were for sale on the streets of the new and chaotic Dar es Salaam.

But our immediate destination was Korogwe, a busy transit town located 234 kilometers northwest of the capital city. Returning Irish aid workers had described Korogwe as a settlement roughly the size of a small midland town back home. There were no accurate statistics available, but an educated guess had put the population at around ten thousand. I, too, would be an Irish aid worker and Korogwe was to become home to my thirteen-year-old daughter,

Kaniah, and me, for the next five years. My three older daughters, who were attending colleges in the United States and Ireland, hoped to visit whenever possible.

❧

I arrived in Korogwe as part of an Ireland Aid project aimed at improving the teaching skills of Tanzania's primary school teachers. The need was monumental because the primary education system in Tanzania was in crisis. In 1960, before independence, the primary school enrollment rate had been 28% of the school-age population. That percentage had risen to 87% by 1984. Then the rate had begun to slide back dramatically. By 1989, enrollment had dropped to 60% and daily attendance records were even worse.

Two main factors had contributed to the decline: the increasing demand for child labor in agriculture and trade and the steadily rising cost of education. Although primary education was theoretically free, in practice, parents were asked to pay voluntary contributions for each school-going child. Parents also had to meet the cost of expensive school uniforms and books.

Severe shortages of classrooms, desks, chairs, chalkboards, and even the humble sticks of chalk, stalked the country. The single teaching aid in most classrooms, when there was a room, was the chalkboard. But most of the boards were so badly eroded that they were virtually useless. In rural areas, staff houses were dilapidated and often dangerous, and teachers' salaries were frequently delayed for months at a time. School inspectors had no transportation. If a car or lorry should ever happen to become available, there was often no money for fuel. Consequently, teachers passed from one year to the next without ever seeing an education officer. How could teachers be motivated to improve their teaching skills or pursue further education when they were forced to go for months without their basic wage?

A national exam was administered to all seventh standard students every year and it was the instrument used to select the best students for admission to the state-funded secondary school system. Only the top ten percent of all students qualified. Parents of successful applicants then had to contribute to the cost of keeping their children at the state boarding schools and they also had to find money for uniforms and books. The remaining unsuccessful students either stayed at home to work on *shambas*, migrated to the cities where they became involved in petty street trade and street crime, or they enrolled in private secondary schools that were even more expensive. The final and least attractive option of all was to become a primary school teacher.

There were four grades of teachers in the Tanzanian Primary School System: Diploma Level and Grades A, B and C. Diploma Level teachers had completed the equivalent of British 'A' Level exams plus two years of training at a Grade 'A' teacher training college. Upon graduation from their training courses, they all became secondary school teachers or subject area tutors at any one of the forty training colleges throughout the country. Grade 'A' teachers had 'O' Level exam results plus two years of training at a Grade 'A' college. They became primary school teachers at the highest rate of pay. Grade 'B' teachers were those with seventh standard primary school education and two years of training at a Grade 'B' college. Grade 'C' teachers were those who had achieved the poorest standard seven results and had no teacher training whatsoever. Mercifully, Grade 'C' teachers were slowly being upgraded and would eventually be phased out.

When I first arrived in Korogwe, I asked my Tanzanian colleagues, "What happens to Grade 'B' or Grade 'C' teachers who return to training colleges for upgrading? Do they return to their original primary schools upon successful completion of their courses?" Their incredulous reaction, to my very naïve question, really startled me.

"A newly upgraded Grade 'A' teacher returning to a primary school? Mama, what are you thinking? That would be unbelievable! Don't you know that primary school teachers are despised?"

I was struck speechless. Although I was aware that Tanzanian English was often quite formal and could be very different from colloquial English usage, I did not expect to hear anything as harsh as 'despised'. In this case, it really meant 'looked down upon,' and not 'hated'. Nonetheless, the incident served to illustrate the full scale of the challenge that lay ahead.

☜☞

The town of Korogwe was a sprawling place, physically divided into two sections by the Pangani River. Old Korogwe sat on the south end and Manundu, the new town, was located to the north. The two sections were separated by a kilometer of spectacular potholes, two petrol stations that could take in up to a million Tanzanian shillings a week during the rainy seasons, and the town jail. Whenever the rains arrived, the potholes swelled to the size of lakes and the service stations did a roaring trade by salvaging sinking buses. That accounted for the million shillings in a good wet week.

Fellow aid workers, whom I had met at a volunteer training program in Dublin, had told me that I would be delighted with the historic Old Town of Korogwe. So I pictured those winding roads, so dear to the hearts of all travel writers, climbing up into green verdant hills. I pictured the little thatched huts and maybe even one or two stone houses with their quaintly shuttered windows.

But, there were no green hills, stone houses, or shuttered windows in Old Town. And while I could well imagine what it must have been like before independence, when Indian and Arabesque houses had graced the hillsides, only crumbling ruins swayed there now - with their tiled roofs scattered to the four winds and their latticed verandas hanging on by a few rusty nails. Silent men sat in their shaded doorways, sewing - the soft hum of their machines and the rustle of trees barely stirring the stillness all around them. Old Korogwe sat up there on the cool mountainside, like those wise old men - unconcerned and untouched by a rapidly changing world. And its venerable railway station still saw an occasional train chugging through, taking an occasional moonstruck traveler to that strange new world beyond.

The seat of the Anglican Church in Tanga Region and the Anglican Mission Hospital were located on the road leading up to Old Korogwe. Two English missionary doctors, Hazel and Richard, were in charge of the hospital. They were a married couple in their mid-thirties and they had two adorable little girls who were indistinguishable from their Tanzanian playmates. Jessica and Grace spoke Swahili, climbed trees, collected nuts, and chased monkeys – and they had become as Tanzanian as any other village child.

Hazel and Richard had been working in Korogwe for two years prior to our arrival and had been the only medical service available to a cluster of neighboring towns for several years prior to that. Every year they returned to England to raise money for medicine and hospital equipment, and to find funds for their own salaries.

The life of a mission doctor was harsh at the best of times. The lives of these particular doctors were complicated by the fact that they both worked full-time at the hospital. Their living quarters were in a rambling barn-like structure that was buried deep into the side of a mountain. A single faucet sat in the front yard and gave water during the rainy seasons. Two one-hundred-gallon plastic drums were filled with river water whenever the faucet went dry. A family of chattering monkeys inhabited the trees and bushes surrounding the house. When the town's electricity went off every evening, the house fell into darkness. The house had recently been burgled and the doctors were robbed of their emergency gas lamp and their only fan. If all of that hadn't been enough to contend with, their personal vehicle, which they had been using for hospital work, had finally given up the ghost and died. They were now *kwa miguu* – on foot with babes on their backs.

These doctors worked with the most basic supplies and equipment and they were locked in a constant struggle to train local women as nurses' aides. But the work of a nurse was hard and the hours were long. Invariably, the trainees, who had their own families to feed, *shambas* to till, and water to find, gave up and looked for something less physically demanding.

Despite the lack of rest and constant demands, Hazel and Richard loved Africa and they planned to stay in Tanzania for the rest of their working lives. People like them lived and worked quietly in every village and town up and down the length and breadth of the continent. Their daily toils went unnoticed, and largely unheralded, by the rest of the world. Nonetheless, their 'ordinary' lives were truly heroic.

❧

The new town of Manundu was a brash and bold youngster by comparison. It had been built in 1952 during the dying days of the British Empire. Its construction had signified a last-ditch effort to hold back the impending death throes, and, at the same time, to celebrate the coronation of Britain's new young queen.

Manundu's concept had been quite grand in design. Sewage drains had been dug and lined with layer after layer of carefully cut stone. A central post office and several smart stone council buildings were constructed in the middle of an elegant, tree-lined town square. A spanking new tarmacadam road connected the old town with the new. But the land was low - and not even engineers were able hold back the rain. Consequently, during rainy seasons, Manundu became a malarial trap.

Fifty years later, there was no trace of the road and the drains had become vast breeding grounds for mosquitoes. The gentle, swaying foreign trees had disappeared. Streets and houses now baked under the scorching mid-day sun. Only the post office remained as a fading, haunting reminder of Britain's colonial past.

Malaria was the number one killer disease in Korogwe. The average villager could not afford pyrethrum-treated mosquito nets for their beds, or screens for their doors and windows. When the heavy summer rains arrived and the mosquitoes multiplied, it was virtually impossible to escape the deadly disease. Infants became infected so often that their blood weakened and they died. Older children and adults had a better chance of fighting off the illness but repeated attacks of malaria left them severely debilitated. Chloroquine was the only available cure, and if families didn't have enough money to purchase it, they too died. There was no solution to this malaria scourge because the town was situated in the wrong place. And the people of Korogwe had been paying for that fatal miscalculation every day since then.

❧

The river that flowed under the new bridge at the entrance to Old Korgwe was home to a family of seven crocodiles - four grown ones and three small ones. "How on earth do they keep track of crocodiles?" I asked myself. There were no gamekeepers in town and no wildlife personnel of any description in the entire Tanga region.

It was the dry season in Tanzania when we first arrived and the town had been without water for over a month. Normally, water ran down from the surrounding mountains in metal pipes and was collected into large holding tanks for distribution to the public pump and private homes. But the holding tanks were pepper dry and the only other source of water was the Pangani River.

At sunrise every morning, male prisoners from the town jail walked two-by-two to the riverside, with their wrists strapped tightly together. They carried bright blue plastic buckets on their heads. They joined crowds of women and children at the river's edge, all busily washing, bathing, and drawing buckets of drinking water. These prisoners were conspicuous as the only male folk engaged in a "females only" domestic task. Incarceration was the easy part of their prison sentence. Public humiliation was the other.

Eight children were currently in the mission hospital suffering from crocodile gashes and several women, minus their fingers, were hospitalized there as well. I had seen crocodiles floating farther downstream but I had not yet spotted one lying directly under the bridge. This led me to wonder why nobody had devised a simple system for lowering buckets into the river by rope. "Why are small children still swimming in the river despite the obvious dangers?" I asked myself. People seemed to have a remarkable facility to hear some dreadful news, like a neighbor's child being eaten alive by a crocodile the previous day, and then proceed to put themselves in the exact same danger. There seemed to be a long-suffering sense of fatalism in everything that the people of Korogwe did, or did not do.

❧

The local bus stand was the social and commercial heartbeat of town. A collection of cardboard, tin, and wooden shacks surrounded another dirt patch on the road to Manundu. Fleets of coaches heading north to Nairobi or south to Dar es Salaam roared into the bus stand all day and all night - raising clouds of suffocating dust when the weather was dry and volleys of thick, black mud whenever it rained.

The phenomenal consumption of cooking oil, all over the developing world, was well documented. Hotels served chips swimming in it, chickens were coated in it, and cabbage soaked in it. But the one positive spin-off of that culinary phenomenon was that the discarded five-gallon oil drums could be pressed flat and used for roofs and sidings for thousands of houses. Consequently, the friendly face of an Italian chef, beaten down but still smiling, beamed forth on schoolchildren, office workers, food diners, and bus travelers all over Africa.

Practical uses for various recycled tin cans were limited only by the extent of the individual imagination. They became decorative planters for flowers, feeding troughs for goats and cattle, office and household furniture, storage tins for harvested maize, and a wide array of ingenious toys for young children. We, in the North, were mere neophytes in the art of recycling, when judged by standards such as these.

Orange skins, banana peelings, and eggshells littered the ground around banks of battered buses – their noisy engines idling and their languid passengers steaming. But the discarded refuse didn't remain on the ground very long. Cats, dogs, goats, and chickens scratched in it, licked it clean, and strayed off to feed in various dumps that surrounded the nearby market. But with the coming of the rains, the whole place became a muddy lake; and it could only be a matter of time before one of those killer crocodiles crawled out from the underbelly of an idling bus!

The rains in Korogwe were like nothing I had ever known. The brutal force of a mid-day downpour was absolutely terrifying as it thundered down onto the village of tin roofs. The whole village seemed to shift under its onslaught. Sometimes it felt as though the homes and huts might all just float away down the Pangani River.

With water, water, everywhere, there was frequently not a drop to drink. Because there was no filter system for Korogwe's water supply, what went into the pipes was precisely what came out, when it managed to come out at all. If it didn't rain, the pipes were dry. When it did rain, the pipes were clogged.

I came home from work one day, dripping with sweat and panting to get into the shower. But there was not a drop of water, black or clear, to be had. All the neighbors had water but there was not an ounce for me!

I flew off in search of the college maintenance man. I was really freaked. Heat could do terrible things to you - heat and no water. Joseph said that he would send a man to look at the problem. So I waited and waited and waited some more; clothes stuck to my skin and rivers of perspiration ran down my back.

Finally, at my wits end, I trailed across to my neighbor's house.

"What did they do when I had water and you didn't?" I asked. Water discrimination was a frequent and almost criminal occurrence in this part of the world.

"They banged on the pipes," said she.

"That's it? That's all they did? They banged on the pipes?"

Well, apparently so! It was as simple as that!

"Right, Kaniah! Get the rolling pin and turn on those taps."

With rolling pin in hand, I proceeded outdoors and began smashing and banging on the pipes for all I was worth. One way or another, we were going to have running water that night.

"Anything happening?' I roared above the din.

Kaniah was manning the faucets but nothing was happening.

I continued my onslaught, undeterred. I'd either bust those pipes or I'd get water; or I might just about manage both.

"Hey, Mom," she shouted from the innards of the kitchen. "It's hissing."

And sure enough, the pipes sputtered and spat and shuddered and shook. Then they emitted an almighty blast - and out spewed a venomous tide of tar. The pipes had been completely blocked with thick, black mud.

My African neighbors must have thought that all *wazungu* were mad. The week before the water episode, I had been out in the pelting rain putting plastic bags over my tomato plants. The tiny seedlings had just begun to peep through the soil, and I was not about to lose the fruits of all my hard work to a savage downpour. The neighbors asked me why I was putting hats on my plants. Next, I was out in the sweltering heat, belting the living daylights out of water pipes. But I'd have tomatoes when no one else had them and they would all be asking for some of my plastic hats!

◦◦◦

In Korogwe, day became night at precisely 6:30 p.m. every evening, rain or shine, summer and winter. And our nights grew very long when the lights went out.

We had miraculously surmounted the water drought, but Kaniah and I were now facing into another long, dark African night. So we decided to head off for the Village Inn. Although the rain had stopped, the road was still swimming in mud.

The nicest part of the day in Korogwe came right after sunset. That was when scores of little stalls set up for the evening trade. We could buy barbecued cobs of maize, tiny cups of sweet *chai*, mangoes and oranges, batteries and music tapes, and we could even have our photographs taken. The day's work was done and life's small pleasures were about to begin.

Oil lamps flickered under the cover of night. Old men sat on their hunkers, scratched their beards, and silently surveyed the passing scene. Young men ambled along, laughing and joking and attracting as much attention as they could from the village women. Children flitted up and down the road - chased by barking dogs, skipping over steaming garbage tips, and greeting the passing *wazungu*. "*Habari za jioni, Mwalimu,*" they called out. Every foreigner in Korogwe was thought to be a *Mwalimu* – a teacher. It was a whole lot better than, "Hi there, soldier!" No doubt about that. But very little activity was happening that night. Severe mud conditions had seriously curtailed the evening's rituals.

Kaniah and I stumbled along in the dark, beaming our flashlights in front of us while we tentatively slid one foot in front of the other. Car wheels had gouged foot-deep ruts into the road and we were in constant danger of toppling into them. If we weren't very careful, we could easily end up in body casts.

The Village Inn was an imaginative collection of thatched *vipanda* corralled behind a split-log fence. The Inn attracted the older clientele of the village. Venerable old men clustered close together in the smoky dark. The faint light from rusting oil lamps flickered away on the wooden tables in front of them and the fiery tips of their lighted cigarettes pricked the inky night. There, in the quiet of the deepening night, they whispered conspiratorially, ruminating moodily about the changing world around them. The younger generation, those *new* men with loose change in their pockets, had no interest in the Village Inn. They wanted glamour and excitement. So they spent their time, and their money, in the *dangerous* new establishments that kept springing up along the main road - establishments filled with flashy city girls, loud music, and adjoining bedrooms.

At the Village Inn, we could sometimes get beer, sometimes Coke, and sometimes Sprite; but we could never get all three at the one time. This was a beer and Coke night. We could have Safari but not Pilsner and we could have our beer served hot or cold. "Oh, cold, if you don't mind, and do you have any food on offer tonight?' Great! They had *mbuzi*. The charcoaled goat at the Village Inn was always a veritable feast.

We went up to the brazier and chose a slice of goat from the slabs of meat that were hanging from a hook. Only an occasional flame from the simmering fire disturbed the night. The sharp blade of a flashing knife shimmered as the stoical *mpishi* flicked his machete skillfully through the still air. Then he soaked the slices of meat in beer, rolled them in salt and pepper, and dropped them onto white-hot coals. He worked with a casual grace, a grace so casual that it was hypnotic. The crackling fire and the sizzling meat, the muted sounds from a radio far off in the distance, and the whispered voices of the old men created a peace that was pure magic. "Why am I worrying about muddy water on a night like this?" I asked myself.

After placing our orders, Kaniah and I returned to the obscurity of our little hut and waited in the darkness for our tantalizing meal. We had plastered ourselves with insect repellent before leaving the house, but the mosquitoes were vicious that night and they were biting right through our clothing. I had forgotten to wear ankle socks, so "the mossies" were on the attack from all sides. In desperation, I pulled my bare legs up under me and sat on them. And Kaniah and I continued to wait.

Waitresses in Tanzania had the disconcerting habit of joining one's company whenever and wherever they chose. It was a slow night at the Village Inn so our waitress pulled up a chair, sat with her head in her hands, and stared silently across the flickering lamp right into our faces. I tried to distract her attention with a patter of every day conversation.

"Why don't the villagers do something about that road?' I asked her. "We nearly broke our legs coming down here tonight." We all knew that within one day of the rain stopping, the road would be baked hard and the ruts that were at present just a squishing ooze would become permanent features until the next rains arrived. Nobody would be able to walk the road without risking life and limb and vehicles would proceed to carve new tracks ever closer to the village houses. At the moment, the ground was so soft that a gang of men with *jembes* could level it in a few hours. It would be no more difficult than icing the top of a cake.

"Maybe somebody will come and help us to fix the road," said the waitress, without a moment's hesitation.

"Really? Like who?" I asked.

"The construction workers on the main road," came the disconcerting reply. To her, the solution was patently obvious.

"But the construction crew is made up of aid workers," I said. "Surely, they are not going to come up here to level a muddy road."

But she was right and I was so wrong. A week later, the construction crew arrived with huge earthmovers and leveled the road. The road crew would be long gone when the next rains arrived, and the road would return to its dangerously pitted state. What would happen then? "Just wait for another rescue." Apparently, one always came!

ᕕᕗ

Kaniah, attended the local primary school attached to the teacher training college. She was in seventh standard, which was the final standard before entering secondary school. The age of her classmates ranged anywhere from thirteen to sixteen, depending on the age at which they had first entered school.

Two of Kaniah's classmates were our closest neighbors. Vero was aged fifteen and Paulina was a year younger. Both girls were preparing for their standard seven exams and both hoped to be among the handful of successful candidates who would progress into the state secondary school system. If they made it, they would attend Bungu Secondary School located high up in the Usambara Mountains. They would travel by bus and stay at the school residences throughout the year, returning home only for school breaks and national holidays.

Electric power, when it was available, was far beyond the financial reach of most villagers. They cooked on firewood outside their family homes and they used kerosene lamps for sewing and reading. This had been a bad month for both families, so their electricity supplies had been disconnected for non-payment of their bills.

I had heard the murmured voices of the two girls outside our front door, late one night, and had peeked out to investigate. Normally, families were all in bed by 9:30 p.m. They needed to be up long before dawn to get their chores done before leaving for school or work. So, late night reveling was out of the question.

I found Vero and Paulina sitting under our outdoor security light, surrounded by swarms of mosquitoes and studying diligently for an English exam they were due to take the next day.

English was one of the most important subjects on the standard seven exam and the girls would need high marks to entertain any hope of getting into secondary school. Kaniah knew that and offered to coach her friends for an hour every evening.

They had been working on split infinitives in school that day. This really meant that they had copied reams of notes from the chalkboard into their notebooks. Teachers wrote copious notes on the board, students copied the notes, and then the students memorized the notes. The next day, teachers tested the memories of their students.

Kaniah quickly became swamped by the intricacies of this coaching business. She asked me how she could explain the following conundrum to her friends:

Mary sleeps on the bed.
Mary is in bed.
Mary is on the bed.

The question simply read: "Which sentence is correct?"

This, along with split infinitives, was pretty sophisticated stuff. Especially for students who didn't know the difference between a noun and a verb and who could not construct a simple English sentence. So they carried on as before, simply memorizing everything.

❦

Vero was the eldest sibling in a family of five children, with another baby shortly on the way. Her mother's unmarried sister and her baby daughter, Lucy, also lived with them - along with her mother's nephew, Alan, who was thirteen.

Vero went straight to the family *shamba* from school every day, where she worked in the fields until dusk. This work could mean planting the seeds, watering them, weeding the plot, or harvesting the crop – all according to the season. When she returned home at sundown, she had to prepare the evening meal. She set and lit the fire outside the house and cooked *ugali*, a basic maize-based mash. After that, she bathed the younger children and put them to bed. Finally, if there happened to be any time at all left before complete exhaustion took over, she studied. She was up again to face a new day at dawn. Her routine never changed, except on Sundays when she attended church. As far as she was concerned, the longer the service lasted, the better. Sunday was her only day of rest.

Boys in Korogwe had only one job. They sat in the *shambas* from dawn to dusk screaming. If they were attending school, they went to the *shambas* right after school and stayed there until dark. Their shrill, high-pitched screams were meant to scare off predatory birds and, thus, protect the family's crops.

Every now and again, the Nkigi family managed to collect a supply of discarded plastic bags from the local markets, and they considered it a stroke of good luck if they managed to find any salvageable ones at all. They washed and disinfected the reusable ones and hung them on the bushes to dry. The freshly laundered plastic bags soon became storage bins for the family's rice and maize. But the unredeemable ones were relegated to the *shamba*. There the *shamba* boys tied them onto long bamboo poles and created ghostly white scarecrows that crackled wildly in the wind.

Vero wanted to be an airline pilot. She had never been outside the region of Tanga and she could count on one hand the number of times he had been as far as Old Korogwe, but she wanted to be a pilot. While all children had their fantasies, wanting to become doctors, film stars, astronauts, and singers, "What real chance does Vero have?" I often wondered. Who would help her to follow her heart's desire?

Nonetheless, Vero struggled on, sitting out there under our security light, swatting mosquitoes and puzzling over split infinitives. Vero, who wanted to be an airline pilot! She too had her dreams and the first step to realizing them would be to get accepted into a state-funded secondary school.

❧

Kaniah woke up at 6:00 a.m. every morning to eat her breakfast, get dressed, and meet up with her pals for the half-mile walk to school. Every student was expected to bring a strong twig brush and be present on the grounds at least forty-five minutes before classes were due to begin. Their first duty was to sweep the dirt-packed yard and all the classroom floors, and have them ready for the arrival of their teachers. When clean-up was finished, one of the students would bang a strip of iron hanging from a tree branch with another block of iron, and the students would all race to line up for physical drills. They would, then, march around the neatly swept field behind the schoolhouse in military fashion, under the ever-watchful eye of a switch-bearing teacher.

Discipline was tight. Control was maintained with the crack of a sharp switch across the backs of bare legs. The same technique was employed in the classrooms for correcting mistakes or for rewarding impertinent questions. Dialogue between teacher and student was actively discouraged and teachers were always right.

For the most part, Tanzanian students were remarkably well behaved, mannerly, obedient, attentive, and eager. Unfortunately, the same could not always be said for their teachers, whose salaries were so abysmally low that many of them did not feel it incumbent on them to turn up for school at all.

It was not unusual to find a classroom of students sitting unattended for an entire morning, flipping through notebooks and studying lessons they had copied from the chalkboard; lessons they had not understood when they had first been presented and lessons they would never understand, no matter how long they sat and stared at their baffling notes. Nonetheless, they struggled on, learning everything off by heart and hoping to regurgitate it successfully for those fateful state exams.

When planting season arrived, the entire student body became an army of farmers. The school *shamba* was situated right behind our staff house and it was used for the cultivation of rice.

Children would begin to arrive at the fields at dawn and their work would continue on at a steady pace, in the blazing heat, without drinks or rest, until 10:00 a.m. The switch-bearing teacher was ever at hand, ready and willing to light upon suspected malingerers.

First, the fields had to be completely cleared of the suffocating weeds that invaded every inch of arable farmland. Children would break up acre after acre of the stony earth with their bare hands and, if they were lucky, they might have the help of an occasional *jembe*. This vital piece of farm equipment looked like a hoe, but it had a much stronger steel blade and the children wielded it like an axe. There was not a single piece of mechanized farm machinery in all of Korogwe.

One line of students led the operation, breaking and turning the soil, with their swinging *jembes* flying dangerously close to bare hands and bare feet. A second line of students followed, pulling the loosened weeds and scrub-grass up by hand. A third line brought up the rear, stacking waste and debris in neat bundles and carrying it away on their heads. They worked on in this fashion, clearing section after section of land until the entire acreage had been thoroughly cleaned and neat furrows had been prepared.

The next step was to plant and water the seeds. There were no such conveniences as hoses for these children. They drew water from faucets located several hundred meters away and carried the heavy buckets back to the fields on their heads.

Break came at 10:00 a.m., when the students were allowed to stop and go home for *chai*. They had thirty minutes to eat, change into their school uniforms, and report to school for the rest of the day. They were then expected to concentrate on their regular lessons, after having spent four hours of backbreaking labor in the hot fields. These were all children aged from nine up to sixteen years of age.

One day, at the peak of the planting season, Kaniah returned home from *shamba* duty and collapsed into a heap on her bed. She was a part-time student at the village school, where she studied

Swahili, music, history, and geography. She pursued the rest of her studies - English, Irish, French, and Math on her own, at home.

I tried to tell her that she really didn't have to go to *shamb*a because she was not a full-time student. Her teachers didn't expect her to be there. But she insisted that she must. If she didn't turn up and do exactly what everyone else was doing, the rest of the students would make fun of her. They had already begun taunting her about her faltering Swahili. "You are an *mzungu*," they jeered. "You are weak. You can't do it." So she battled on until the end of the planting season.

Some weeks later, when the crops had broken through and were in need of weeding, the whole grueling process began anew. At that stage the work became even more severe, because the rains had arrived and the flooded fields were infested with leeches. Kaniah finally conceded defeat. The students could laugh at her all they liked, but disgusting leeches trying to suck blood from her bare legs was the last and final straw.

It was not difficult to see that several weeks of learning were lost, every year, to the rice and maize crops. This type of *shamba* work took place in every primary and secondary school and in every training college in Tanzania. It was an outgrowth of Julius Nyrere's policy of self-reliance. Theoretically, every school was responsible for raising enough rice and maize to feed the entire student body for the year. However, primary school children lived at home and did not eat at school; so what exactly was the purpose of all this intensive farming?

The answer became very clear at the end of school term when, following a bountiful harvest, one meal of rice and *mchuz*i was prepared for the students and they enjoyed their meal at school. The remainder of the harvest should have been sold at the markets and the money put towards badly needed school materials such as books, paper, and chalk. In fact, the rice and maize found its way into the homes of the school staff, and if any of it ever did reach the markets, only the teachers made a profit.

Examples of this kind of student exploitation were legion. Free school textbooks provided by foreign donor agencies were available only to those who could pay for them. Other valuable aid resources, such as medicines and computer supplies, were for open sale on the streets and in the markets of most towns. Many of the people in policy-making positions paid only lip service to the needs of the students. They saw solutions to the education crisis in the form of more foreign funds, when practical solutions could be found much closer to home.

The whole system of teacher training needed to be re-evaluated and revalued. Selection needed to be from among the brightest and best, not the weakest. Teacher training colleges needed to be serious institutions of learning and not part-time farm camps. Primary education needed to become a national priority with serious political commitment. This would necessitate an overhaul and reallocation of the national budget, since education currently received only two percent.

⸙

Kaniah was making a remarkable adjustment to living within the African community but because she was so uncomplaining about it all, it was easy to lose sight of the fact that she was not African and did not share the same cultural priorities or values. However, I finally began to grasp a glimmer of what she was going through when I witnessed a heart-breaking incident involving her pet kitten.

Sugaa was the abandoned cat of former VSO workers (British Volunteer Services Overseas) and she was the cat that would eventually cause almighty consternation in our household.

When the VSO volunteers had completed their assignments and were preparing to return to England, they had given Sugaa to Vero's family. In the fullness of time, Sugaa produced a litter of kittens, all of which were promptly adopted by neighboring families who were anxious to have them as mouse catchers. But the runt of the litter was left, and Sugaa wanted nothing to do with it. She abandoned the miserable little scrap to its fate, leaving it lying in a heap under a bush.

I knew in my heart what was coming next; Kaniah would want to adopt it. I told her that she couldn't afford to get too attached to the kitten because we would eventually be going home to Ireland and her adopted kitten would be discarded exactly as Sugaa had been. Furthermore, if we did take her in, she would never learn to fend for herself. And the wild was a dangerous place for abandoned pets.

While Kaniah understood the reasoning behind everything I said, she insisted that she only wanted to feed it, to help it along until it could survive on its own. "How many times have I heard that song before?" I asked myself.

But I surrendered. Kaniah bundled up the little bag of bones and named it Trinket. She kept it safe from predators, tucked up in a box in our hall. At first Trinket looked terribly ill, with her crusted eyes glued tightly shut. But Kaniah nursed her faithfully, feeding her every few minutes through a baby-doll bottle, cleaning her eyes with cotton wool, and stroking her bony little limbs. Miraculously, little Trinket began to thrive.

The neighboring children were fascinated by Kaniah's devotion to this puny little throwaway. They were clinically practical. In their eyes, animals only existed to be eaten, or to work. These children lived at survival level and, as far as they were concerned, an animal's only purpose was to sustain human life. If animals were not fit for consumption, or if they couldn't work, then they could have no value. And strangely to us, the children didn't seem to accept that animals could feel pain or suffer when injured. It just didn't seem to enter their consciousness.

Sadly though, Trinket's miraculous recovery was short-lived. One day she just stopped eating and began to fade away. It was a truly heart-rending ordeal. Trinket could barely lift her head but she managed to limp on wobbly legs towards Sugaa and fall at her mother's side. But Sugaa deliberately ignored her dying kitten. She roused herself from her comfortable slumber and moved away to the far end of the room.

Kaniah exploded in fury. She now loathed Sugaa for deserting her own. She hunted the uncaring mother from the house, cursing her and swearing that she would never again let her inside the door.

She lifted little Trinket into her lap and tried to comfort her, holding the kitten close to the warmth of her own body. Tears streamed down her face, and then the pathetic little parcel of bones began to convulse. That was too, too much! Our friend, Rachel, who was a Peace Corps worker, had been visiting us, watching and quietly helping. When she could bear the pain no longer, Kaniah thrust the trembling little parcel into Rachel's arms. Our friend hovered over it, stroking its belly softly and listening for its breathing. Then Trinket suffered one final seizure and died.

At that point, we were all crying, but relieved that the suffering was over. Kaniah rooted through her belongings and selected one of her softest woolen vests to wrap the little bundle in. After putting it in its box, she carried the box outside to bury it in the garden. Her eyes were red and swollen and she was still crying.

When her friends spotted Kaniah in the garden, they came rushing over and clustered around the fence. They suddenly realized that Trinket had died and that Kaniah was upset. Then they did the most awful thing. They began to tease her, jeering her, crooning out loud, "Angalia, Kaniah. Angalia! Trinket, Trinket." They rocked back and forth, pretending to cradle the kitten in their arms and laughing uproariously while they did it.

Kaniah was devastated by their blind cruelty. She ran back into the house and began pleading with me to let her go home to Ireland.

"I can't stay here anymore, Mom. I don't understand these people. They have no feelings. They just want to hurt me. Please let me go home!"

I tried to explain that pets were a luxury these children could not afford, but nothing would explain their calculated, hurtful behavior. They were supposed to be her friends.

Later on that night, when Kaniah was sitting with Vero under the security light, I could hear her talking about what had happened that day and about how unhappy she was in Korogwe. She told Vero that she didn't want to have anything more to do with them. They had hurt her to her very soul. She wanted to go back home, where people were like her, and where people understood her.

Vero had not been with her brothers and sisters earlier in the day. As usual, she had been out in the *shamba* working. She was older and more sensitive than her siblings, and she had been a really good friend to Kaniah ever since that first day when we had arrived. She turned on the others and I could hear her scolding them.

"You did a terrible thing today when you made fun of Kaniah. That was not a joke. Don't you understand that it is sad when anything dies? Don't you understand that you are not supposed to laugh when other people are suffering? You have hurt Kaniah badly. You must not laugh at her. Her ways are not our ways and you should be more careful."

It helped a little that Vero could see things her way and Kaniah began to recover some of her usual buoyancy. But then, several nights following the Trinket incident, she came racing into the kitchen, screaming for a knife.

"What's wrong?" I asked, suddenly alarmed at her panic. "What do you want with a knife?"

She was frantic and began spilling the cutlery drawer out onto the floor, and diving for a sharp knife.

"Alvin has caught a little bird and has tied its leg with a piece of string. He throws the bird into the air and when it flies up, trying to escape, he snaps the string hard and the bird comes crashing down. He keeps doing this, over and over again, and everyone is laughing. They think it's funny."

She ran out with the knife, intent on freeing the captive bird. One of the older boys caught the bird on the pretext of showing it to Kaniah. Then he took the knife from her and cut the string. The frightened little bird fluttered off into the night.

"Why do you do horrible things like that?" She screamed at Alvin, her eyes blazing and her body shaking with rage. "You were hurting the bird. You were torturing it and making it suffer. How would you like it if someone did that to you?"

Alvin was nonplussed. To him it was all very simple.

"It was in my *shamba* eating my corn. So I took it!" There was no more to say.

Beatrice was my house-girl. She had two daughters and no husband. He had left her when the children were babies. She had received information that he now lived in Moshi with a second family but she never heard anything directly from him. Beatrice supported her two daughters, her mother, several older brothers, and a younger sister from the produce of a small *shamba* that sat on a hillside far outside of town. There she grew maize, beans, and cassava, and she had a few orange and banana trees. If she managed to harvest the bananas before the monkeys ate them, the family occasionally enjoyed a treat. But a successful maize crop was crucial to their lives.

If the rains came on time and the harvest was good, the family had enough *ugali* to keep them fed until the next planting season. If not, they all went hungry.

Tanzanians did not starve. The land was rich and fruits grew wild, but not all kinds in all seasons. There was sometimes an abundance of food and at other times there was hunger. The difference between a good rainy season and a poor one made the difference between having a full stomach and an empty one. But, in Tanzania, starvation was rare.

Like most of her neighbors, Beatrice's life was a hard one. Her two-roomed mud was scrupulously clean, but it had no water and no electricity. The main room had a wooden bench that ran along the wall, a table, two chairs, and two small stools. The table was covered with a bright, checkered cloth, and the stump of a candle stood in a *Blue Band* tin in the center. In the second room, two foam mattresses lay on the dirt-packed ground. There was no bedding of any description. Beatrice cooked outdoors on a fire of sticks. She had two blackened pots; she used one for cooking *ugali* and one for boiling water or making *mchuzi*.

Beatrice had been working for ten years as a house-girl for VSO volunteers. They normally arrived in Tanzania, from Britain, on two-year contracts. And when each pair departed, Beatrice was retained by their successors. However, due to policy changes within the organization, there were no plans to replace the current couple. Because they were caring people, they had been having sleepless nights worrying about what was going to happen to Beatrice and her family, dependent as they all were on that single wage.

Some months prior to their departure date, the volunteers asked if I would be willing to take Beatrice on as my house-girl and keep her in a job. I told them candidly that house-girls or house-boys were not really my scene and, furthermore, I was not at all sure how long I would be in Korogwe. I could not guarantee Beatrice a job for any definite length of time, but she would be welcome to come and work with me for the duration. If Kaniah and I could get used to child-eating crocodiles, water droughts, malarial mosquitoes, and *ugali*, we figured we should be able to handle the notion of a house-girl.

Neema, Beatrice's eldest daughter, attended a private secondary school in the neighboring town of Mombo. She was in that school, not by choice, but only because her standard seven results had not been good enough to secure her a place in a less expensive state school. Beatrice was determined that Neema would get a good education and have a better life than she ever had. Insanely, a woman who lived in a mud hut had to pay high fees to a private school for her daughter's education.

Anytime that Beatrice came into our sitting room and settled into one of our two armchairs, straightened her *kanga* on her lap, and silently looked at the floor, was the time that I knew I was heading for big trouble.

One day Beatrice came to me with a *shida kubwa*, a big problem. She needed to pay Neema's school fees and she had no money. She also needed money to buy a new school uniform and books.

Beatrice earned about 120,000 Tanzanian shillings a year and out of that, school fees alone would devour 60,000 shillings. To put that into perspective, a kilo of rice cost 200 shillings. There was no way on God's good earth that Beatrice could pay out so much money for school fees and still feed herself and her family. I explained the whole economics of the situation to her and Beatrice sat in the chair, mopping her eyes and crying bitter tears. There was no way of reasoning with her. "I must keep my child in school," was all she was prepared to say. Beatrice was a lady who was not for turning.

Beatrice was a Pentecostal Christian. She firmly believed that God always answered her prayers. He healed her when she was sick and He sent her money when she needed it. Now, He had sent me. I was His answer to her prayers. She fully believed this. I would have to give her the money for Neema's fees.

Now I had the *shida kubwa*. I wanted to help her. Really! I did! It was more than admirable that she was so determined to give her daughter an education and a real chance in life. But if I handed over the money without some undertaking from Beatrice that she would plan for the future, would I be helping her or helping to continue a crippling cycle of dependency? Neema would be safe for the first term, but at the end of that, Beatrice would be back to me again and again and again. And if I happened to be in Korogwe when her next daughter, Juliana, reached secondary school age, the story would be repeated. But I would eventually leave Tanzania and Beatrice would be out of a job. What would happen then?

I puzzled over this *shida kubwa* for a long time and I offered her a solution.

"I will loan you twenty thousand shillings to cover the first school term, but for the next four months you will receive a little less pay to make up for the loan. But I will also help you to find ways to earn additional money. If you can make a success of anything at all, we will continue like that into the next term and so on until the end of the school year. That way, you will have the money for Neema's fees and maybe even discover a new business at the same time. But my problem is this. Do you think you will be able to manage with a cut in wages for the first few days?"

Beatrice's face lit up. *Hamna shida.* No problem. She was thrilled and delighted. Her faith had paid off in the end. God would never let her down.

So we embarked on a training scheme. Kaniah began by teaching Beatrice how to make chocolate biscuits. We bought her the flour, sugar, margarine, milk, and cocoa and gave her free reign over our kitchen. She prepared the biscuit mix every morning right after she arrived for work and put the trays into the oven to bake. Then she continued with her chores. When she was ready to go home, the biscuits were ready for sale.

We calculated that if she baked and sold three-dozen biscuits for five days, she would earn a profit of a thousand shillings a week, after expenses. That would more than compensate for her reduced wages, and if things happened to go really well, she could even make a tidy profit.

The first few days of trading proved to be a roaring success. All of the children and neighbors had heard about the chocolate biscuits and Beatrice sold the whole lot before she even left our house. She was absolutely over the moon. She began calling herself a *mwanamke biashara*, a businesswoman. But the initial success began to pale when the neighbors' extra shillings were no more and the customers no longer came calling to the door.

Shida kubwa, intoned a crestfallen Beatrice, as she wrung her hands and straightened her kanga, despondent once again.

"What do you mean, *shida kubwa*?" I retorted. "It's not a problem. Sell your biscuits to the *dukas,* or go down to the bus stand and sell them on the street like everyone else does. These are great biscuits. Nobody else in town has anything like them. You can sell them all easily." I gave her a huge sales pitch. I felt like one of those demented used-car salesmen from Texas. But Beatrice was not moved.

"When can I do that?" she moaned. "I am always here or in the *shamba.*"

I was not about to be defeated on this. "Then send Juliana," I persisted. "She can sell them in a few minutes after school."

"She doesn't like to do that," was all Beatrice had to offer. This was the biggest riddle of all to me. Juliana was dreadfully spoiled - and downright lazy into the bargain. Her mother worked all the hours that God sent and Juliana did absolutely nothing but pout. And to my amazement, Beatrice silently accepted this shameful behavior.

So now we had another problem. Beatrice continued to make the biscuits and sell them all back too me. When I had overdosed on chocolate and had distributed biscuits to all my friends and neighbors, and Juliana had eaten the remainder, Beatrice no longer made them. This was definitely not my idea of a *mwanamke biashara.*

In fact, Beatrice was no better off than when we had started out on this escapade several weeks previously. What were we to do now?

I knew that Beatrice kept a few chickens, so I asked her if they laid eggs.

"No," came the swift reply, "because I don't have food to give them. Without food, they don't lay."

That gave me a bright new idea.

"OK," I said, brimming as ever with entrepreneurial glee. "Here's what we will do. Every Friday evening, I'll give you additional money to buy chicken feed. Then when the hens lay, you can sell the eggs at the hotel. Every egg with fetch seventy-five shillings and that's a lot of money for one egg."

It was settled and once more the businesswoman was delighted with herself. She bought the chicken feed and began feeding her hens. Success was not long in showing its welcome face. The hens were great layers and Beatrice even got them to hatch eleven eggs. Now she had thirteen fowl. She planned to keep some as layers and raise some to sell as meat. This looked like becoming one of my better ventures; it was very promising indeed.

But hold on! A black cloud was hovering above us. Suddenly, Beatrice told me that the chickens had contacted fowl disease and she needed another thousand shillings for *dawa*. I was beginning to feel like a cash dispenser. I gave her the money and I also bought one of her chickens for dinner, along with six freshly laid eggs. "Funny thing though," I thought to myself as I plucked stringy feathers off the bony chicken carcass. "I seem to be her only customer, once again."

A few days later, as I was setting off for a trip to Dar to purchase supplies for the aid project, Beatrice intercepted me and put in a request for *special dawa* for her chickens. Beatrice was good at this. She seemed to be able to judge exactly the right moment to catch me unawares. She had written down the name of the *dawa* for me, so I would be in doubt about what was needed, and I left. *Kinga kwa ndui kwa kuku*, said the little yellow slip.

After completing my project work in Dar, I began to trudge around the city from chemist to chemist, looking for someone who might sell the elusive *dawa*. Finally, I located a chemist on India Street who stocked all sorts of animal concoctions. But now I needed to get a thermos.

"Why?" I asked, getting more agitated and vexed by the minute. I was hot and I was tired and I was very, very hungry. I wanted to get on the road and be back in Korogwe by nightfall. "Because it is a live vaccine," said the chemist, giving me that blank stare reserved for uncomprehending and facile *wazungu*.

"Right!" Away I went, bought the thermos, and returned to collect the precious *dawa*. On my journey home, I began puzzling over this recurring chicken problem. "What on earth can be wrong with those fowl? They seem to have no end of mysterious problems." So I dug out my Swahili dictionary when I got back to Korogwe, and oh yes, there it was – *ndui*.

"Sacred Heart of God! Can this be? It's no wonder I have been the only customer. Those chickens have some form of smallpox." And I had been eating both the chickens and their wretched eggs for weeks."

⌒⌒

At the end of the month I paid Beatrice her wages. She was very confused.

"Where is the rest of it?" she wanted to know, horrified, all agog with stricken face and wringing hands.

"Holy Mother of God, help me! After all my effort, this cannot not be happening." But it was happening, indeed it was!

I struggled to find the right Swahili words to explain the arrangement that we had struck. "I gave you a loan for Neema's fees. And you are meant to be earning additional money with your baking and with your chickens and their eggs. That makes up for the initial loss of wages. Don't you remember our agreement?"

She shook her head vehemently. She did not comprehend what I was on about. Furthermore, she was deeply hurt. How did I expect her to manage on so little money? I felt like screaming and tearing out my hair – or better still, hers. I tried again to explain, but it was all in vain. She nodded her head dejectedly and left, totally convinced that I was a terrible person who had cheated her out of her just pay. I decided to ask Kaniah to talk with her. Since her Swahili was far better than mine, maybe she would make a better fist of it. Maybe this time Beatrice would understand.

Oh, yes! Kaniah must have done a brilliant job – very persuasive! Because Beatrice then came to me, smiling, and asked me if I could now give her enough money to put a new roof on her house.

◌◌

We lived in a normal staff house on the college grounds. Each house had a plot of land attached to it for garden farming, and those plots were really quite big. Various aid workers had occupied our house over the years but none of them had actually cultivated the land. Consequently, our Tanzanian next-door neighbors had appropriated it and planted spinach, tomatoes, cassava, and beans on it. They also kept chickens, pigs, and goats. The staff houses were all attached and everything was free range, including the children.

Goats grazed under our windowsills, pigs were slaughtered in the open air by candlelight, and cocks that couldn't tell time began crowing at three o'clock in the morning. Children shot mangoes and oranges out of our trees with slingshots. According to one of my *wazungu* friends, it was like having a bed-sitter on Noah's Ark.

Because of recurring food shortages in the region, I decided to reclaim part of my allotment and plant a vegetable garden. And I struck another deal with Beatrice. If she would help me to clear and weed the plot, she could have half of my harvest. She could also retain part of the land to grow beans for her own family. I didn't like beans but they grew quickly and were a good source of protein. And I figured that they would be a great supplement for Beatrice's family. Once again, she seemed to be very happy with the arrangement. We set out to work.

I planted a little of everything and I examined my crops every morning before going to work. We had tomatoes, sweet corn, potatoes, radishes, carrots, and beans. They were all blooming and we were entirely delighted.

Then one morning, without warning, I went out to the garden as usual, only to discover that overnight some class of vicious bug had attacked the beans. The once healthy green leaves had become a mass of chewed–up vines.

"Beatrice," I howled, unwilling to believe my own eyes. "Come and see the beans. What can we do?"

Beatrice came, and looked, and pronounced, *shida kubwa*. Then she turned on her heels and sauntered back into the house.

"That's it? Your whole crop is decimated and all you can say is *shida kubwa*?" I was stunned. But Beatrice just looked back at me with a blank stare.

I called my poor persecuted Kaniah and told her to bring out a bucket. Then we began picking the beans that had survived. I figured that we could shell and dry them in the sun. They wouldn't be as good as if they had had a few more days to ripen on the vine, but they would at least be edible. Then I mixed water and washing-up liquid and sprayed what was left of the plants. It might do them no good at all but there was nothing to lose at that point. I could only kill them or cure them.

The overwhelming sense of fatalism that permeated everything from crocodiles to malaria and on to dying crops was paralyzing. I decided that it must derive from a lifetime of warring with the elements and losing the fight. Hunger or plenty depended on the rain and the bugs. In good times, it was a case of "eat and eat" with no thought of tomorrow. Storage bins for surplus maize and rice were expensive. Mice and insects attacked uncovered bins. Soft fruits and vegetables had a short shelf life in such intense heat. Tomorrow would bring its own troubles. So, "Live for today, for tomorrow we may die."

❧

At 3:00 in the morning, I conceded defeat. I knew there would be no sleep for me that night. The heat was unrelenting. I felt like I was trapped in a hippo's body, with arms and legs as heavy as lead. They actually hurt; it was painful to move so I tried to lie quite still in my coffin-like mosquito tent. If I stripped away the netting, those malarial pests would eat me alive. But not even a whiff of air could reach me in there. "Who could imagine that such a flimsy net like this could practically suffocate you?" I asked myself
. The mattress on my bed was my cross of crucifixion, a slab of foam rubber that sucked me into a sweltering, airless pit. I sat up with my back to the damp wall, pulled my knees under my chin, and tried to put as much distance as possible between me and that object of torture. The wall was sopping wet and lively geckos leapfrogged across it in the dark. It had begun to rain and the rice paddies were alive with millions of croaking bullfrogs. In my ignorance, when I had first come to Korogwe, I had thought that the *mahindi* mill behind my house had been left running - such was the furor of noise emanating from the frogs. The tangled bush was also home to billions of crickets and grasshoppers, and their unrelenting buzz sawed across my fragile nerves. I could hear Kaniah tossing and turning in her heat-disturbed sleep. We had no electricity and even if we did, we had no fan. My eyes were sore and swollen and I knew I would be like a zombie in the morning. I pitied insomniacs. This night wandering was demonic.

❧

The population of Korogwe was roughly half Muslim and half Christian. On our first Sunday morning after arrival, the tapping at our bedroom window had begun at sunrise. *"Hodi, Hodi! Unataka kwenda kanisa?"* sang out a chorus of unseen voices. We had received invitations to accompany our neighbors to a host of churches including Anglican, Lutheran, Jehovah Witness, and Pentecostal. Muslims hadn't approached us as yet, but I wondered if, perhaps, Muslims weren't into active *wazungu* evangelization.

Religion was a big part of the daily lives of the people. The dominant Christian religions in the Tanga region were Lutheran, Anglican, and Catholic, with Pentecostal churches making serious inroads into the established terrain. The Lutherans and Anglicans had arrived during Tanzania's colonial past and the Catholics had come by way of Irish missionaries.

Every evening our Lutheran neighbors gathered in their sitting room and we could hear them praying and singing softly before going to their beds. It was all very comforting. Prayers were as much a part of their daily lives as cooking and eating. Their religion was simple and uncomplicated. They believed in God and the Devil, and in good and evil. They prayed mainly to ask God for special favors and to ask for His on-going help. Interestingly, I learned that the Swahili word *kuomba* meant to beg, to ask, and to pray.

I sometimes wondered if, with our own intense intellectualizing, we had lost a lot of the comfort that comes with a simple faith - faith that can sustain its people through incredible hardships. There were dangers in that simplicity, to be sure. There was the danger that God could become a giver of gifts and if we prayed often enough and hard enough, we wouldn't need to do much else. Much like my own friend, Beatrice! It was the age-old argument of religion becoming the opiate of the people. Prayer without understanding could indeed become just that. But I couldn't help wondering if my neighbors would be any farther along the road to happiness without their sustaining faith.

At 4:00 a.m. every morning, we could hear the Muslim call to prayer rising from loudspeakers mounted on the roof of the nearby mosque. Muslim women in Korogwe did not dress in *buibuis* or *chadours* – those long black cloaks and hoods that became so familiar to people in the North during the Afghan and Iraqi wars. Korogwe was inland, and the farther inland one traveled, the less rigid the dress code became.

The coastal town of Tanga was much more traditionally Muslim. I was standing in a bank queue in Tanga one day with several Muslim women in front of me. It was 33 degrees Celsius and I was dripping sweat, even though I was dressed in a light cotton blouse and skirt.

The Muslim women were wearing black headdresses that completely covered their hair and were strapped firmly under their chins. A solid black veil covered everything but their eyes. They wore full-length black acetate cloaks, with regular street dresses under them. Effectively, they were wearing two full sets of clothing.

Black absorbs heat and acetate sticks to the skin like cling-wrap. Those ladies were melting. One of them had elaborate lace-like tattoos imprinted on every inch of visible skin, which granted, wasn't much. But when she raised her hands to wipe her face under the veil, and her coat sleeves slipped back, I could see those lace tattoos snaking all the way up to her elbows. Her feet down to her soles were also covered, as were the backs of her hands and her fingers. I could only surmise that such elaborate tattoos were her way of displaying her vanity. We did the same thing with carefully applied make-up, fashionable hairstyles, and trendy clothes. But their physical discomfort, in such searing heat, must have been excruciating. Even the long white robes that Muslim men wore would have been less oppressive.

❦

Korogwe was a hotbed of gossip. *The Village of Squinting Windows* was only trotting behind our *Village of Whispering Winds*. The ever-churning rumor mill had begun to grind out a fantastic yarn concerning one of the foreign aid workers who, upon completing his contract in Korogwe, had returned to his home in Germany. This young volunteer doctor had served his time in the district hospital for two years. Because he had been so highly regarded in the community, the hospital administrators and the village council had thrown an impressive farewell party for him, just before his departure. All the important community leaders had attended. The *mzungu* doctor had departed in a blaze of glory.

He had only been gone a few short weeks when the vicious rumors began to fly. From the petrol stations to the markets, from the *shambas to* the schools, from the training college and into the banks, the rumors had spread. The rumors went like this.

The poor unfortunate doctor had gone home and been asked to undergo a series of medical examinations. The results were HIV positive. The doctor took a second test. He tested positive again. He was distraught. He shot himself. The poor doctor was dead.

I was in Dar es Salaam some weeks after that particular rumor had grown legs, and I was having lunch at a small café. A European gentleman approached and asked if he could join me. We started chatting and after discovering that my home base was in Korogwe, he said, "I heard that tragic story about the young German doctor. What a terrible thing to happen."

Fortunately, I was able to tell him that the rumors he had heard were exactly that, nasty rumors. One of our friends had just received a letter from the presumed deceased assuring us that he was alive and well. Obviously, some demented mind had started the scurrilous tale and it had taken on a life of its own. Speculation was growing that a disappointed lover was responsible, a lover who had been left behind. There I was, more than 200 kilometers from home base, chatting casually with a complete stranger who, upon hearing the name Korogwe, connected it with the HIV positive foreign doctor.

Curiously, HIV, locally known as *Ukimwi*, was a taboo subject in Korogwe. There were no statistics, official or otherwise, concerning the numbers of people infected or the numbers of people suffering or dying from Aids/*Ukimwi*. We had statistics for every other communicable disease from malaria to smallpox, but nothing for HIV. People died from tuberculosis, typhoid, pneumonia, and malaria but nobody ever mentioned *Ukimwi*. The whole fascination with the supposedly infected *mzungu* doctor caused me to wonder if perhaps, by repeating the story, the people had found a way to bring the dreaded topic out into the open. The readiness of people to talk about the disease, when it was related to an *mzungu*, was very revealing.

Another story doing the rounds concerned a certain local clergyman who was involved in some shady business practices and who had been using the official church vehicle to facilitate his nefarious enterprises.

It was common knowledge that a lucrative trade in bootlegged Kenyan beer flourished right across the northern part of Tanzania. The close proximity of Korogwe to the border made successful evasion of import duties a real possibility, particularly when key officials were willing to look the other way for a few thousand *shilingi*. There were regular police checkpoints from the border all the way south to Dar es Salaam, but they too could be negotiated for the right price. It made me wonder about what kind of profit could possibly be made after all those palms had been sufficiently greased. But smuggling must have paid handsomely because smuggling was rampant.

The community first began to suspect illegal activity when the church vehicle appeared with newly tinted windows, making it impossible to see into the van from the outside. The local police sergeant paid an informal visit to the reverend gentleman concerned and had a quiet word in his ear. However, the reverend gentleman chose to disregard these growing concerns and carried on with his illicit trade. I have no doubt that he had also failed to thank the police sergeant adequately for his concern. Consequently, the reverend soon found himself paying dearly for that little oversight.

Two men appeared at the clergyman's door late one night and requested assistance to take a sick relative to hospital. The clergyman did the charitable thing and obliged. The route to hospital took them through a large sisal plantation, with miles and miles of deserted track. Somewhere deep inside that lonely plantation, the reverend gentleman was knocked unconscious and dumped into a ditch. Plantation workers discovered him, badly beaten and heavily drugged, when they arrived for work the next morning.

The villains had absconded with the truck and, presumably, had crossed the porous border into Kenya. There, with the license plates changed, the vehicle would have been sold. Local wisdom also said that those responsible for the kidnapping had been associates of associates from the bootlegging business, associates who had not received their anticipated cut of profits. Furthermore, the police were showing very little interest in investigating the crime. That alone lent great credence to all manner of salacious gossip. The clergyman had been severely injured and taken to the hospital he was supposedly heading to in the first place. He had not yet resurfaced in town. And so the intriguing saga continued.

☙

"When does being your brother's keeper spill over into minding your brother's business?" Unhappily, Kaniah and I found ourselves at the center of just such a riddle, when we started to attend Sunday morning mass.

The Catholic Church close to the college campus celebrated Sunday mass at 8:30 a.m., and it finished anywhere between 10:15 and 10:30, depending on the staying power of the celebrant and the enthusiasm of the congregation. The church was stifling hot, there was little or no air, and the church pews were always tightly packed. It was close to impossible to breathe. So Kaniah and I decided that if we arrived for mass somewhere around 9:20, we would be in plenty of time to hear the final words of the priest's homily and participate in the offertory and communion. In other words, we would arrive late and stay until the end instead of arriving early and leaving early. It also seemed the sensible thing to do since our Swahili was not up to scratch and the homily could rage on for forty-five minutes, leaving us drained and nearly comatose by its conclusion.

So we began to put our plan into action. We drove up to the church grounds, but parked quite a distance from the entrance so that noise from our car engine would not disturb the mass in progress. We then waited outside the church, in time-honored Irish fashion, until the end of the homily, and entered quietly. We thought we had everything under control.

Such was not the case. Everything was out of control. One Sunday, after we had returned home from mass and were going about our normal lives, minding our own business, a neighbor approached Kaniah and demanded to know why we always arrived late for mass. The priest had delivered a blistering sermon that day deploring the behavior of certain individuals who could not manage to get to church on time, even with the help of a car! Of course, we hadn't heard the attack since we had been sheltering outside the church door at the time. Worse luck!

The following Sunday, we arrived at mass as usual. As we took our places outside, along with a substantial crowd of other latecomers, a very officious, sash-bedecked and irate young lady strode up to us and in a voice filled with righteous indignation boomed, "You are late again! Why are you always late?"

Well, hold on there just a little minute now! What was this? The Spanish Inquisition on the steps of the church? Cultural differences and all that aside, I was going to have a really hard time with this one. As calmly as I could manage, but shaking with barely contained rage myself, I told her that I thought my Sunday morning activities were my concern and none of hers. Kaniah leapt in to make our excuses, once again explaining about the heat and the language and so on and so forth. The rest of the doorstep congregation listened in with rapt attention. This was certainly different! This was good!

We said no more and stayed on until mass was over. But I was still fuming. "I don't think they'll be seeing us in that church again, either early or late," I muttered to Kaniah. "We'll find another mass, even if we have to drive all the way to Tanga. But it seems to me that whether I go to mass or not, and at what time I go to mass, is nobody's business but mine."

I thought over that incident a lot during the following week. Maybe the priest thought that the *wazungu* were setting a bad example for his people by coming late. If so, he could have told us in private and given us a chance to explain. But censure by public exposure seemed to be the order of the day. The voice of authority, whether it was in government, business, school, or church was never meant to be questioned.

As it turned out, we didn't have to drive to Tanga after all. There was another church in Old Town, high up on a hill, where the air was cool and where mass normally lasted for little over an hour. Mercifully, the parish priest was blissfully unconcerned about our comings and goings. We were in complete and perfect harmony.

Even by Korogwe standards, we had just experienced a seriously bizarre day. The drama that eventually erupted had its roots in a litany of cultural misunderstandings and damaged pride. Malevolent forces that had been swirling around the protagonists for a very long time had been lying in wait for just the right moment to engulf their unsuspecting victims. And the consummate moment had just arrived.

Positions of authority were sacred; that was a given. And there was a strict pecking order and accepted ritual for just about every aspect of daily life. In a typical domestic household, the cook sat majestically on the top rung of the ladder. Then, under him came the house-girl, or house-boy, then the watchman, and finally the gardener. If a nanny happened to be employed to look after the children, she took her rightful place ahead of the cook. This was never the case in my household. I was all of those people - kind of like back home in Dublin. However, in Africa, this was the order recognized by the workers themselves and they resisted any attempt to interfere with it.

Problems relating to these positions of authority had recently come to a head in the home of one of my friends, problems between the cook and the watchman. The cook was feeling seriously offended because the watchman regularly questioned his instructions. The cook approached the householder and asked him to intervene; in other words, to put the watchman firmly in his place. He wanted everyone in the household to acknowledge and respect the correct line of authority.

My friend had some difficulty with this because he completely failed to understand the hierarchy of positions. To him, the workers were all individuals with their own jobs to do. Only their rates of pay defined their higher order of skills. He just wanted them to get on with their jobs and keep their petty squabbles to themselves. But according to the cook, and everyone else on his staff, the householder himself had been the cause of the disharmony, because he had failed to set up the correct order of command in the first place. So in order to re-establish peace in his house, the *mzungu* had to put aside his own feelings and speak to the watchman. With that done, peace was quickly restored.

Similarly, in any business or institution, directives from anyone in authority were accepted without question. Children learned this pattern of compliance beginning with their first days at primary school. That behavior was then reinforced in secondary school and eventually the young adults carried it out into the workplace.

The head of one of our local institutions had certainly developed an exaggerated sense of his own authority, along with grand illusions of self-importance. He had no idea whatsoever about what a genuine exchange of views might mean. There was only one way to think about, or to do anything, and that was his way. Those who even dared to question his authority quickly found themselves transferred to the outer bush. Consequently, all of life within that particular institution had become deadly boring.

Our vexatious little drama began to unfold against just such a cultural background. Ann and David were two British aid volunteers. They were both qualified primary school teachers. However, their home organization had inappropriately assigned them to teach English to third-level students, and, as it happened, the English Department of the training college in question was adequately staffed with its own Tanzanian English tutors. So the aid volunteers soon found themselves superfluous to need. They had no real role to play within the community and were simply called upon to fill in whenever and wherever they were needed. Frustration quickly set in.

However, in a brave attempt to redefine their roles, the volunteers set about compiling some novel ideas to enrich the English language program and they presented them to the college head. They offered to launch an English language newspaper. They offered to organize a current events debating forum. They offered to run a series of skills-training workshops, hoping to develop a library of audio-visual teaching aids. But every suggestion that they put forward hit a brick wall. The standard responses from head office never varied; they ran from "no time," to "no interest," to "no money," and "no materials." There was never any discussion about possible fund-raising campaigns or possible reorganization of the school timetable. The more the volunteers persisted in their efforts to enrich the program, the more obstinate the administration became. Ann and David became thoroughly demoralized. They were wasting two years of their lives and accomplishing nothing.

Eight months into their contracts, Ann struck on the brilliant idea of opening a pre-school facility in a disused building close to the school campus. Miraculously, her idea proved to be a winner from the start. The administration was very interested. Ann submitted an impressive proposal to her home organization, in which she defined the needs of the local community and local input of venue and staff. She then requested funds to rehabilitate the building, train the staff, and equip the school. The proposal was approved almost immediately. Vital funds were allocated, work on the building got underway, and, in a flurry of excitement, the pre-school opened to a warm reception from administration and the community at large.

Ann's project became a resounding success. She was an excellent teacher as well as a strong organizer and a stimulating teacher trainer. She set up a parents' committee to encourage home involvement in the children's education and she developed training workshops for potential classroom aides. The project went from strength to strength. Even the critical factor of meeting recurring expenses was resolved when Ann's organization agreed to provide a small but regular injection of funds. But this was the rock upon which a very worthy project would founder. Who would administer the funds?

The head administrator instructed Ann to deposit all of her project funds into the institution's central bank account. Immediately, for Ann, alarm bells began to ring. She could see her pre-school funds being swallowed up in short order, never to be seen again. So she proceeded to open a separate account in her project's name, and she soon found herself facing a wounded bear in head office.

Although the daily operations of the school continued to flow smoothly, the working relationship between Ann and those in head office deteriorated markedly. Ann's independent bank account became a festering wound. A litany of complaints began to reach her, along with insistent demands for more reports and more accountability. Constant stress, tension, and pettiness became the order of the day. Meanwhile, David's contributions to the English Language

Department remained negligible. He found himself sitting in the staff room reading novels, with his active teaching hours few and far between. After eighteen months of growing frustration, they decided to throw in the towel and return to England.

Undoubtedly, strong personality clashes had played a big part in increasing the tension. The volunteers were young and inexperienced and perhaps they had not seen the potential for creating serious misunderstandings by their outspoken behavior. At the same time, the head administrator was fiercely intent on nailing down his own authority. If the *wazungu* succeeded in flaunting his authority, would that then open the gates to dissension among his own staff?

Although Ann and David had been a very popular couple with the local community, their decision to depart prematurely surprised no one. They hosted a big going-away party for the neighbors and their children and they spent the last few days of their service videotaping the families, their co-workers, and the neighborhood. Their chief adversary in head office rose above their private differences and hosted a splendid farewell dinner on the eve of their departure. All seemed to be sweetness and light. Easy-going banter carried the evening. The head had done the gentlemanly thing and if the young *wazungu* were determined to leave in a disgruntled mood, well he could not be blamed. He had tried to be the peacemaker.

The departing couple had everything organized. They were set to leave Korogwe on the 9:00 a.m. bus for Arusha and catch a connecting flight from Kilimanjaro to London the same evening. But their last order of business was to videotape the school choir, which rehearsed every day before classes. They planned to edit the entire tape when they got back to England and send a copy of it back to the college, as a parting gift.

That was the point at which everything started to go disastrously wrong. David appeared at the choir's morning rehearsal with his camera and he began to film. Instantly, a message was fired across campus from head office ordering the choirmaster to cease and desist all operations and report to administration immediately. David was also ordered to appear with his offending tape.

The head administrator was enraged. This was the same

gentleman who had so generously hosted the farewell dinner the night before. When the three baffled cohorts arrived at his office, he suspended the choirmaster on the spot and ordered him to immediately vacate his staff house. Furthermore, he ordered the beleaguered choirmaster to write and sign a full confession admitting his complicity in undermining the authority of the head by staging and recording a school performance without prior approval from his superior. So there!

The head proceeded to confront the departing pair, demanding that they hand over the unauthorized recording. They, in turn, insisted on their right to retain what was their private property. All hell broke loose. A full frontal screaming match erupted with the head insisting that Ann and David had overstepped the boundaries.

"What boundaries?" they roared, confused, perplexed, and bewildered.

They had not sought permission from the authorities to record a school session.

"Where are the regulations governing this procedure?" they demanded to know.

He had full authority to make and impose all such regulations at any time and their ignorance of the fact did not excuse them for this vulgar display of gross misbehavior.

What in fact had the couple done wrong? There were notices posted at police barracks and military installations all over the country prohibiting photography. These were security precautions, respected by everyone, because cameras were impounded on a regular basis for contravention of such restrictions. But school property was not a sensitive location. It was an educational institution and there were no warning signs anywhere. The couple had photographed their friends, colleagues, and students - the mountains, trees and bushes - the school building and the local community. Visiting tourists took similar photographs every day. David had done nothing different.

But the head would not back down. He insisted that he had full authority to confiscate this unauthorized tape. He compared himself to "the captain of an ocean going ship," responsible for the good name and reputation of his institution and his country. He would not allow these people to leave Tanzania with such an offensive piece of propaganda. He went into full flight, threatening to call in the police and have Ann and David detained if they persisted in their refusal to comply with his orders.

The volunteers were stunned but they also knew that they were defeated. They had lived in Korogwe long enough to recognize that they were clearly outgunned. Maybe the head hadn't a leg to stand on, but should they risk everything by involving the police? What kind of Pandora's Box would that open? Would there be some sort of interminable enquiry? If that were to happen, they could be stuck in Korogwe indefinitely.

The standoff ended with David throwing the offending tape across the headmaster's desk and storming out of the office in a blind rage. Ann followed, crying with fury. It was a heartbreaking way to end their contentious stay.

Tears of frustration were mixed with tears of farewell as the pair left Korogwe village. The humiliated choirmaster was left dangling for weeks, uncertain of his fate. His first confession was roundly rejected. He had not adequately acknowledged the depths of his transgression and had not fully expressed unconditional remorse. His confession had to be rewritten. This he did. Then he spent several more days gathering allies from within his colleagues to act as emissaries to the head, to speak in his favor, to plead for his reinstatement. It was a ghastly experience. The unfortunate choirmaster had been reduced to the point of groveling for his livelihood. When the head was suitably convinced that he had firmly imprinted his indisputable authority on everyone, he magnanimously relented. The newly chastened choirmaster was allowed back. And there could be no doubt in anyone's mind, who was the boss.

The unhappy incident did not rest there. Ann and David related the whole sorry incident back to their organization when they returned to England. The organization subsequently held an interview with the concerned head, recovered the tape, and then severed its more than twenty-year relationship with the institution. Would the repercussions have any lasting effect on the administration's management style? It was doubtful. More than likely, it would be considered little more than a slight irritation in the grand scheme of institutional life

❧

I had my first real encounter with the shadowy world of bureaucratic roguery shortly after that. As a foreign national working in Tanzania, I was obliged to apply for an official resident's visa and I had to produce a sheaf of documents to support my application. These included introductions from the Office of the President of Tanzania, bilateral government agreements, employment contracts, education credentials, character references, and Lord knows what else. I had collected all of the required paperwork and duly appeared for my appointment at the inspector's office in Tanga. But I was a raw novice at this game of bureaucracy and I was in for some big surprises.

I asked to see Edward, my contact at the regional office. He promptly appeared, warmly greeted me, and ushered me into the regional inspector's office. However, the greeting I received there was distinctly lacking in warmth; in fact, it was downright chilly. The inspector was rushing out to another appointment and couldn't see me. He curtly informed me that I should come back some other time, "maybe next week". Never mind that I had just driven 70 kilometers on a dirt road to make that particular appointment.

"But I can't do that," I protested. "I am on my way to Mombassa to collect my daughters who are arriving on the Nairobi to Mombassa train."

The inspector was singularly unimpressed by my urgent need for a visa.

"Why can't your daughters come to Tanga on the bus?" he asked, while busying himself with a reef of papers and visibly unconcerned with my plight.

"Because this is their first time in Africa and they are expecting me to be at the train station. I have no way of contacting them to advise them to do otherwise."

"This is very strange," I thought. "Why am I standing here apologizing for my daughters' means of travel?" Moreover, I was puzzled because my project manager had personally arranged this appointment just the day before, when he had obtained his own visa without any apparent difficulty.

The inspector curtly dismissed me with a mumbled suggestion that I might try another government department, and see another government inspector, and get another letter from him. He offered no explanation as to why I might need this new letter. I just had to get it, and in the unlikely event that I actually succeeded, I could return to his office and perhaps I would be seen.

I then embarked upon a dizzying round of offices, officials, questions, blank stares, half-answers, and lots and lots of waiting, waiting, and more waiting. I began to wonder if I were actually making history. "Surely," I thought, "they must have gone through this procedure hundreds of times before me, considering the numbers of foreign nationals that are working in the Tanga region. Why then the mass confusion, the non-comprehension, the utter bewilderment at my simple request for a resident visa?"

"Why do you want a resident's visa?" I was asked, again and again.

The answer to that question was obvious. 'I am a foreign aid worker and I have to comply with government regulations. I need a visa today in order to travel to Mombassa and collect my daughters."

"But you don't need a resident visa to re-enter Tanzania. Just show your passport," I was told.

I was seriously beginning to question my sanity. "What about the car I am driving? Won't I need a re-entry permit for it? And my daughters? Won't they need some documentation to prove they are staying with me?" I was not about to head off into Kenya without the necessary papers. I had heard too many gruesome tales about intrepid travelers who were rotting in jails throughout Africa, victims of missing documentation.

Everyone I met seemed to be utterly baffled. What could I possibly be talking about? Then I discovered something very interesting. They all presumed that I didn't speak or understand Swahili. Granted, I was not totally fluent, but I could understand enough to make sense out of the following exchange.

"She wants a resident visa because she doesn't want to pay the tourist rates."

I knew there were three currency rates in force throughout Tanzania. The highest rate for accommodation was the tourist rate and a good standard hotel would cost about one hundred dollars per person, per night. That was way, way out of my league. The next rate was for foreign residents and that came in at about half the tourist rate. The lowest rate was for Tanzanian nationals. As a foreign aid worker, my family and I were entitled to the second rate and I needed a resident's permit to verify my status. But to these officials, all foreigners were rich; so all foreigners, including this one, should be classified as tourists.

After a great deal more discussion and procrastination, another official entered the picture. Officials were ten-a-penny in that building but this one proved to be much more helpful and understanding and he issued the necessary letter.

Armed with what turned out to be no more than a second letter of introduction, I returned to the original office. The chief inspector had not returned. I was shown into a crowded waiting room. The brown-streaked walls were lined with benches and lifeless bodies; all were wedged together and glued with sweat. The eternal waiting game had begun anew. People grew old in Africa, just waiting.

I returned to see Edward. There he sat, his chair propped back against the wall, casually reading his newspaper. A roomful of people sat outside his door - all waiting; waiting for something to happen. But nothing was going on in Edward's office! Nothing, that is, until an obnoxiously loud *mzungu*, tall and skinny with knobby knees sticking out from beneath his khaki shorts burst in, brandishing a few bottles of cheap gin. He went through a thoroughly disgusting, backslapping routine with the office clerk, proclaiming his gifts to be "good stuff". He must have been a familiar face in there, judging from the broad grins and delighted reception he was receiving. And then the penny dropped. "What a thick I have been! This is all about *baksheesh*."

My patience was at an end. I had been running around like a fool for two and a half hours and I was getting nowhere fast. I was being, very pointedly, ignored.

"Do I have to pay you something in order to get this visa?" I asked, looking straight at Edward.

He was thrown into confusion, suddenly confronted by such a direct and awkward question. Clearly, one was not expected to be so open, so ungracious, and so rude. One was meant to offer a subtle gift. Considering all the officials that I had encountered that morning, I would have needed to be Santa Claus to satisfy them all.

Edward began shuffling papers around his desk, opening and closing desk drawers, and getting terribly busy, all of a sudden. Then he got up and abruptly left the office, leaving me sitting alone at his desk. He returned a few minutes later and without another word, took my passport and stamped it. Visa granted! I never did see the big man, the inspector, again. He had just been another bit player in the overall performance.

Chapter Two
TWO WORLDS COLLIDE

It was a sixty-five kilometer trek from Tanga to the border of Kenya on the Indian Ocean and it had taken us four and a half hours to cover that distance. It was easy to picture David Livingstone hacking his way through bush like that and ending up with jungle fever! Dense and tangled vegetation swamped a road that looked like it had just been bombed. What we really needed was a tank!

We joined a creeping immigration queue at the border post in Horohoro. Three buses had reached the border before us and every single one of those passengers had to clear immigration and pass through a rigorous customs check. We had the additional problem of temporarily exporting a car, even though we intended to return in the same vehicle within three days.

The extraordinary patience shown by armies of travelers, forever on the move all over Africa, mystified me. Or was that extraordinary patience really a case of despair? Had all those happy wanderers just given up and were they all just helplessly succumbing to every indignity hurled their way? Kaniah and I meekly shuffled along with the crowd, curbing all our simmering, anxious tendencies. We certainly did not want to become the legendary ugly foreigners!

Every room we entered along the way was choked with bundles of dog-eared, yellowed, and termite-eaten logbooks. They were bursting out from cupboards that looked like they had been there for centuries. Still more of those blighted scripts were stacked against the walls, with some of them tumbling over onto chairs and benches. The customs girl sat perched on top of another wobbly stack. The rooms were dank and dusty. Endless queues of faceless travelers went through the same motions, day after day, with their names and numbers dutifully recorded in the bulging ledgers. What would happen when those rooms filled to capacity? Would they carry on building more shacks, to house more ledgers? Would they eventually create some macabre Ledger City? That was another conundrum – just one more in a growing litany of Africa's imponderables.

Entire families seemed to be traveling with all their worldly possessions crammed into canvas sacks. Most of the family groups were Asian. Men traveling solo were usually Tanzanians and Kenyans, but I noticed a large contingent of lone males carrying Yemeni passports. My Kiswahili teacher had told me that many Omani and Yemeni citizens of African origin were beginning to experience growing levels of discrimination in those countries. Some of them had obviously decided to try their luck back on the African continent.

Most of the tourists at this border post were weather-beaten European backpackers. Some had been on the road for months and some for years. They had no itinerary and no timetable. They picked up and moved on whenever and wherever the fancy took them. Curiously, though, they rarely seemed to be enjoying any of it. It was a grim test of endurance, this dogged trek through Africa, then Asia, and finally South America. It was a doggedness that I found hard to understand, and I wondered about all these things as I passed from one officer to the next and as I encountered more dark rooms and more bored faces.

A few hundred meters down the road and the whole tedious process began anew - on the Kenyan side. It was a dose of grim endurance in spades! Finally, we passed through a chain-link fence and drove on to a stunningly sound, hard-topped tarmacadam road.

This was a true revelation – another world! We passed through acres and acres and mile after mile of carefully tended and gracefully swaying coconut palms. Neat little tourist towns with quirky little craft stalls peppered the coastline. Within less than one hour, we found ourselves on the approach road to Mombassa by way of the Likoni Ferry.

Long queues of cars moved swiftly onto the barge and foot passengers squeezed themselves up against the rails. The anchor lifted and within another ten minutes we were deposited onto the island of Mombassa. The sudden and unexpectedly cool efficiency of the whole operation took my breath away.

The Old Town of Mombassa had all the Arab influences of Zanzibar combined with the additional flavor of a long Portuguese presence. Fort Jesus, a towering circular stone edifice, dominated the harbor. In 1593, the Portuguese had established this colony on the East African Coast in order to consolidate their trade with India. Fort Jesus had fallen to the Omanis in the late seventeenth century and Mombassa was now a solid Islamic city. An impressive arch spanning the main artery of Moi Avenue exhorted one and all to: "Honor Allah and Read the Quaran."

The British Empire had followed on the heels of the Omanis, and a strong touch of colonial England was still evident everywhere. English brand names eclipsed all others on the market shelves, and the old colonial-style hotels were still the choicest in town. Winding, polished oak staircases, rambling flag-stoned corridors, four-poster beds, and rose-covered courtyards all harked back to an opulent colonial past. Unlike Tanzania, where the ascetic socialism of Julius Nyerere decried colonial soft living, Kenya lovingly embraced it.

Mombassa was an assault on the senses. Traffic was grid-locked and the heat was unrelenting. Street traders crammed every corner. Swarms of black-cloaked women, looking exactly like their 'black spider' namesakes, hurried through the crowded streets. I half expected to see rivers of sweat flowing in their wake.

Geraldine Ann, Aisling, and Breifní stepped off the train, bursting to begin their African saga. They had not slept a wink on the ten-hour train journey from Nairobi and had hardly slept at all since departing London. Nonetheless, there was not a minute to spare. We were about to wage a full-scale assault on the city.

We decided to begin with a leisurely stroll through the city center so we could take in all the exotic sights along the way. Breifní suddenly began to buckle under the intense heat of the noonday sun. She wasn't wearing a hat, which was almost suicidal if you happened to be a very fair-skinned redhead. But she recovered, bought a straw hat, and was determined to press on. After wandering around the old town for several hours, and in search of some respite, we nipped down a laneway and into a cool, dark *duka*. Breifní leaned against a wall, turned ash while, and slid down the wall into a heap on the floor. She looked, for all the world, like an ice-cream cone melting. It was time to call it a day.

◖∽◗

We were on our way to Lamu, one of the oldest centers of Islam on the East African Coast. A friend of mine, from Wales, had worked there as a VSO in the 1970s and she had returned with her family the previous year. It had been her first return visit since she had left - all those years ago. She was married to a Muslim man from Lamu. Her story cast a different light on all the stories I had ever heard about Christian women and Muslim men. This was her story, as she told it to me.

◖∽◗

"I was a pretty typical small town girl from a village outside of Cardiff. All the things you've ever heard about Wales, from the slag heaps to the chapel meetings, defined me. I expected to become a teacher and return to the village primary school, or if I really went mad, I might find a good public school in Cardiff. In fact, I was quite happy to do either. I was not a madcap. I was a good student. I didn't drink or do drugs and I had a steady boyfriend. We were totally compatible; we had the same religion, same nationality, and same culture."

Her best friend at college, Jean, was as wild as a March wind. She managed to stay at college because she was born to be clever. When Elaine had to sweat to get through my exams, Jean could cram for a week and sail through. And like Elaine, Jean also knew where she wanted to go after college. That meant anywhere in the world outside of Britain. In fact, it meant anywhere in the world that the VSO wanted to send her.

Elaine continued, "The closer I came to finishing my training, the more I felt that it would be fun to go away for a year to some really exotic spot before settling down to the house, the husband, and the children. So, when Jean received her assignment for Nairobi, I was right there beside her."

Nairobi was everything that the two young teachers had expected, and more. They were appointed to a large English-speaking state school where they were short of nothing. The safari parks and lakes were within an hour's drive from their school and there were scores of expatriates within the Nairobi community. When their two-year contracts came to an end, they applied for extensions and were relocated to Lamu.

"It was like going to another planet," explained Elaine. "Lamu was an old, old town with a long history of Arabs and Muslims. This time we were at a Muslim school. We didn't speak much Kiswahili. The first day I met the head teacher in the hall and said, "Good Morning," as I passed. "I was summoned to his office later that afternoon."

"If you want to work in an Islamic school," he told me, "you should learn to speak our language. And you can start by greeting me correctly. You must say '*Shikamoo*' – to which I will reply, '*Marahaba*.' Is that understood?"

"I agreed." It was understood.

But that wasn't all. "You must cover yourself properly," he continued. "Ask one of the teachers, Fatuma, to take you to her aunt's house after school. The *shangazi* will make some dresses and veils for you. Please wear them."

"That was it," continued Elaine. "I had been thoroughly chastised. The meeting was over. I don't know if I was frightened or intimidated at the time, but it never occurred to me not to do what I had been told. I knew it hadn't been merely a suggestion to be followed or disregarded as I might choose. If I wanted that job, then I had no choice. But I thought to myself, what of it? It's only a dress! It didn't make a lot of difference to me what I wore. The veil covered my hair but not my face. I figured I could live with that."

She went on, "But it made a huge difference at school. Before I put on the long dresses and took the veil, the local teachers had been very cold to me. They would be sitting in the teacher's room talking and gossiping, but when I came along in my western gear, all the chat dried up. Now, with me dressed in traditional style, they began to draw me into their conversations and my Swahili began to get better and better."

The *shangazi's* house soon became the center of Elaine's life. Unmarried Muslim girls were not allowed to walk out alone without a male escort. But because she was an *mzungu*, and not a Muslim, she was able to go the *shangazi's* house on her own. It was a meeting place for all the unmarried female teachers in the locality.

"A married man and his wife could eat together, but unmarried men and women could not. So all the single women in a family prepared and cooked their evening meal together. Then they would sit about on the floor, eat their meal, and gossip. And I began to join them. That was literally all we did. We ate, and talked, and sewed. You will find this hard to believe, but I had more fun in that room than I ever had before or since. The barrage of gossip was absolutely wild. Some of it wasn't even true, and we all knew it, but it was like telling tall tales – the more malicious the tale, the better we liked it. We talked and laughed about wives in Lamu, wives in Oman, wives on Pemba, and mistresses in Zanzibar. We would be falling about the place in complete hysterics, inventing more and more outrageous yarns for hours on end."

It so happened that Jean had a British volunteer friend, named Andy, who was on the school's soccer team. And Andy had a local friend named Mbaraka.

"Mbaraka's sister was about to get married and we were all invited to the wedding party. Since weddings were very big, very important social occasions, all the women needed new outfits. We were in a state of high tension for weeks before the wedding, busily planning the dresses, purchasing the fabric, and visiting dressmakers. My outfit turned out to be a red-flowered, loose fitting, floor-length dress with a matching gold head veil. It was by far the simplest garment on display that day. All the other women wore dazzling creations made from organdy and lace, with sparkling sequins and glass beads sewn on everywhere. They even strapped silver tinkling bells around their ankles. Although they were completely covered by black *buibuis* for the ceremony, later at the party that night, the *buibuis* came off and those sedate lady teachers went absolutely berserk. You may think that Muslim women are a suppressed lot, but I never saw such wild abandon in all my life!"

Elaine met Mbaraka at that wedding. He was a fisherman and he owned his own boat. Every Saturday morning after their initial meeting, Elaine would ride her bicycle down to the wharf to collect her fish from Mbaraka. They were immediately attracted to each other, so, with the help of Andy and Jean, they began to arrange a series of exciting secret encounters.

"Jean and I lived in a large apartment building that looked something like those communist complexes that were built all over North Korea and East Berlin. Every evening as the sun went down, I would creep nervously up onto the dreary roof. And there would be Mbaraka, patiently waiting for me. Talk about romantic! Just try to imagine a sultry night, a star-studded sky, a mellow moon, and two young lovers looking out over a shimmering sea. Was it any wonder that I was captivated?"

They started getting bolder and bolder, eventually arranging clandestine meetings at the cinema in Mombassa. "Andy would buy two tickets and he and Mbaraka would walk into the theater alone. Then Jean and I would follow, also alone. Once inside, we would meet up together. This was the way of Muslim life. Everything was possible with a little skillful planning. And honest to God, it made life so much more exciting."

Elaine's second mission contract ended and she reluctantly returned to Wales. Mbaraka kept on writing, saying he would soon be able to visit her in Britain. Of course, she never thought it would really happen. After all, how could he afford to buy a ticket to England on a fisherman's earnings? Nevertheless, he worked and saved and after two years' effort, he was getting steadily closer to his goal.

When his travel plans began to take shape, and when it looked like they might become more reality than fantasy, Elaine began scouting around the bucket shops in London for bargain airline tickets. However, long distance arrangements such as these often became snared in endless complications. Mbaraka needed American dollars to purchase the tickets and, because tight currency exchange restrictions were in effect at the time, there was no legal way to get his hands on the dollars. But, love conquered all. With some shrewd back-street trading in Mombassa, Mbaraka overcame the second hurdle. He now had the necessary hard currency for the fare.

Then the almost insurmountable task of trying to get a valid passport began, with a mountain of documentation to accumulate and awkward questions to answer. "Why are you leaving the country? Is anybody sponsoring you in England? How much money are you taking out of the country? Are you carrying any gems, drugs, or precious metals? Will you be studying in England? Do you have tax clearance?" Nine months later, and following multiple applications and repeated interviews, Mbaraka was finally on his way.

But he nearly didn't make it out of Heathrow Airport. As soon as he had disembarked, Mbaraka was led away and detained by immigration authorities. They suspected that he was an illegal immigrant because he was carrying very little cash. Elaine meanwhile was outside the gate, trying frantically to find out whether or not he had been on board. All the other passengers had exited. To make matters worse, Mbaraka's English was so bad that he wasn't able to explain about his British girl friend.

In desperation, he produced a letter from Elaine that outlined his travel itinerary and had further instructions about what to say to the immigration authorities. Unfortunately, it was all written in Kiswahili and the officials would not believe that a Briton had written it. After an hour of frantic enquiries, Elaine discovered Mbaraka's predicament and rescued him from imminent deportation.

Elaine had secured a permanent teaching post in Cardiff and Mbaraka joined her there. When his tourist visa expired, she accompanied him to the immigration authorities and requested an extension on grounds of a family crisis. This was the start of a two-year process, always petitioning the authorities for additional visa extensions. The whole situation became very fraught because Elaine was not sure, even at that stage, whether or not she wanted to marry Mbaraka.

When Elaine had lived in Lamu, she had thrown herself headlong into the Muslim way of life. It had been fun - exciting and exotic. Furthermore, she always knew that it would come to an end. Now on home ground and under the gray British skies, things looked a whole lot different. Her family had initially welcomed Mbaraka as a friend of their daughter, but as his stay began to extend indefinitely, they became more and more anxious and far less welcoming. Mbaraka was thoroughly unsuitable as a marriage partner for their daughter and they wanted him out of Elaine's life forever.

Mbaraka supported himself by working as a casual laborer on the docks and on various building sites. But times were tough in Britain, in the 1980s, and illegal immigrants were not in general favor. They were competing with local men for a few scarce jobs. "Would anything short of true love drive a man to leave a magical tropical island and choose to live in a climate as hostile as ours, and under such depressing conditions?" wondered Elaine, as she pondered her future. Mbaraka had had a good life in Lamu. He'd had an independent livelihood, his Islamic culture, and the support of a loving family. They were not poor and he had not been persecuted. His life had been good. Nonetheless, he had given it all up in exchange for the life of an illegal, unemployed, and unprotected immigrant in Britain.

Mbaraka's big break finally came when he secured a job as a waiter at a well-known Arabic restaurant. He soon discovered that he had a natural flair for cooking, and he swiftly moved up the ranks to the position of assistant chef. That gave him the courage he needed to enroll in a formal cookery course. He began to study English seriously. Elaine, too, found her courage. She decided to marry Mbaraka.

It was now eight years later. They had two small children and Mbaraka and Elaine had returned to Lamu for the first time in eleven years. They had spent a small fortune on gifts before leaving Britain – dresses and shirts for the children, bolts of cloth for the women, and shirts and jackets for the men. They were leading very modest lives in Cardiff. They lived in a council house and drove an old banger of a car. But because they lived in Britain, they *had* to rich. That was a given; that was what everyone in Lamu wanted to believe. Furthermore, the family expected Elaine and Mbaraka to solve all the financial problems of the entire extended clan. They were, after all, the rich new Britons.

Elaine struggled to explain the absurdity of those misconceptions.

"They have no idea, no clue, how hard we work in Britain. Our lives in Lamu were so simple. We went to work and we rested in the afternoons when it was too hot to work. We bought what we needed for the day. If we couldn't afford something, we did without it. We were not rich but we weren't poor. Life was simple, uncomplicated, and peaceful. But in Britain, we never stop working. I am gone from home for the entire day, five days a week. Mbaraka works nights and sometimes he works on weekends to top up his earnings. We want to buy a home on the outskirts of Cardiff but we were saving for six years to pay for this trip. We probably won't be able to do it again for another ten."

It sounded tough enough. Did she have any regrets?

'No way," she replied. "Both sets of parents accepted our civil marriage. Mbaraka's family knows that he didn't become a Christian and they are happy with that. And I didn't become a Muslim."

And what about Mbaraka? How did he feel about it all? Did he have any hankerings to return to the simple life at home?

"There are no regrets there, either. He doesn't think he could go back to his old ways now. We have good friends in Cardiff and he thinks that there is a better future for our children there. He still sits on the floor to sew, he still cooks some of his old dishes, and he still speaks Kiswahili, now and then. But now he speaks English, too, and he carries a British passport."

Mombassa and Lamu; they were East Africa in microcosm. There was the rigid Muslim world of the town, and some would say, the decadent western world of the beaches - the black spiders on Kenyatta Avenue, where not an inch of flesh was revealed, and the skimpy bikinis on Ngali Beach, where hardly an inch was covered. There was the daily struggle for survival outside the gates, and the lazy indulgence of those within. It was a murky but true picture of the newly emerging and very complex Africa.

Chapter Three
SAFARIS

Our fortnight's Christmas holiday sprint across Tanzania had begun.

❧

Moshi is Kiswahili for smoke, and it is also the name of the town at the foot of Mount Kilimanjaro and base camp for all those intrepid climbers about to embark on their valiant quests to scale her peak.

That was, undoubtedly, a lofty endeavor and I had nothing but admiration for all those so inclined. I could only imagine their exhilaration as they stood on her snowcapped summit, within a hand's reach of the heavens, looking down upon the world at their feet. Alas, I was not made of such stern stuff. From among this confederation of five women, my four daughters and myself, Geraldine Ann could have made the strongest challenge. But that would be another day's work. We were on our way to Tarangire National Park and we had decided to break our journey in Moshi. It seemed blasphemous to be so close to this world class natural wonder and not pay due homage, if only for a short while. So we detoured at the junction for Arusha and headed eastwards towards the great mountain.

The entrance to Kilimanjaro National Park was obscured by thick groundcover and meandering trails. This colossus of a mountain was towering above us, yet we were unable to find out how to get to it. That should have been a red flag alert for things to come. Were we actually having trouble finding an access road? But we carried on circling and marveling at the absurdity of it all, until we eventually happened upon the right trail.

We entered a vast car park close to the gates and were instantly set upon by hoards of mountain porters offering us their services. It was already mid-day and any self-respecting climber had long since departed. It would take three days to climb to the summit and two days to descend. We, on the other hand, were mere dilettantes. We knew our limitations, so our goal was to reach the first resting point. "We hardly need porters for such a modest expedition," we thought.

However, at the reception desk we were informed that climbers could not enter the park without a guide - no matter how brief their intended climb. After some consideration, we decided, well, yes, that did seem reasonable. There was no telling how or why people might wander off from the designated trails and become lost for all eternity in the vast wilderness. And we were also relieved to see that we were not the only wimps around. There were a lot more philistines stumbling about, just like us, setting off for a comfortable, leisurely afternoon's stroll.

But the outrageous demands from self-appointed guides were downright laughable. The first "official" guide asked for $70.00 per person, with a straight face – and there were five of us. Although I must say, he did look every inch the part. But did we? Now, honestly, did we look like mountain climbers? While he was wearing a bottle-green quilted cotton vest over a long-sleeved denim shirt, faded blue jeans, and some very classy looking climbing boots, we were all dressed up in trailing cotton skirts and rubber-soled runners. However, our discordantly genteel appearance didn't seem to faze him at all! He was game to take us wherever we wanted to go. "I'll just point you in the right the direction and we will be away." When we enquired about the duration of his prospective climb, without any packs of any kind, he coolly responded – one hour up and one hour down.

We laughed out loud! Three hundred and fifty dollars for a two-hour stroll! I didn't think so! He didn't see the humor in any of it and indignantly took himself off to seek a set of more agreeable clients, clients with more honest and sincere intent.

Within a few short seconds, another string of would-be guides was jostling around us. They were not nearly as impressive a sight and we were not at all sure we wanted to be accompanied by such fair-weather guides. After all, they looked frighteningly like ourselves, all dressed up in their Sunday best with slip-on shoes, white socks, and soft, billowing trousers. "How can these be guides?" we asked ourselves.

They were all talking together, shouting into our faces, haggling and badgering us, and we were rapidly reaching the conclusion that we really didn't need to do this after all. What was the big deal about Kilimanjaro anyway? Hadn't we already seen her peak as we drove through the gates that morning? Then, in the middle of all the confusion, Kaniah rushed in to our rescue, and with her now flawless Swahili she managed to put a whole new spin on things. "How could they possibly have mistaken us for rich tourists? We were poor volunteers." They were all apologies. The price of the tour plummeted to ten dollars apiece. "Now you're talking! We'll take it."

After paying the park entrance fee and the guide's fee, we started off, feeling more and more like imposters with every step we took. We wore no mountain boots, no flak jackets, and no bulging backpacks. Haggard but triumphant climbers passed us on their way down, stark relief and self-satisfaction stamped all over their confident gaits. We demurely walked on, thinking out loud, "This isn't what anyone could call a climb - yet." I was beginning to think that I might have been selling myself short all along. The girls were sprinting on ahead of me but I had not even hit the panting stage.

"What makes these climbers think they're so great?" I mused. "We could really do this if we put our minds to it." We were beginning to enjoy this adventure, chatting amongst ourselves, joking and laughing and observing everything that was going on around us. We passed a park ranger who was coming off his tour-of-duty on the back range. He had been out tracking poachers on the far side of the mountain. We took that to mean the Kenyan side.

"What were the poachers after?" we enquired, innocently.

"Lions," came the reply.

"Oh, I see." Well, let's just think about all of this again.

Within no time at all, we were at the first resting point. We kept a respectful distance from the genuine mountaineers who were deep into technical conversations with their climbing companions. "We could go on like this for another hour – or two," we thought. "It's been no punishment at all." But alas, we had other plans. "Maybe we'll do it another time." And we sailed off to the descent, returning to base camp feeling just great. True philistines to the last, that's what we were! Roll on, Arusha!

Our real interest in going to Arusha National Park was to see the flamingoes. Somewhere along the line, I had picked up the misguided impression that flamingoes were an endangered species and I thought we should see them before they disappeared off the face of the earth - like the dinosaurs. So there we were, standing at the gates of the park when we had the great good fortune to meet up with a group of Danish foreign aid workers. They were spending a few weeks studying at a Swahili language course in Arusha and they cordially invited us to join them. They had four of the most extraordinarily well-behaved young children I had ever met, in their group. And I wondered, not for the first time, what was it about Africa that had this magical, tranquilizing effect on every single child?

Arusha National Park was more renowned for its natural beauty than for its prolific wildlife, so the small number of animals in sight did not disappoint us. We climbed up to a designated observation post overlooking a small crater and were able to view scattered herds of elephants, zebras, gazelles, and giraffes grazing contentedly in the far distance. We caught the wistful whiff of summer jasmine in the air and heard the rhythmic tap-tap-tap of a busy woodpecker. Willowy corn lilies swayed in the gentle morning breeze.

We reboarded the van and drove on, most of us slumbering off into a heat-induced trance. The hill trails were heavily forested and squadrons of chattering monkeys swung through the trees. Then we turned a bend on the hill, and suddenly a hemorrhage of brilliant pink appeared in the far distance. Millions of flamingoes were watering at a lake, but the water was completely buried beneath the blanket of downy feathers. "Where did I ever pick up the demented idea that flamingoes were an endangered species?" I wondered to myself. Sometimes I confounded myself with my own misinformation.

Having accomplished our modest mission and photographed that incredible sight just in case I might have been right, we bade farewell to our companions and set off to spend the night at the Uruhu Lutheran Hostel in Moshi - a scrupulously clean and friendly · establishment that offered a full dinner menu including steak, fresh fish, and ice cream. What more could anyone want?

◦◦◦

Arusha was the jewel of the north and the epicenter of Tanzania's safari industry. In the heady days following national independence, Arusha had become a thriving business town complete with gracious parks, fashionable tourist hotels, and a bright new international conference center. However, over the intervening years, much of Arusha's glow had tarnished, caught as it was in the general economic downturn of the country. But it was valiantly fighting back. Although it, too, had all the usual pot-holed streets, broken footpaths, and shops screaming for a coat of paint, the maniacal disorder of Dar es Salaam was not shrilly evident.

Arusha had the calm, quiet step befitting its regal surroundings. In the early morning light, long before billowing white clouds descended over the snowcapped peaks of Mount Meru and Kilimanjaro, Arusha slumbered. Zebra-striped safari vans filled hotel car parks, and khaki-clad tourists roamed her streets looking much like the herds of game they had come to see. Arusha was the closest I had come, so far, to the picture stored away in my mind's eye, of Africa.

Our destination was Tarangire National Park. It was the 23rd of December and the temperature stood at thirty degrees Celsius. Although this was marginally cooler than it had been in Korogwe, we were still covered in dust and dripping with sweat.

December was one of the busiest months on the tourist calendar and we had made no prior arrangements for accommodation. We had tried, but attempting to communicate by telephone from Korogwe had been a dead loss. Then, when we finally managed to get through from Arusha, the receptionist told us that the park was already fully booked. But the girls were determined that they would not leave Tanzania without seeing some serious animals. So we decided to press on and chance our luck. If all else failed, we could possibly get a day pass into the park and return to a hotel in Arusha for the night.

The road leading up to Tarangire Park had none of the splendor that we had seen on glossy tourist travel brochures. Tanzania was not Kenya and Tanzanian parks remained largely unspoiled. Dirt tracks disappeared off the main road and wove their way through vast expanses of natural scrub and dense undergrowth. The coarse, wild grass was like shrunken brown straw, and the wind-battered trees were sparse and gnarled. We did not meet a single vehicle along the entire stretch of road. "How on earth can that be?" we asked one another. "Weren't we just told that the park was completely full?" So when we turned into the reception area and approached the desk, we were feeling a little more hopeful.

Our hopes were instantly realized! The receptionist offered us two luxury, tented lodges. We would have been thrilled out of our minds to get a regulation tent in the campsite. But lodges? Now that was something special. Merry Christmas! We were deliriously happy!

⟨∽⟩

*Safar*i is the Swahili word for a journey, and for *wazungu* that journey usually meant circling around a wildlife park in a zebra-striped van looking for and observing animals. Our *safari* started the next morning, Christmas Eve, at daybreak. We skipped breakfast. We had lost our appetites in the savage heat, and anyway, we wanted to be on the prowl when the big animals set out for the kill. Although we had lucked out royally with our accommodation, we had not been quite as fortunate with the guides. All the *safari* vans and their guides were indeed fully booked, so we decided we were up to doing this *safari* thing for ourselves. After all, hadn't we surpassed all our own expectations on Kilimanjaro? With a reliable vehicle under us and with five intelligent women guiding the way, what could go wrong?

We had not driven five hundred yards out of the lodge gate when a golden lioness lumbered out of the bush and crossed directly in front of our car. It caught us so unaware that we didn't know whether to stop stock-still and stare or crawl along as quietly as we could and follow her. That was the defining moment for the rest of the day. "Go on! No, stop! Shh! Be quiet! Who has the camera? Get off my bag!" Before we could settle on what we should be doing, the imperious lion made his appearance and passed so close to us that he practically brushed the front fender of our car. He proceeded to follow on after his mate, across the brittle plains, with his tawny mane rippling in the morning breeze.

We were gripped with an almost uncontrollable urge to flee the van, steal across the road, crouch under a bush, and watch. But that would have been the height of pure madness. Those animals had appeared from out of nowhere. This was their turf. Tourists in fully equipped *safari* vans, complete with open-topped roof hatches, were able to observe the largest, most dangerous animals in complete safety. We, on the other hand, would have to content ourselves with craning our necks and jostling for position inside the cramped interior of an ordinary passenger vehicle.

The lioness and her mate settled down under the shade of a spreading jacaranda and were soon joined by another lioness and several cubs. More than likely, they had already dined on their kill and were now settling down to pass the heat of the day. We couldn't believe our luck. If we had passed that way just a few minutes later, we would have missed them altogether. And we didn't spot another cat for the rest of the trip.

All the wilderness trails were clearly marked out with arrows, so we were feeling reasonably confident. In truth, we turned out to be more like the Keystone Kops than *safari* trekkers. We drove up blind alleys, backtracked, reversed, and lunged ahead again, only to find that we were going in circles and in grave danger of invading some dozing animal's private space. Every one of the girls had her own ideas about what we should be doing, and how we should be doing it. But there was one really thorny problem impeding progress. We couldn't agree on any one of the ideas. So we bashed on regardless, the blind leading the blind. Fortunately, there were so many elephants, giraffes, zebras, wildebeest, gazelles, buffalo, monkeys, and baboons under every bush and in every tree that we would have to have been deaf, dumb, and blind to miss them.

Every twist in the road revealed a new and more awesome sight, eliciting stunned gasps and loud shrieks of joy. Giraffes, with their impossibly long, sleek necks, towered above the trees, their dark, doleful eyes fixed languidly on the staring strangers. Platoons of monkeys, with babies clinging to their backs, swung gracefully through the trees. Mighty baboons preened and groomed one another under the shade of spreading branches. Streams of silky gazelles pirouetted through the air. Ungainly wildebeest moved in tight packs, attempting to stay out of harm's way, while daintily striped zebras grazed peacefully on tufts of coarse grass. Herd after herd of elephants lumbered along, the perennial search for water guiding their way.

The first rush of excitement began to wane as the intense heat of late afternoon began to take its toll. We decided that it would be a good idea to return to the lodge for a cool drink and an evening rest.

That was easier said than done. We had become so thoroughly disoriented in the vast wilderness that we couldn't find our way back to the lodge. Every bush and every tree that we had noted as a marker looked identical to the one that had come before it.

"I'm dead certain that we passed that tree on the way out. I remember the bare branches on the windward side," offered one expert in the group.

But then, we passed half a dozen carbon copies.

Or, "Wait! There's the termite hill. Yes, this is the right way! I'm sure we passed it earlier!" offered another.

Of course we did. We'd been back and forth that road at least a dozen times already. "On exactly *which* journey did we pass it the first time? And in what direction had we been going? And where should we be going now?" I asked. There were no answers.

Every herd of elephants looked familiar and every baboon had a face we'd seen before; every giraffe lurking behind a tree was the one that we had seen first thing that morning. On top of everything else, we were running dangerously low on petrol. We'd been circling around the same spot, like hungry jackdaws, for an hour or more, and we were digging ourselves deeper and deeper into the bush. We hadn't passed another vehicle in all that time. I began to worry about what might happen to people who got lost out there. We didn't have an official guide, so who would know if we never returned? How long would it be before some startled tourists found our bodies fried in the blazing sun, with hungry lions tearing the doors off our car? I was beginning to hallucinate.

Suddenly Aisling leapt up in the back seat of our car. She'd had an apparition.

"Hey guys, look, there's the lake! Remember the one we saw on the map at the lodge this morning? It's straight ahead of us."

And sure enough, there it was, the lovely lake we had seen on the map, shimmering away in the afternoon heat.

"Well, since we've come all this way, we should drive on and make the day complete. We'll just go to the lakeside. It can only be another few hundred yards more, and the guide book says that rhinos usually water at this lake." For once, we were all agreed. We hadn't seen any hippos or rhinos and the day was rapidly coming to an end.

We drove on, and on, and on. The water was just there. Aisling could see it. It was right in front of us.

"Keep going, just a little farther." Gamely, she urged us on.

The mountain range that had been in the far distance kept coming closer and closer but we had not yet hit the lake.

Geraldine Ann decided that it was time to stop and take stock.

We all piled out of the car and looked back over the way we had just come. There was nothing to see but the lonely tracks of our car trailing across the dry, parched sand. We were in the middle of a desert. Or not quite – we were in the middle of a dried-up lake – and we had been following a ghostly mirage.

It was one of those," Good God Almighty," moments. There was not another living, breathing soul around, neither man nor beast. There was not a breeze in the air, nor a bird in the sky. There was absolute and complete silence. It felt like we were the only people on earth. We were just about overcome by the power of the moment.

But, back to reality. Light was fading fast and we had to get out of there.

"Right. Seriously now. Who knows the way back?" I demanded. There were no takers.

"Dear God, we should never be let out alone. And I should never be allowed behind the wheel of a car. I couldn't find my way our of a paper sack with a compass. But since I am the only one insured to drive this thing, we are stuck with me. We are a seriously pathetic lot," I moaned, and barreled on.

"Were the mountains on our right or left when we left this morning?" I asked. That gave some indication about the level of our orienteering skills; right, left, up and down. After that, we were lost.

"Breifní, just cut it out! This is no time to start hyperventilating!" I heard from the back seat.

"Geraldine Ann, get us to hell out of here!" whispered a very chastened Aisling.

And miraculously, she did. We had a few false starts, a few bad turns, a few skids, a few narrow scrapes with hideous mountains that kept coming our way, but nothing much to talk about. As a blazing sun went down over the African plains and as daylight turned to night, we cruised blissfully through the gates of our lodge, with our petrol tank on empty.

It had been a very dry season and there was very little grazing land left for foraging animals. Our parkland tents sat on top of a promontory that overlooked the Tarangire River. In the quiet of the evening light, we sat out in front of our tents, listening to the sounds of the bush. Giraffes loped along, with their long graceful necks silhouetted against the setting sun. A herd of thirsty zebra watered at the shrunken river. We had been warned not to bring food back to our tents, as prowling animals could be very dangerous. We had already seen a family of baboons sniffing around our tents earlier that evening. They had shown no fear. They boldly stood their ground and spat viciously at us as we passed by.

It was Christmas Eve and the park staff had prepared an outdoor barbecue for the lodge guests. A golden thorn-needle tree, draped with twinkling fairly lights, sat in the middle of dozens of flickering candles. The air was filled with intoxicating smells. The anarchy of city life was lost in the timeless order of Tarangire. Noise, fumes, speed, and strain succumbed to the brooding stillness of the African plains.

We returned to our tents and to sleep. The next day would be Christmas.

Sometime around dawn, I woke up with a start and lay dead still on my cot - listening. I could feel the cold presence of something outside our tent and I could barely breathe with fright. Kaniah stirred. She was also awake - tense and listening. Then we heard the deep rumbling growl of a lion.

We were frozen to our beds, straining to catch the sound of the animal's movements. We could hear him, or her, panting heavily as it padded and brushed against the tent. I knew that Kaniah was rigid with fear but neither of us stirred. I heard the muted sounds of a car revving up in the distance, and then silence fell once again.

We lay motionless for what felt like hours, listening and waiting. The movement had stopped. Dawn broke and I tentatively unsnapped the screened window flaps on our tent. All was still. Whatever had been there was now gone. We could see only the orange glow of another brilliant sunrise creeping over the horizon.

The three girls in the other tent had heard nothing. At first, they dismissed our ravings about prowling lions with veiled suggestions of heatstroke. But the discovery of incriminating tracks outside the back of our tent corroborated our story. My heart palpitations receded. Everything looked better in daylight.

As we passed our neighbor's tent on the way to breakfast, he stuck his head out of the flap and shouted, "Merry Christmas!" It sounded so nice. But this was certainly a strange way to spend Christmas morning.

Our neighbor was from New York City and he had just attended a cousin's wedding in Uganda. He hadn't been able to convince any of his family to accompany him on his *safari* to Tanzania, so he had come alone. He, too, was missing the cold and snappy Christmases back home.

Over a breakfast of tangy tropical fruits and creamy hot chocolate, we compared the virtues of Christmases past. There was no place on earth like New York City for the holidays. The dazzling windows on Fifth Avenue and stylish skaters in Rockefeller Center. The biting cold, the snow-packed streets, the roasted chestnuts, and busy shoppers. Santa Claus on every corner and Christmas carols in the air.

But nothing could compare with Christmas in dear old Dublin. Holly wreaths on Grafton Street and Cheeky Charlies at the fairs. The stinging rain, the hot whiskeys, the sticky buns, and Christmas puddings. Charity boxes on every corner and cathedral bells in the air.

❧

Christmas Mass in Arusha turned out to be more than we had bargained for. As soon as we appeared at the back of the church, we were immediately ushered into an already jam-packed pew. *Silent Night* sounded every bit as joyous as at Midnight Mass back home, and we settled comfortably into attending the morning service.

Then, as the Offertory Procession assembled in the middle aisle, a parish usher appeared at Aisling's side and invited her to carry the chalice. A look of sheer panic shot across her face and sent the rest of us into convulsions. This was a very kind and gracious gesture offered to us, as visitors, and Aisling absolutely had to oblige. But Aisling would have been the last one of the girls to ever step into the limelight. Kaniah and Breifní, on the other hand, would have taken it all in their stride.

We dared not look up as she came back down from the altar, for fear of exploding into gales of undignified laughter. Then, as Aisling regained her seat and we struggled to compose ourselves, a Tanzanian woman who had been standing directly behind us, reached over and dropped a newborn baby into Aisling's lap. She turned and disappeared.

At that stage, we became nearly helpless with suppressed laughter. Horror was written all over Aisling's face. What was she meant to do? Did Tanzanian women offer their babies to the first *mzungu* who came along? Was this meant to be a generous Christmas present? The baby, blissfully unaware of the commotion he was causing, went on gurgling and chewing his fist as Aisling's eyes grew bigger and bigger.

Mercifully, the baby's mother returned before the end of mass and, without a word, calmly retrieved her child. Where she had gone, and why, God only knew. We left the church weak in the knees, with Aisling fleeing ahead of us. God forbid she should become ensnared in anything else! And we were about to begin an unforgettable journey home.

There was a long stretch of road between Arusha and Moshi that was absolutely treacherous. It was covered in loose gravel, and speeding cars hurled storms of tiny stones up against our car windows as they hurtled along. I was driving a reasonably new Land Cruiser and I was crawling. But I was taking no chances. This journey demanded one hundred percent concentration. The cars that sped past us looked like they were held together with sticky tape – and they were traveling like rockets. We all breathed sighs of relief when we finally hit the hard top with our windscreen still intact. Then just as we began to relax, the car skidded violently and swerved clear off the road. Right at the entrance to town, we had busted a tire.

What rotten luck! We, who had been inching along at a snail's pace, had busted a tire, while those desperadoes in beat-up jalopies whizzed right on past us. As soon as we jumped down from the cab to have a look, a small crowd of shouting, jostling men descended on us. They were like a swarm of locust. It was Christmas Day and the only service station in town was closed up tight. But, "Not to worry," called Geraldine Ann as she dug out the spanner and the jack. "We can handle this ourselves."

We thanked the crowd of excited men for their concern and their gracious offers of assistance, but we assured them that we were fine. Really, we were! We were well able for this task. It was no more than a minor inconvenience. But their offers were becoming more boisterous, and more insistent, and the small crowd was beginning to grow. In fact, it was actually ballooning!

We wanted to get the tire changed, *go tapaidh*, and get the blazes out of there. So we continued to unlock the tools and position the jack. They were suddenly wrenched from our hands. Men began grabbing at the tools from all sides, aggressively demanding money to change the tire. Unfortunately, we had unlatched the spare from the back of the truck before the turmoil had begun, and Breifní was trying desperately to hold onto it. In fact, she was sitting on it. She knew it was in terrible danger of disappearing down the street. Everyone was shouting and pushing and the whole scene was rapidly careering out of control.

The temperature was soaring and the crowd was growing ugly, getting nastier and more frightening by the minute. "Africa for Africans," was the chilling pronouncement that we heard coming from one of the ringleaders.

Geraldine Ann spotted the white uniform of a policeman who was watching the melee from a distance, but who showed no inclination to intervene. So she sprinted off in his direction. Surely, he would come to our assistance. Surprisingly, he was in no great hurry to help. He slowly shuffled up to the vehicle, cast a quizzical eye over the four of us, who were now surrounded by a very hostile crowd, and snarled:

"What is the problem here? Don't you want to pay to change the tire?"

We were slightly taken aback by that, but Geraldine Ann rushed on to explain that we didn't really need help. If they would all just move back and leave us to it, we could manage the job ourselves. We were grateful for their concern, but we had all changed tires before. It wasn't a very difficult task.

Kaniah was locked in the car with the purses, the suitcases, the Christmas presents, and the cameras; and she was suffocating in there. But we were afraid to open the door to let her out.

This crowd had become a mob and the policeman seemed to be part and parcel of it.

The jack and the rest of the tools had, by now, been yanked from our hands and one of the men was under the car, jamming boulders under the axle in a fruitless attempt to set the jack on the boulders and raise the truck. In my frantic mind, I could see him smashing the jack and leaving us stranded in that inhospitable place, with the car and all of its contents thoroughly looted.

So I turned to the policeman and suggested that if he agreed to send the crowd away, I would pay one man to change the tire. He promptly turned on the crowd and snarled again, but this time he was delivering orders. Reluctantly, the crowd dispersed, leaving us with only the policeman and his chosen candidate for the job.

I asked him how much the job would cost.

"Forty-five US dollars," he answered, without turning a hair. And Tanzanian shillings would not be accepted. Only US dollars would do.

We knew that it was now out of our hands. It was a case of pay up or they would strip the car.

It took half an hour to get the simple job done. The policeman and his pal had enjoyed a profitable day's work and we couldn't get out to town fast enough. We resumed our long drive home in silence. We were physically and emotionally drained. We wouldn't forget that Christmas Day anytime soon!

We spent two quiet days in Korogwe, regrouping and regaining our senses, before starting off on the next leg of our trip – to Dar es Salaam and Zanzibar.

A steady stream of bewildered-looking tourists passed along the harbor at Dar es Salaam, dragging themselves and their backpacks through the sweltering heat. We melted into the herd, all dreamy travelers drawn irresistibly to the mysteries of the Spice Islands.

The ticket agent offered us a choice between first, second, and third class accommodation on the "Flying Horse" catamaran, or the deluxe "Sea Empress," a modern hydrofoil that promised us a "speedy, superior experience". We opted for the latter and found ourselves imprisoned in dwarf-sized seats that left us gasping for air We hadn't been told that passengers on the hydrofoil were required to remain seated for the duration of the journey and that there was no air-conditioning on board. And we hadn't thought to ask. We then enjoyed seventy-five minutes of blood-curdling violence, as dismembered bodies flashed across a giant video screen directly in front of us. Our fellow passengers laughed and clapped as cars crashed, arms and legs smashed, and heads rolled in this made-for-export, triple-X rated movie. We decided that we would take the slow boat back to Dar.

❦

Following independence in 1964, Tanganyika, on the mainland, had joined with the islands of Zanzibar, Mafia, and Pemba to form a new nation called Tanzania. So, upon our disembarkation at Zanzibar, we were surprised to discover that we were required to present our passports for inspection and comply with all the usual immigration procedures, even though we had already done all of that on our initial arrival in Dar es Salaam. We were even more surprised to discover that, although mainland Tanzanians were also required to follow the same regulations when entering Zanzibar, the reverse did not apply. Zanzibaris were permitted free and unrestricted travel to the mainland. It seemed, to us, to be a glaring case of double standards. We decided that mainland Tanzanians had to be among the most extraordinarily tolerant people in the world!

Pandemonium reigned at the immigration office. We struggled valiantly to complete our landing forms while our bags were wrestled off our backs. We were slowly catching on to the fact that traveling in Africa amounted to a running series of battles to hold onto one's possessions. The fewer the possessions - the fewer the battles that had to be fought. Once that little lesson was learned, life became considerably easier.

One overly zealous "culture guide," attached himself to us and accompanied us, uninvited, to our hotel in Stone Town. Short of being downright rude, it was virtually impossible to shake him off. He wanted to plan our days and nights for us, book our tours for us, hire taxis for us, and buy treasures for us. We decided to give him the silent treatment since our consistently polite, "No, thank you," was having no effect at all, at all! It worked. He eventually tired of our blank stares and left us in peace.

Our hotel was a little jewel wedged in among a psychedelic collage of Arabic ruins. Age and decay were the very ingredients that had lured us there. So many European cities were now interchangeable with their cold, clean lines of glass and steel. The rubble and ruins of places like Zanzibar hinted of dark secrets from the past, just waiting and tempting us to unearth them. Invariably, we rose to the bait.

Shadowy figures slithered along dark alleys. Black-hooded Muslim women flitted in and out of magnificently carved and brass-studded doors. Grizzled old men squatted in darkened doorways, silently sucking on their pipes - and watching. Twisted laneways opened into dirt-packed squares where clutches of men and boys gathered under the starry sky, their long white robes iridescent in the feeble gaslight. And a haunting call to prayer boomed out from the minaret of a nearby mosque. We were bewitched.

We had booked a spice tour of the island for the next morning. Our guide, Muhammad, met us in the small reception area of our hotel. He had left his taxi at the end of the lane because the passage was too narrow to accommodate a car. His taxi was, quite literally, falling apart. We had to keep a firm hold of the passenger door to prevent it from flying off. But Muhammad, himself, was the second jewel that we found in Zanzibar.

Either he truly loved his job or he was a brilliant actor, because Muhammad glowed with the joys of life. He smiled and chatted, he climbed trees to fetch fruits, he greeted every islander as a friend, and he gave us the grand tour. He plunged us deep into the interior and intoxicated us with the tastes and smells of cloves, nutmeg, peppers, ginger, aniseed, swamp apples, and pineapples. We sampled them all. We sipped fresh juice from coconut shells and stopped at a roadside stand for freshly ground, deep rich coffee. We ate donuts fried in sizzling coconut oil. We painted our nails with henna. We stopped to talk with little boys returning from Friday morning mosque and had our first lesson in the truths of the Quaran.

The history of Zanzibar was inextricably linked with the history of the slave trade. In the early part of the nineteenth century, the Omani commercial empire had spread its influence into East Africa and onto the islands of Zanzibar and Pemba.

The reign of Sayid Said bin Sultan began in 1806 and ended with his death in 1856. During that time, he acquired large tracts of land, which he put under private cultivation. He also encouraged the immigration of other wealthy, land-hungry Arabs in order to consolidate his power. By the year 1837, he had moved the capital of the Omani empire from Muscat to Zanzibar.

The basis of the Sultan's wealth lay in the intense cultivation of coconut and clove plantations. Coconuts were grown to serve the increasing world demand for oil, and cloves were an essential ingredient in Arabic and Indian dishes. Both crops flourished in Zanzibar's fertile soil and under its hot, tropical sun. Furthermore, both crops produced several harvests every year. But since the success of this plantation economy depended upon a continuing supply of cheap labor, a growing slave trade from the mainland began to fill that need.

Long before the coming of the Arab traders, indigenous tribes of Africans had forged their own trails from the interior of Tanganyika to the Indian Ocean - engaged in an active trade of ivory and salt for glassware, hoes, and other farming implements. The Arab caravans of the early nineteenth century began to follow those long-established native routes, traveling to the interior with cloth, firearms and beads and returning with ivory and slaves.

African chiefs sold local criminals, captured prisoners of war, and anyone else who posed a threat to their power, into slavery. But when the demand for slaves began to increase and those usual sources could not meet the demand, widespread kidnapping ensued. The kidnapped slaves were transported to the coast under brutal conditions. They endured relentless forced marches with very little food or water, and were shackled together in iron collars and heavy ankle chains. Those who survived were either sold to Arab plantation owners on Zanzibar or shipped onwards to the Arab states in the North Indian Ocean. The more fortunate of them went south to plantations on the islands of the Seychelles. .

One of the main trails started at the interior settlement of Tabora and headed east to the coastal town of *Bagamoyo*: Swahili for "lay down my heart". And it was from that heart-breaking port that the cruel, but lucrative, slave trade to the east had burgeoned.

By the middle of the nineteenth century, more than half the population of Zanzibar was made up of slaves. And by the year 1850, seventy percent of the inhabitants of Bagamoyo had converted to Islam.

Slavery was officially abolished in Zanzibar in the year of 1897, but a clandestine slave trade continued to flourish along the coast well into the early part of the twentieth century. The economy of the island would have collapsed without it. After abolition, however, the living conditions of freed slaves became worse. As slaves, they had been treated as valuable investments. It had been in the interest of the plantation owners to keep them well fed and healthy. Following abolition, however, those same masters hired back their former slaves but paid wages so low that the freed slaves could scarcely survive. So, although slavery had been technically abolished, the brutal reality of exploitation on a scale even worse than before continued for generations to come.

Clove and coconut plantations remained the foundation of the island's economy right up to the present time. The site of the old slave market was also preserved, looking much as it had when those benighted souls of long ago had stumbled off mainland *dhows* and fallen into its underground chambers. And it was there that they had awaited their fates on the auction blocks.

After showing us the slave chambers and the slave market, Muhammad took us up to the highest point on Zanzibar. It was all of twenty-feet above sea level. From this vantage point, the Sultan Sayid could view the harbor and the ocean and enjoy the company of his harem when the temperatures and humidity of town became too oppressive. The ruins of what had been an elaborate compound, with opulent open baths for his numerous wives and concubines, remained intact, and confirmed the reality of what otherwise might have appeared to be no more than a royal fantasy.

⁓

It was hard to get a true fix on Dar es Salaam, because it had so many faces. The most obvious one, and the one that really jolted, was the cold and brutal face of poverty living side by side with conspicuous wealth.

Shortly after our initial arrival in Dar es Salaam, we were sitting in the middle of a massive traffic jam, suffocating with the heat. I had rolled down the side window of the project vehicle and stretched out to see if there was any hope of imminent release. What might have been a cat or a dog, but in fact was a human cripple, was crawling painfully between the cars, his hands and knees bound in worn rubber pads. Impatient drivers, including myself, in their spanking new Land Rovers and Land Cruisers, honked and bleated their horns, oblivious to his very existence. I was stupefied. That most wretched of men slowly and ponderously dragged his shrunken legs after him, while fashionably dressed young men in their baggy silk trousers hurried past, self-absorbed, throwing him not even a glance.

I could have driven right over him. My stomach lurched and

sickening bile retched up into my mouth. I saw similar sights many times after that. Every town in Africa had its share. But each time was like the first time. I got a helpless, piercing stab in the pit of my stomach. It was like hurtling down into a dark and terrible chasm, a pit that was black with guilt. "Why do we have so much and do so little?"

The population of Dar was growing at a frightening rate and neither housing nor public services could keep pace. In 1988, twenty percent of the population of Tanzania lived in cities. By the year 2004, the rate was expected to reach forty percent or more. This phenomenal growth was largely uncontrolled and unplanned. Local municipal and district councils were empowered to allocate large tracts for public housing and sell individual sites for private dwellings. But in reality, government funds for public housing had been abysmally small in the past and were steadily shrinking, instead of growing with public demand.

As was the case in most developing countries, people who had any funds at all attempted to look after themselves. But ordinary Tanzanians seldom had enough money at any given time to begin and actually complete a building. So they ended up buying a site and purchasing sand and cement to make their own building blocks, bit by bit. Whenever they had a few extra shillings to spare, they made a few more bricks. This anarchic approach to the housing problem had created a potential catastrophe. Partially completed, dangerously built structures littered the city and became home to thousands of migrants from the countryside, that floating and homeless population that squatted wherever they could find cover.

Those without any means whatsoever resorted to constructing temporary shelters in the growing shantytowns on the outskirts of the city. These illegal settlements had no sanitation or waste disposal facilities at all. Crude pit latrines served as toilets in the best of circumstances. In the worst cases, squatters used open wasteland and local streams. Garbage dumps grew into mountains and existed side-by-side with human living quarters. The tips became active breeding grounds for vermin, rodents, and malarial mosquitoes. Heavy rains brought the inevitable flooding, with infectious disease spreading unimpeded throughout the settlements.

Another intriguing facet of Dar es Salaam was that, although there were no large or modern type department stores, it was possible to purchase just about anything I needed, provided I had enough money and time. The most unlikely looking little *duka* could house just about everything from the proverbial needle to the anchor. One had to take precautions, however, when flitting in and out of those *dukas*. A careless *mzungu* on a shopping spree could attract all kinds of unwanted attention. I had often experienced the uneasy sensation of someone breathing down my neck, and had to swiftly nip into a nearby hotel or cafe to thwart the impending theft.

Horrific scenes of mob justice were being played out, almost every day, in central Dar. The *Daily News* carried a story about a number of suspected thieves who had been burned alive in the middle of the city. The avenging crowd had draped rubber tire tubes around the necks of the perpetrators and then set the tubes alight. *Flaming necklaces* was the common street name for that brand of summary justice.

The same newspaper carried a series of photographs relating to another ghastly incident. The first photo showed an accused man lying on the ground, being kicked and stomped on by a gang of youths. A large crowd had gathered around to watch. The commentary went on to say that, while another youth had run off to get petrol in order to set the victim alight, a passing traffic policeman had rescued him. The alleged thief had been suspected of trying to rob a car mirror.

◦◦◦

The Indian community owned the vast majority of trading establishments in the capital city. Only the food industry seemed to be in the hands of black Tanzanians. This was the obvious and somewhat startling pattern in most cities and towns throughout the country.

The Indian community in Dar es Salaam was, generally speaking, well-educated, wealthy, and influential. They tended to live and socialize in close proximity to one another and exclude all outsiders from their intimate circles. They supported their own private schools and places of worship. Although they spoke their native languages at home, they were also fluent in Swahili and English and could easily switch into the language of choice for business purposes. Unfortunately, this culture of self-imposed isolation was beginning to foster a growing sense of resentment among the black Tanzanian community. It was a disturbing and unhealthy development for the Indian community in Tanzania - and for Tanzanian society.

◦〜੭)

The fortnight's Christmas holidays sped past and Geraldine Ann, Aisling, and Breifní were heading back to their colleges. As their departure day approached, our college principal invited us to attend a "Chat" party at his house, to say good-bye to the girls and wish them *safari nzuri.*

Another golden sunset was slipping slowly over our reclaimed *shamba* as we made our way through the maize fields to the home of our host. The guest list included college administrators and teaching staff, plus the only other Ireland Aid family in Korogwe, the Gaynors. We were all looking forward to a stimulating and enjoyable evening.

The principal's wife had arranged the grass area in front of the house in a very formal manner, with a column of straight-backed wooden chairs lined up along the rear fringe of grass. Two more rows of classroom chairs extended forward from both ends. Several long buffet tables, laden with soft drinks, beer, local *pombe,* and lashings of food faced the rear column and completed the rectangular formation.

I had a sudden premonition that this was going to be a night to remember as soon as I spotted a delegation of smartly uniformed students lining up to greet us at the entrance to the house. As they escorted the members of our party to newly upholstered, red velvet chairs, I spied an unbelievable sight from the corner of my eye. It was a television set. There it sat, in all its glory, out in the open air, in the middle of the buffet table, with a VCR propped up beside it. I hadn't seen a television anywhere in Korogwe, up until then, and I was utterly transfixed at seeing one suddenly appear in such an extraordinary setting.

As guests of honor at this very impressive gathering, the two foreign families were seated front and center, with members of the college staff spreading outwards in descending order. We were slightly overawed by the formality of it all. We had been expecting something far less regal. Unfortunately, we were unable to make out the faces of any of the people seated at the far ends of the rectangle because it had suddenly become very dark. We could, however, catch the hushed murmur of their voices.

There was one glaring problem with this precise configuration. We could only converse with those who were sitting on either side of us, and those individuals happened to be members of our own families. We could, of course, raise our voices and shout out along the line of guests. But that seemed distinctly inappropriate on such a grand occasion. Consequently, the free flow of chat was severely limited.

When all the guests had been seated, our gracious host slowly began moving along the line of chairs, greeting each visitor individually and extending heartiest salutations. A bevy of smiling college students followed closely behind, deferentially serving drinks. Our host then urged us to *feel free* to help ourselves and partake of his amazing feast. When we had all returned to our seats with overflowing plates of rice, *mchuzi,* and charcoaled goat, our principal took his position beside the television set. We were astounded to discover that we were about to view and enjoy a ninety-minute video documentary on the papal visit of Pope John Paul II to Tanzania.

A pulsating air of uncertainty began to permeate this august gathering. Were we meant to sit in respectful silence and listen to John Paul? Were we allowed to chat, as had been suggested on the invitations? Could we leave our designated seats and circulate among the guests?

A steady stream of smiling students kept appearing and the

beverages kept flowing. And with this considerable consumption of Stella Artois and local *pombe*, the initial respectful silence began to give way to raucous hilarity. By the time the video had reached the final papal blessing, the orderly formation of tables and chairs had completely collapsed. And on to the VCR leapt the gyrating, frenetic, and half-naked bodies of *Zairian Bosi Bosi* dancers!

I often got the feeling, out there in Africa, that I had wandered into the twilight zone.

❦

By ten o'clock that night, with the beer flowing and the chat buzzing, the girls and I rose to take our leave. We had an early start in the morning and the drive to Mombassa would take at least six hours on a very rough road. But at least this time our papers were all in order. So we said our thanks, bade our farewells and departed. Our host and his guests had been warm and generous. It had been nothing short of an exhilarating evening.

There were only two bedrooms in our staff house, with a single bed in each; and we had five people to accommodate. It was impossible to put sleeping bags on the floor. Armies of cockroaches, spiders, ants, and lizards were on nightly patrol. So we had set up an extra bed in the sitting room for Briefini, and Geraldine Ann and Aisling had been sleeping at the house of neighbors who were away on holidays. Everything had been working like a dream.

Those neighbors, the VSO volunteers mentioned earlier, owned a pet cat that had been surviving on scraps of food from our house, · while its owners were absent. But unlike most native cats that knew how to survive in the wild, its *wazungu* masters had ruined this one. They had been feeding her a diet of *dagaa*, tiny dried fish that were meant for human consumption, and another unheard of luxury, cow's milk. So with her owners in temporary absence, the spoiled cat had been crying outside of both houses and driving all of us crazy.

A few minutes after leaving our house to retire, the girls returned. They needed the key to their kitchen. Every door in every house had an individual key, and every door was routinely locked in order to prevent certain theft. The girls thought that if they could lock the howling cat into their rear kitchen, perhaps they could get some sleep. So they took the house keys, which had been entrusted to me, and left. Once again, I locked my front door.

They were back again within seconds. None of the keys fitted the kitchen door. "Can you keep the cat for the night?" they asked. I took it, deposited it in my kitchen, and the girls left, again. Breifní moved into Kaniah's room, to spend this last night. I switched on the security light outside my front door and retired to my bed for the third time that night.

At about four o'clock in the morning, Breifní tapped on my bedroom door. "Mom, why is the front door swinging open?" she whispered.

She had got up to go to the bathroom and had spotted the front door wide open. I turned on the light in the sitting room. Everything was gone. Breifní's mattress, sheets, pillow, and mosquito net - our only two chairs, my short-wave radio, clock, and hurricane lamp - and all of Kaniah's Christmas presents were gone. Only the bed, that was now jammed half way out the door, was left.

Thank God, before going to bed, I had put all the handbags into my bedroom, along with the suitcases. I cannot imagine what had prompted me to do that because I am not especially cautious by nature. In all the confusion, with the girls coming and going throughout the night, I must have forgotten to lock the front door the final time. No doubt, someone had been lurking in the bushes, and watching.

Breifní and I roused the rest of the family and we all stood in stupefied silence, looking from one to another and then at the empty room. I was shattered by my own carelessness. We couldn't even make a cup of tea because the kettle and all of our dried food was also gone. A fat lot of help that foolish cat had been. *She* was still there, circling and pawing and scratching around our feet, and meowing up at us like mad.

I peered into the darkness outside to see if I could spot our watchman. Sure enough, there he was, curled up on a chair in the corner of the *shamba*, snoring. He looked like a hedgehog, with his head tucked tightly inside the collar of his jacket. His bow and poisoned arrows lay uselessly beside him. Those prowling bandits had found us easy picking. Luckily, our *askari* had not awakened; otherwise he could easily have been killed.

We waited until first light, pacing the floor and wringing our hands; and then Geraldine Ann and I drove off to the project manager's house to report the robbery. As we approached the main road, we became even more alarmed. Armed policemen were poised on all corners. That was not a common sight for Korogwe. Petty crimes we had a-plenty, but full battledress? Definitely not!

We turned into Frank's driveway and his *askari*, an old warrior if ever there was one, came hobbling down the lane to meet us. With arms and hands flying in all directions, he delivered a torrent of information about robbers who had burst into their neighbor's house in the middle of the night. The thieves had battered the *askari* unconscious, broken in the door, and tied up all fifteen of the building's inhabitants. Since the householders were major Indian merchants in town and had not yet banked the weekend takings, the thieves had escaped with several million *shilingi* in cash. And to make certain that they had thoroughly terrorized the family, the intruders had fired several rounds of bullets into the roof and walls.

My little story about stolen Christmas presents began to pale in light of this one. It had definitely been one hell of a night in Korogwe - from the papal visit to naked dancers, petty larceny, grievous bodily harm, and armed robbery.

⌒⌒

With the Christmas holidays over, the girls gone back to their colleges and jobs, and only Kaniah and myself left in Korogwe, life returned to its normal crawl. We discovered the mountain town of Lushoto one weekend when we were casting about for something different to do.

Lushoto was a lovely little town high in the Usambara Range, about a two-hour drive north of Korogwe. During the glory days of the German empire, before World War I had put an end to another imperial dream, Lushoto had been designated as the capital of German East Africa.

A narrow, spiraling road snaked its way up the mountainside, giving breathtaking views of the mist-shrouded valleys below. Even Korogwe looked strangely appealing in the distance. The air was cool and crisp and miniature waterfalls splashed invitingly at every bend in the road.

We felt a wonderful sense of release as we left the muggy suffocation of the lowlands behind. However, the drive meandered perilously close to the edge of unprotected cliffs and danger from instantaneous rockslides lurked everywhere.

The orderly design of the village square harked back to Lushoto's Teutonic past. However, over the intervening years, traditionally thatched *vipanda* had squeezed out the old colonial ruins, and now a tangle of vibrant reds and oranges cascaded over reeds and canvas. Men and boys lazed about on crumbling benches while women scrubbed their clothes and their young children in the streams. Occasionally, a hunter might emerge from the woods, toting a rifle over his shoulder and a fresh carcass for dinner. Children amused themselves by grooming and plaiting one another's hair. Time moved slowly up there in that other world.

The Lawns Hotel was the main hostelry in town. It was a run-down, rambling affair with a typical English rose garden leading from the dirt road up to the front door. Nonetheless, it had the same comforting appeal as an ageing auntie's country cottage.

An eccentric old German couple owned the hotel, but only the gentleman was in permanent residence. With his skeletal shoulders slouched forward and the matted strands of his graying hair falling into his rheumy eyes, he stomped around the Lawns Hotel like a dictatorial baron. He barked out a staccato of unintelligible orders in pidgin Swahili, to young girl servants who studiously ignored him. This appeared to be a familiar routine, judging from the total detachment of the girls and the ceaseless bellowing of the landlord. Neither one seemed to be paying a blind bit of notice to the other.

The dining room was deserted. We were the only guests. Faded prints of European castles dotted the pockmarked walls. A crudely bricked-up stone fireplace stood in the center of the room. The white wicker furniture was scratched and peeling and its cloth-covered cushions were threadbare. The Lawn Hotel was forlorn and forsaken, a lonely place forgotten in time.

The lunch menu was painfully predictable; it would be tough chicken and greasy chips once again. Lushoto supplied the entire Tanga Region with fresh fruits and vegetables, yet there were no vegetables at all on the lunch menu. "Is the food in this hotel so bad because there are so few tourists or is it the other way round?" we wondered.

Whatever about the shortcomings of the local cuisine, Lushoto was a showcase of missionary zeal. It was filled to bursting with Christian churches, the dominant denomination being Lutheran, but with a healthy sprinkling of Catholic and Evangelical congregations pulling up the rear. After lunch, we headed off to visit a German doctor whom we had met in Korogwe and who worked at the Lutheran Mission Hospital.

One curious thing about living in Africa was that foreigners were always delighted to receive visitors. On their home turf, the same people could be cool and aloof, but far removed from the familiarity of home base and cast adrift in Africa, they exuded warmth and good cheer to passing strangers and fellow travelers alike.

Paul and Rena had been living in Tanzania for seven years. They had spent the first four years on the shores of Lake Victoria and had then moved on to Lushoto. They had a family of four children; two were their natural born children, one was an adopted Rwandan girl aged five, and one was an adopted Tanzanian boy aged four. The little girl's mother had died in hospital after crossing the border from Uganda. The boy's mother had also died in hospital, a victim of Aids-related pneumonia. Joseph, the little boy, had been born with clubbed feet and Rena had already taken him back to Germany several times for bone operations. Although he was now able to walk, his feet remained badly disfigured.

We entered the house through a large country kitchen. Most

private homes in Tanzania were very spacious, with high-ceilinged lobbies that created clever air corridors throughout the entire house. A wire-covered hutch stood in the corner of the entryway, with two grown gerbils and half a dozen babies clambering all over one another. Paul immediately asked Kaniah if she would like to take one of the babies home with her. That was a big mistake. I knew we were going to end up raising one of those ugly, ferret-faced little creatures.

I hated rats. When we had first moved into our Korogwe house, we had discovered that we were about to share our home with a full colony of them. Rats had taken up residence in our roof space. We spent several weeks closing up air vents and setting poisoned traps in a valiant effort to live rodent-free. But those foul little creatures just went right on gnawing their way through our ceilings and dribbling wood dust down onto our beds. After several months of tears, torment, and terror, we had finally gotten rid of them; but now we were about to take home a first cousin as a pet!

Paul's hall was dark and cool. It led into a cozy family sitting room, all furnished in dark wood and plump cushions, and with a comforting log fire spitting to life. The children were finishing up their lunch of homemade bread, yogurt, and cheese. It could have been a typical mountain family scene from the Black Forest.

Paul had just returned from Dar where he had been trying to recruit an English language teacher for a proposed international school in Lushoto. Private schools like theirs were springing up everywhere. More and more foreign aid workers were arriving in the country and many *wazungu* wanted to educate their children at home, rather than having to send them away to large boarding schools in the cities. There were eleven potential students in the Lushoto community. Paul and Rena had four, there were three from an agricultural mission project, two children were from a forestry aid program, and two more were the children of local community workers.

Paul and his family were in the throes of planning for a holiday-cum-reconnaissance mission to Zimbabwe. They had decided that the time had come for the family to move into a more settled lifestyle. Their eldest daughter had just turned ten years of age and she had never been to formal school. They were afraid that, if they delayed much longer, the eventual transition from home tutoring to formal schooling would be extremely traumatic for her. They had heard good things about living standards in Zimbabwe and they thought it might hold the answer to their dilemma. They did not want to go back to Europe. They enjoyed the personal freedom and independence of African life, but at the same time, they did not want to sacrifice their children's education for an alternative lifestyle. Perhaps they could find a happy middle ground in Zimbabwe, they thought. But then Paul made, what was for me, a startling suggestion. He calmly said, "Our second choice would be to live in Ireland."

"What was that?" I sat up at attention. "You are seriously considering moving from Tanzania, in sub-Saharan Africa, to Ireland on the northern fringe of Europe? A family with no Irish connections? A family of German-Tanzanians?" Zimbabwe I could understand, but what was this thing Paul had with Ireland?

"I think I'd like to raise sheep, perhaps own a large sheep farm," continued Paul, as he stroked his beard and lifted five-year-old Valentina onto his knee.

I asked him if he had ever been to Ireland. I was hesitant to lay the cruel, hard facts before him and possibly burst his rosy bubble. Ireland was cold, wet, and windy and living conditions could be distinctly inhospitable in the remote sheep-raising regions of that country.

"Not yet," conceded Paul, "But we intend to visit Ireland when we return to Europe next month. I've read everything I can find in German periodicals about Ireland and I think it is a place where we could live quite happily."

I suggested that the Irish climate might be just a bit extreme for African children, accustomed, as they were, to temperatures that never dropped below 15 degrees Celsius. "That won't be a problem. They will just have to adjust. But I *am* a little worried about whether or not they would be accepted," explained Paul. Evidently, they had experienced some unpleasant incidents on previous home visits to Germany, when prejudices had been directed against them because they were a racially mixed family. He wondered how they would get on in Ireland.

"Well, they certainly would be different, no doubt about that!" I said. "You won't find too many young Africans roaming the Wicklow hills or the mountains of north Leitrim. That's where you'll be if you want to sheep farm. But other than the foul weather at times, and the Irish language at school, the children should be perfectly all right."

Paul was enthusiastic about the idea of his children learning Irish. They already spoke German and Swahili and some English. He thought it would be marvelous for them to learn another language. He'd actually like to speak Irish himself. He also thought that we were fantastically lucky to have such a unique language of our own. I couldn't help thinking about all the parents back in Ireland who hadn't a good word to say for the Irish language; "A total waste of time, useless in the modern world, unbankable, and an intolerable burden," to name but a few of the slings and arrows that were constantly being hurled at it.

So, we decided that I would work out an itinerary for him. Rena and the children would remain in Germany while Paul scouted out the general lay of the land in Ireland. If he liked what he found, he would ask Rena to join him for the final part of his visit.

It struck me as very strange indeed, the number of people I had encountered in Africa who were casting about in webs of confusion, looking for somewhere, anywhere, to put down roots. It seemed so terribly odd - all that shiftless and rootless wandering. The bravest adventurers in Africa just didn't seem to have any real understanding of, or any real sense of place.

We returned to Korogwe via a route that took us around the back of the Usambara Mountains and down through acres of delicately scented tea plantations. Those same estates had been established during the period of British domain, but just like with the sisal industry, they had been nationalized by the Tanzanian government following independence. Neat contours of fragrant tea plants coiled around the undulating mountain slopes, gently rising and falling with the hills. An army of local women, dressed in brightly patterned *kangas*, moved quietly over the landscape, expertly plucking the rich, tender leaves and filling their canvas sacks. One could easily forget wars, and famines, and noise, and pollution up there. It put a whole lot of things into proper perspective. And it made it much easier to understand why so many Europeans came to Africa and never left.

All those dreamy stories, like "Out of Africa," and "West with the Night," had been set against backdrops like this. The big sprawling houses of Thika might have disappeared, but it didn't tax the imagination much to picture them up there in the tea estates. While an unprepossessing factory now replaced the lovely colonial house and workers' huts encircled the factory walls, the workers' pay hadn't changed very much in the meantime.

☜☞

The world of tea spanned several continents and had a dynasty of families that continued to work and live according to age-old traditions, generation after generation. We met one such couple, Sam and Pam, when they stopped to pay a brief visit to a friend in Korogwe. They were traveling from a tea estate on the outskirts of Nairobi to the Brooke Bond Estate in Mbeya - a distance of over three thousand kilometers. They intended to reach Mbeya, located in the most southeastern corner of Tanzania, complete their business engagement there, and drive back to Nairobi - all in less than one week.

Distances were totally irrelevant to white Africans. Distances were simply spaces that had to be crossed. These people approached harrowing journeys, such as this one, with scarcely a second thought. They might throw a few extra bits of clothing into the back of their jeep, add several jugs of fresh drinking water, a thermos of tea and a basket of fruit, and away they would go.

Sam and Pam had been born to English parents on the tea estates of Sri Lanka. They had grown up according to comfortable colonial traditions, and in later life, they had passed seamlessly into the cozy world of tea. They had lived and worked on estates all over Asia and East Africa and had managed to hold onto the same carefree lifestyle wherever they had happened to land.

They enjoyed the best of modern housing, easy access to local and imported foodstuffs, excellent boarding school facilities in the UK for their children, and the quintessential local golf club to complete their busy social lives. Domestic servants handled all the household chores and even child rearing became a walk on the beach. Life for the tea plantation dynasties was hassle-free, safe, and secure.

We drove on past the tea fields and began to descend a treacherously winding pass, stopping just short of colliding with a battle-green Land Rover that was swerving crazily all over the road. We discovered Ronald, the owner of the Village Resort Hotel in Korogwe, at the wheel.

Ronald had been the illustrious manager of these tea estates in the good old days, long before the demon drink had grabbed him by the throat. After one particular incident of late-night reveling, and not on tea, he had driven the company vehicle right over the edge. Only a huge boulder straddling the cliff's rim had come between him and all eternity. The boulder had saved his life; but Ronald had lost his job.

So now he dreamed about busloads of German guests arriving at his establishment halfway down the mountainside, wealthy tourists looking for tantalizing day trips to the neighboring rainforests. He could see *Ronald's Hotel* as their trusty base camp and Ronald himself as their courageous guide. "No better place and no better man!" was my immediate reaction. But Ronald would need a substantial injection of money to install standard toilets and continuous running water. After all, he was talking about German tourists! And to do that, he would need to get off the hard stuff. So many brilliant ideas eventually drown in the *water of life!*

Alphonse was Ronald's right hand man. He had been export supervisor at the tea estates during Ronald's reign as manager and, quite befitting the disposition of a loyal subordinate, he had voluntarily left his employment in solidarity with his terminated boss.

We had stopped on the roadside at that point, and both Ronald and Alphonse were effusive in their greetings and in their enthusiasm for a chat.

"So you are from Ireland! Funny that!" mused Alphonse. "I remember the man we used to send our tea to in Dublin. His name was John Fitzpatrick. But that was such a long time ago."

I was completely flabbergasted. I had worked with John Fitzpatrick's brother, Barry, oh, so long ago, at Dublin Airport. Those were the days when working at the airport was as close as anyone in Ireland could get to Hollywood glamour. And I remembered John Fitzpatrick well. John Fitzpatrick, the successful sales representative for a firm of London tea merchants, the man who drove a van when everyone else took the bus. "Good grief," I exclaimed. "I can still see those distinctive wooden tea chests with their exotic black markings stacked in the back of his van." Little did I think, then, that I would one day encounter a former colleague of his, one whom he had never met but who still remembered his name, driving madly along the slopes of the Usambaras. I shook my head in disbelief. "What a strange world we live in."

A few weeks after our trip to Lushoto, Paul and Rena called into our house for a brief word. They were on their way back from Zimbabwe. They had been flagged down on the road into Korogwe by neighbors from Lushoto who had spotted their car approaching. They had wanted to alert Paul, before he arrived at his home with his family, that they would be returning to an empty house. Apparently, a few days after their departure, robbers had struck. A truck had arrived in broad daylight and cleaned out their home – right down to the light bulbs and the bathroom soap. They didn't know any more details but were heading to Lushoto straight away. Rena was in a state of shock. "Imagine arriving back from holidays to find you own nothing but the clothes on your back," she said. Rena was a hardy soul, but this dreadful turn of events had shaken her world.

They had crossed Zimbabwe off their list of possible homelands. "The landscape, with the possible exception of the region around the Zambezi River and Victoria Falls, is hopelessly dull and uninteresting," according to Rena. And now that Tanzania had dealt them such a severe blow, I sincerely hoped that Ireland would be more kind.

❦

The northern suburbs of Dar es Salaam were the preserve of wealthy business and professional Tanzanians, *wazungu* attached to diplomatic missions and the ever-expanding expatriate community. This preserve was not easily penetrated by the average citizen and we were unexpectedly initiated into its rarified world of privilege on the occasion of the annual St. Patrick's Day Dinner.

The invitation we received, as part of the aid community, indicated that formal dress should be worn, and the subscription requested was substantial enough to suggest a very grand affair. The venue was in the fashionable surroundings of Dar es Salaam's Little Theatre.

Electric power was out of service on the evening of the event, so we had arrived at the theatre under the cover of darkness. Kerosene lamps lit the entryway and clusters of very beautiful people stood about chatting, sipping Irish Cream, and nibbling on chunks of Galtee cheese - all specially flown in for this auspicious occasion. An Irish harpist, also flown in direct from Ireland, plucked gently at her harp strings, and soft Irish airs filled the balmy night. The modulated buzz of genteel voices floated above us like silk scarves caught in a gentle breeze.

We were acquainted with only a handful of people at this glittering event. There had been an official Irish Embassy reception the night before and most of the aid workers had already returned to their posts. I was a bit taken aback by that. Since it was a weekend night, I had assumed that they would be staying on for this event as well. After all, the Irish Club of Tanzania, founded in 1932, was hosting the festivities to mark Ireland's national holiday.

Ninety minutes passed and the electricity supply was still out. The soft, gentle buzz of hushed voices had risen a thousand feet. Each candlelit table featured place settings for eight guests, with four bottles of wine, one bottle of Irish Cream, and one bottle of Bushmill's Irish Whiskey on each table. But by the time the power was finally restored, serious inroads had been made into the beverage stock and the buzz had risen to a roar. We noticed that the only men not kitted out in full black tie were at our table. And the only black Tanzanians in the theatre were also at our tables. "How very odd!" I thought. "After all, aren't we living in black Tanzania?"

A black-tied, rugby-built young buck promptly sat himself down at our table and proceeded to take over the drinks detail. He began by filling glasses with everything in sight and lowering most of them himself. He kept up a steady stream of talk - rugby, rugby, rugby - then on to cars - then back to more rugby. He kept jumping up and down and shouting to his mates at other tables - and asking questions that he answered himself. He rambled on incoherently, addressing everyone at once and nobody in particular. The rest of us sat staring at him in stunned silence. We couldn't get a word in.

We gathered that he had been born and raised in Tanzania and had been shipped off to England for secondary school. He was a young man knee-deep in identity crisis.

The honored guests at the head table were on their feet, ready to raise a toast in honor of St. Patrick, but they were severely beaten back by chants of, "We are the champions," that began ringing out across the hall. Apparently, Wales had beaten England that day and those at our table, and the top table, were the only ones out of the loop. Then the champions rose, and with arms wrapped around one another and swaying drunkenly, they began belting out, "The Whippoorwill" – "We are poor little lambs that have lost our way, baa, baa, baa!" Somebody at the head table again attempted to raise the toast, but he hadn't a hope. Nobody was interested.

"Who are these people?" we asked one another. "Are they English or Welsh or African or what? Why are they here? And more to the point, why are we here?" The only thing clear was why those aid workers who had absconded early back to their posts were not there.

Our golden boy from the rugby squad soon departed our table to join the more jocular locker room set. But he returned a little later to swoop down and relieve us of our unopened bottle of Bushmill's. Apparently, we weren't attacking it fast enough, or with sufficient gusto.

Then on came the disco lights and a mad stampede for the dance floor. There was no *bosi bosi* or reggae that night. There were no jigs or reels either. We were being hauled back in time to the 1950s and, "My girl lollipop, she makes my heart go flippity-flop!" Those formerly beautiful people were now out on the floor pummeling one another all around the place. The women were wild; they were roaring and laughing at absolutely nothing. We would have needed crash helmets and shin guards to approach that floor!

I had seen it all, now. This was the settler society and, by all accounts, they turned up at every catfight in town. It could be an affair hosted by the Irish Club, the British Club, The Scottish Club, the Welsh Club, the American, Canadian, or Australian. The settler crowd would be there! They were the young and not-so-young, but definitely the juvenile rich, and they constituted what passed for high society in Dar es Salaam. I would not have believed it, had I not seen it with my own eyes.

Chapter Four
ZAMBIA AND ZIMBABWE

The long, hot months of summer had passed and Kaniah and I were setting off on our first real expedition outside of Tanzania. We didn't count Kenya. That was right on our doorstep. I had decided to err on the side of caution this time, considering Kaniah's tender years and my propensity for losing direction. So we had booked a first class compartment on the Tazara Railway to Kapiri Mposhi.

The Tazara Railway was the legacy of a close brotherhood that had flourished between Chairman Mao's communist China and Mwalimu Nyerere's socialist Tanzania during the early years following Tanzania's independence. By the year 1974, the Chinese had built an international railway that linked Dar es Salaam with Lusaka, in Zambia, and continued all the way south to the borders of South Africa. But due to initial difficulties brought about through inaccurate revenue sharing, all points south had disappeared from the route in double quick time, and now the complete journey ran from Dar es Salaam to Kapiri Mposhi only.

You might be inclined to ask yourself, "Where exactly is Kapiri Mposhi?" I did, when I first heard the name. It was in Zambia, somewhere southwest of the southernmost Tanzanian town of Mbeya. It was not very far from the border of the Republic of the Congo, which until recently had been the former state of Zaire, which before that, had been the Belgian Congo. Land borders and territorial names were changing at a frightening pace all over Africa. Anyway, the Congo was not somewhere you would like to be right now. And, as I came to discover, Kapiri Mposhi was not exactly anywhere you would choose to be either!

The waiting room in the main train station in Dar es Salaam was very impressive. It was expansive and airy and it had ample seating. One could sit contentedly in quiet comfort and pass the time away peering through the platform gates, imagining magical moments to come on this thirty-six hour odyssey through East Africa. Passengers lounged about chatting convivially, and watching one another. Everything was orderly and pleasant.

But strange things happened at all points of departure throughout Africa. I heard nothing. I saw nothing; there was no announcement, no signal, nothing! Yet, there had to be a secret telepathy afoot in places such as this because what had been a very docile and even passive-looking group of people just moments before, quite suddenly became a marauding mob.

The orderly waiting game was over. People came running from all directions with panic in their eyes. The passenger terminal became an invaded football pitch, with a surging mass of people pushing senselessly towards the train platform. Children were squeezed unmercifully amidst the swell of heaving bodies. Bags became jammed, lost, and trampled-on in the crush. We sat on our bench, too stunned to move. What was all the panic about? As far as we knew, everyone there had a ticket, and everyone had been allocated a particular seat.

When the hysteria of the first few minutes had passed and the bulk of passengers had crammed their way onto the train platform, Kaniah and I picked ourselves up and reluctantly joined the remnants of the mob. We were quickly sucked up and swept along by the flowing tide of flesh. We struggled valiantly to hold onto our belongings, and to each other. We fought our way to our designated carriage and climbed aboard. Thank the Lord; our allocated seats were still vacant.

Our first class compartment had four bunks, two up and two down, and a sticky rubber-topped folding table. That was it. Second class compartments were identical to first class, except that they had six bunks. Third class had no bunks. They had broken wooden benches for the elect and standing and squatting room only for the hoi-polloi. Then there were the carriage corridors and lavatories, all of which were already filled to overflowing. People were crowding around the conductors on the platform, shouting and arguing about overbooked seats. Good Lord! What luck! We had actually found our places unoccupied!

We stashed our backpacks under the bunks and settled back to await our two additional traveling companions. The door of the carriage swung open and the conductor solicitously enquired, "Still two?" to which we replied, "Yes, still two!"

"What is going on in the corridor?" whispered Kaniah. "What's all the commotion about?" We could clearly see our conductor in the middle of a scrum, and money was changing hands. But this train had been fully booked two weeks earlier when I had purchased our "last two" first class places. "How can he be selling tickets now?" wondered Kaniah. We found out soon enough when the door swung open and in burst two burly men who promptly hoisted themselves up to the top bunks.

Kaniah looked stricken. We had booked a "females only" compartment. I turned on the two interlopers with a warning snarl. "You can't stay in here. This compartment is reserved for women only. It is absolutely impossible. There are no curtains on the beds and I have a young daughter traveling with me. This is a big mistake."

"In Tanzania, it is all the same," came the bored reply.

I continued on with my ranting and raving, demanding that they leave immediately, but when it started to become obvious that I was getting nowhere, I tore out into the corridor to look for that sleazy fraud of a train conductor. The interlopers, sensing impending *mzungu* madness, jumped down and followed me. They found the conductor before I did and immediately whipped themselves up into the wizardry of doing another deal.

Back in the compartment, we waited, now nervously watching the door. In came an English lady and her nephew. The lady was middle-aged and white. The nephew was thirty-ish and black. She wanted him to share the compartment with us. Kaniah got that stricken look again.

The lady, called Jane, explained that they had brought this

wonderful food basket to enjoy on the journey and it would be so much more convenient if her nephew could stay in our compartment. "Just think about it," she suggested, "all that needless trekking up and down corridors for meals and so on." She whined on and on, all beseeching eyes and wheedling voice, but we were having none of it. We had expelled the first two intruders in short order and this one was about to join them.

Mercifully, when the door opened once more, a Zambian lady, Naomi, stumbled in. She carried an official ticket for herself and one for her four-year-old daughter. The earnest young nephew reluctantly withdrew, following Naomi's husband to a compartment in second class. He was not a happy man, but we were happy campers. At long last, the sex configurations had been satisfactorily sorted out.

There were two lavatories on this first class carriage, one at either end. One was a flush toilet, but it had no water. The other was a squat toilet and it was awash with water. The foul smell that was emanating from both toilets confirmed my suspicions about the slippery mess that was already covering the floors. And our journey had just begun. I decided I could wait. It would only be thirty-six hours!

We began to get acquainted with our new traveling companions. Jane, the English lady, had been living in a suburb outside of Lusaka since 1964. "My God," I thought. "She must have seen some amazing changes in the region in all that time."

Jane was now a Zambian citizen. She told us that she had arrived in Dar es Salaam the week before, on the Tazara from Kapiri Mposhi. She had been up to Dar to visit her in-laws, and as incredible as it seemed, that had been her first visit to Tanzania. I filled her in on what we were doing. I was working on an aid program in northern Tanzania and Kaniah and I were spending the summer holidays traveling. I then enquired if she could tell us anything about the places we were going to visit: Livingstone, Victoria Falls, and Bulawayo. Once again, she confounded me when she vacantly commented, while gazing out of the window, that "No," she had never been to Zimbabwe. "What about South Africa?" I asked. It was "No," to that as well. She had been living in Zambia for thirty years and she had never visited the neighboring countries? "What does that say about the old colonial mindset?" I asked myself.

Jane really wanted to have a window seat. There were only two of those particular items in this carriage and we had got there first. I had fought a pitched battle to get those seats. But Jane moaned and sighed and lamented her bad luck. She kept looking longingly at Kaniah who was settled by the coveted window, reading. And Jane's mournful eyes began boring holes through the pages of Kaniah's book. Eventually, Jane won. Kaniah relinquished her comfortable seat and climbed up to the top bunk.

Jane was overcome by the passing landscape of Tanzania. She sat glued to the open window, staring and sighing over every bush, hill, and clump of trees she saw. The wind was blowing in my direction and whipping around my face. "Isn't this wonderfully invigorating?" she asked, again and again.

It was now pitch black and we could see nothing but the stars in the sky, but Jane was transfixed. I began to have some dark thoughts about Zambia. Tanzania was, indeed, an enchanting country with its snow-capped mountains, lush plantations, scented fruit groves, and vibrant colors. It varied from the blazing yellows and reds of the tropics to the stately blues and purples of the mountains. It had the Serengeti Plains, Ngorongoro Crater, and Mount Kilimanjaro. What we had been passing for the past few hours had been nothing more than scrub and bush. Yet Jane was deep into it, fascinated, peering into the dark. Finally, I suggested that we close the window. My face was turning to stone. She grudgingly complied and prepared herself for bed. She had brought a downy sleeping bag and a fluffy pillow. We had brought nothing.

Naomi was also Zambian and her husband worked as a porter on the Tazara Railway. They were returning from a shopping trip to Dar. Naomi had stuffed several huge bags of patterned cloth, cleverly camouflaged with bunches of bananas, under her bunk. She planned to sew the material into dresses when she got back home and sell them for a tidy profit in her business. But I doubted if the customs men would be conned by the clumps of bananas. From what I had witnessed on the train platform that morning, she would need to offer a few cans of beer or a few thousand *shilingi* to get her material through that crowd of shysters.

◦∿◦)

Naomi's husband arrived at the door with half a case of Stella Artois. Naomi popped open one of the cans and shoved the rest of them under her bunk, along with the bananas and the cloth. Over the next thirty-six hours, the cans would disappear, one by one. Problems like *baksheesh* and the precious rolls of material became only a distant memory to Naomi. But she looked none the worse for her spectacular indulgence. She lolled back leisurely on the hard bunk, only rising now and again to seek out the lavatory. Her little girl busied herself by twisting off the legs of a yellow-haired baby-doll named Kelley.

Kaniah and I were now beginning to feel real hunger pains. We had eaten nothing since early morning, except for a few miserly sweets, so we enquired from Jane about the dining room and the meal schedule. She informed us sweetly that she would not be eating in the dining room because she had brought her own provisions, but meals would be announced by the conductor, whenever they were ready.

At ten o'clock that night, the conductor stuck his head around the door and asked if we would be needing any food.

"Yes, please, and hurry," came our weak replies. We had just about given up hope of getting anything to eat before morning.

"What do you have?" we wanted to know. But there were no surprises in store. The menu for that night was chicken and rice.

"Can we have some drinks?" we boldly enquired.

"No! You must go to the dining car for that. But the dining car is not open tonight."

"Oh? Why not?"

"Can't say." That put a rapid end to that conversation.

So we would eat in our room and we wouldn't have drinks. How glad I was that I had washed off that sticky table.

At ten forty-five, the food arrived. We now knew the reason behind Jane's brimming food basket. The chicken was as tough as an elephant's hide and the rice was a cold glutinous glob. "Oh well," we comforted ourselves, "only thirty more hours to go."

The conductor reappeared to take our plates and to enquire if we needed bedding. "You bet we do!" And surprise of surprises! He presented us with freshly laundered white sheets, clean pillows, and blue woolen blankets. Things were beginning to look decidedly better. If we had just used a little foresight and had tucked some tasty sandwiches into our backpacks, this expedition wouldn't be half bad!

There then followed a fitful night of trying to sleep. Kaniah's bunk was lopsided and she got wedged between the bunk and the wall every time the train lurched. Since that kept happening with monotonous regularity, she spent most of the night trying to extricate herself from each bruising encounter and cursing that Jezebel, Jane, who was sleeping like a baby beneath her.

Then we stopped and stood still, on the tracks, for what seemed like hours, somewhere, out there. When the train started up again around dawn, we discovered that we still had only thirty more hours to go. Somewhere, out there, we had lost six hours. No one knew how or why!

We spent the next day leaning out of the window, scanning passing stations and hoping to God we would spot someone selling real food. But at every stop the story was the same - more bananas and oranges. As we continued farther south, local women began to appear with enormous baskets of fresh tomatoes and the Zambians were snapping them up. So we added miniature tomatoes to our daily diet of oranges and bananas.

Meanwhile, Jane and her nephew spread the rubber–topped table with a white cloth every few hours and tucked greedily into their sumptuous meals of tinned meat, boiled eggs, rolls and butter, and even jam! Then there was the fresh fruit and coffee. They even had powdered milk with them. But they were not parting with a morsel. Not even the little girl with the yellow-haired doll was getting a crumb. And a blissfully unconcerned Naomi carried on happily popping can after can of Stella Artois.

With twenty-four hours left to travel, the train ran out of water. This was another mystery to puzzle upon. Surely, it must have been possible to fill up the tanks at any one of the stations along the way. We could see long hoses spilling out oceans of water onto the tracks. We asked the conductor why they didn't do something about it. We couldn't brush our teeth or wash our hands because the train had no water. He said they *were* doing something. They were saving what was left for the morning. The stench of urine in the corridor had become something awful. We were not hungry anymore. That particular trial had passed.

Our approach to the town of Mbeya, perched high on the mountainside, was a lovely sight. The small, terraced farms wound themselves around verdant hills like the coils of a snake. The land was green and lush and fertile. Jane swooned in rhapsodies of joy, on a full stomach and on the home stretch. As we inched closer and closer to the Zambian border, I decided to ask Jane what she knew about Kapiri Mposhi.

Would there be transport available at the train station for Lusaka? That was my main concern. I wanted to continue our journey without breaking it in Kapiri. We'd had enough surprises on this train to last a lifetime, and my child needed a proper bed.

Jane told me not to worry; she assured me that there would be no problem at all. There were always loads of buses on hand to meet the train and the trip into Lusaka would take about three hours. She added that, although the road could be better for the first few miles, it improved considerably once it reached the main Lusaka motorway.

According to Jane, Zambia was much more developed than Tanzania. Tanzanians were, in fact, abominably lazy. Every Zambian house, no matter how poor, had a cultivated flower garden out front, not like in Tanzania where the concept of flower gardens was unknown. "Tanzanians don't even know how to thatch, for the love of God! They throw the fronds at their huts in any old fashion. My God, they don't even trim the thatch." And the huts were all the wrong shape, to make matters even worse. Why were Tanzanian huts rectangular and square? Why were they not all round, like in Zambia?

After this heated tirade against Tanzania, she proceeded to offer a few cautionary words of advice about her own country.

"You need to be careful about your purse, but you know that; there are thieves everywhere. We Zambians have terrible problems with Zaire. There is no sense of order in that place at all. They are all bandits over there. They come across the border and no one is safe. They snatch everything. Don't even think of driving a car anywhere near the border. It will be snatched at gunpoint. But you've traveled. I'm sure you're used to all that."

Well, not really! I hadn't contemplated driving a car on that trip and, notwithstanding our little Christmas adventures, I wasn't all that used to bandits. But I'd be sure to bear it all in mind.

❦

We spilled out onto the railway platform and the mad rush for the gate began anew. This time we were competing for seats on buses.

Anarchy reigned. Buses were squashed onto the forecourt of the train station in helter-skelter fashion. Most of them had cardboard signs hanging off their cracked and broken windscreens, indicating the proposed destinations. We spotted one heading for Lusaka and were propelled towards it. Luckily for us, most of the crowd seemed to be heading there too. Otherwise, we could have ended up in Angola.

The bus was falling apart. The crowd was so thick around it that it was impossible to be sure, but there didn't seem to be any headlights on it. The windscreen was smashed out and most of the glass was missing from the side windows as well. But it was definitely going somewhere because a man stood at the front opening, grabbing fares.

We didn't know whether to get on or not. Surely to God, this disintegrating heap of junk could not be the bus – our bus.

Heavy decisions like that were so often taken right out of our hands. The crowd was relentlessly into its pushing mode and we were up on the steps before we had a chance to escape.

The bus was already full. People were jammed into every corner, arms and legs twisted and contorted, sacks and baskets trampled underfoot. A fistfight broke out behind me. One man emerged with a bloody nose. Kaniah had, by now, disappeared into the bowels of this monster and the man at the door was demanding his fares. I couldn't get my hand around to reach my safety pack, which was tied onto my waist. When I did reach it, there was another hand inside. In the suicidal crush, the man behind me had opened the zips on the pouch and only the grace of God had saved our passports. I didn't know if he had taken the money because I couldn't see.

I let out an almighty scream. "Get your effen hand out of my bag."

Now all the rest of the passengers were yelling at him. But this was a man, not a mouse. He made a final desperate grab for my hold all as he was being pushed off the bus. Then the irate conductor reprimanded me soundly, telling me not to be "giving" money to filthy vagrants. "Oh, merciful God, what have we gotten ourselves into?" I moaned.

The saints preserve us! Now they were passing a monstrous wheel, not a tire but a wheel, rim and all, over my head. "Where in the name of all that's holy do they intend to put it?" I gasped. There wasn't even space for the mouse. My leg was caught between bags and cases and I would have toppled over if there had been any room. People were smashed up against one another and against the seats. The wheel became lodged in beside the driver and three people promptly sat on it. With a series of squeals and belches, the bus lurched forward and waddled onto the road.

I forced my way down the bus to get beside Kaniah. She was ghostly white and felt sick. She was absolutely petrified. The heat was suffocating and there was no air. None at all. The stale odor of sweating bodies all around us was nauseating. The road was a mass of potholes, but that did not deter this driver. He plowed ahead straight into them. Kaniah had slumped down onto her bag. I was riven with guilt. What sort of lunacy had I dragged my innocent child into?

After about an hour of sheer hell, some of the passengers got off and we were able to squeeze onto half a seat that had the springs sticking through. But at least we were out of the crush in the aisle and our bags were stacked safely on our laps.

"Holy Mother of God!" I could not believe what I was seeing. A young man was trying to make his way from the back of the bus to the front. He couldn't squeeze past the passengers because it was so jam-packed. So he had crouched down and had begun walking along the backs of the seats; and he was hanging onto the roof by his fingertips. His "fly on the wall" performance was taking place while the bus roared through brush and bush and bounced in and out of gigantic potholes.

And still he hung on. But realistically, where could he have fallen? In the worst-case scenario, he would have had a very soft landing.

We ducked our heads as he scrambled over us. All the while, the bus careered crazily along the cratered road. This mobile wreck threatened to overturn as it rounded a series of bends, but it gallantly righted itself and barreled on. Passengers took it all in their stride. Babies lolled impassively at their mothers' breasts while they were belted around unmercifully in the rattling tin can. Our three hour journey took six hours; like the thirty-six hour train ride had taken forty-six.

"The road could be better," how are you? "When did Jane travel this road, in this style, last?" I asked myself. We were wrung out like dishrags by the time we finally reached the capital.

Thankfully, Lusaka appeared to be a proper city with its tree-lined footpaths, paved streets, and modern office buildings. Our spirits began to rise. Maybe we could find some place to have a hot meal, after we sorted out a room for the night. We asked one of our fellow sufferers for advice and she pointed us in the direction of the Lusaka Hotel on the main street.

"Be careful of your bags," she called in parting.

Surprise! Surprise! There was no room at the inn.

"But if you want to wait around until 18:00, maybe something will come up," suggested the receptionist. Since we didn't have a clue where to look next, we resigned ourselves to leaving our bags with the porter and went off in search of the coach that would take us to Livingstone in the morning.

Lusaka was a proper city, alright, with footpaths, streetlights, and modern buildings; but it also had some very sketchy-looking characters lurking on every street corner and under every business awning. After our harrowing experience in Kapiri Mposhi, I made certain to cover my money belt with my windbreaker, but I still didn't feel entirely safe. That was, no doubt, because we were walking around blindly looking for the bus station.

Whenever we stopped someone to make enquiries, we were ourselves asked, "Which bus station?" Evidently, there were several. "The one with the coaches to Livingstone," we replied. We were directed to the wrong one. We were in some very seedy part of town at that stage. It was the markets area and it was a den of thieves. Some very suspicious-looking characters began following us and we had no idea which way to turn. We didn't want to appear lost, so we kept on walking, more quickly now. Then we spotted two ladies walking together in our direction and stopped them. "It is very dangerous for you to be wandering around town alone," they warned us, and they proceeded to accompany us to the nearest bus station. They were going clear out of their way to see us there safely.

We felt dreadful about that. It was a roasting hot day and they were on their way home from work when we had intercepted them. Each one walked on either side of us, for protection. I half expected to see steam rising from Kaniah and myself, wrapped as we were inside our airtight windbreakers. We finally reached the bus station, which we would never, ever, have found on our own. It was buried behind a barricade of market stalls and empty crates and cartons.

The bus station was empty. The sinking feeling I got when I saw the vacant waiting room and vacant sales hatches was fully justified. A scrawled notice on the wall said it all: "All coaches to Livingstone sold out for the next two days".

We could book seats for later in the week. "But do we really want to spend three more nights and two more days in Lusaka?" I wondered. We asked our lady friends for advice. They suggested we try another coach company, not as reliable as this one, but we were willing to take anything. After another fifteen-minute walk through the blistering heat, it too was booked out. "Is everyone trying to flee Lusaka? Is there something about this place that we should know?" we asked ourselves.

The ladies, kind as they were, had had enough. They hailed a taxi and directed the driver to a third company. Too bad! When we got there, they didn't go to Livingstone. "Would you like to go to Harare instead?" asked the helpful attendant. Even he seemed to want us out of Lusaka.

"Jaysus," we thought. "Maybe we do." We were really deadbeat. Between the drama in Kapiri, the hellish bus ride, the sweltering heat, and the pulsating tension on the streets, we too had had enough. But we had to go back to the hotel first to collect our bags. And praise the Lord! We had a room.

"We'll have dinner," we thought, "and deal with this tomorrow." Scarlet O'Hara had nothing on us.

There were no restaurants in Lusaka, at least none that we could find. There was not a single one on the main street and we were not about to venture farther than that again. There were no take-aways either. "Where do people in Lusaka eat? Do people eat at all? What do people eat, if they do eat?" Kaniah was at a ravenous low.

We finally found a place called The Roasted Chicken, crammed in behind a newsstand and a used-shoes stall, but they didn't sell chicken. They sold curry, scones, and cream donuts filled with a gluey white sludge. And pork pies. But, no drinks. Defeated, we crawled back to our hotel.

"Oh, Thank God," the hotel restaurant had now opened. And yes, this was definitely where the beautiful people of Lusaka must eat. It was perfect; it had starched white tablecloths, attentive waiters, candlelight, and good food. Had this awful day really happened?

We were up at the crack of dawn, determined to get out of Lusaka. We were too early for breakfast so we knew we were in for another lean day. Anyone needing to lose a few surplus pounds should give some serious thought to touring Africa. The daily hunt for transportation leaves no time for such trivia as eating.

We hailed a taxi and asked the driver to take us to wherever we could get a bus for Livingstone. We had made a remarkable discovery the night before, while chatting with one of the hotel residents. Buses were different from coaches. Coaches booked seats and buses didn't have seats. They had protruding springs that threatened mortal injury with every bump in the road. We had taken a bus from Kapiri Mposhi. We would have had to book a coach. So now we knew. We were becoming truly enlightened world travelers.

Our taxi driver was a prince among men. He suggested we try the trains first. That sounded like a really good idea; after all, we had had such a fascinating experience on the last one. But Rats! It was booked out. "What now?" we asked.

"Let's try the buses," he said, as we sped off in a cloud of dust. Why hadn't we thought of that?

We pulled up opposite a bus station. It could have been any bus station, but it looked painfully familiar. Battered and bruised tin hulks leaned drunkenly on bald tires. "How on earth do they manage to move?" I wondered. That was one of the great mysteries of life. "Why does my car break down and refuse to budge when a nut comes loose and these wrecks just barrel along forever?"

Our taxi driver advised us to sit tight. He would go across the yard and check things out. We thought that was very nice of him as we were not yet fully primed to face the day's tribulations. He returned to tell us that we were in luck. Hallelujah, there was space! That meant space, not necessarily seats. But who cared? We'd take it!

He took our money, we followed him, he bought our tickets, and we thanked him. We were on our way.

Well, this didn't look too bad. We'd seen worse. A very nice young couple made room for us on the back row of seats. Now there were nine people sitting where there should have been six, but nobody complained. They just made themselves smaller.

We had a chance to study the local populace from the vantage point of our window seats and this was decidedly different. We would not have had to worry about covering our legs in Lusaka. There wasn't a *kanga* or a *buibui* in sight. There were miniskirts encasing bodies so tightly wrapped that they must have threatened asphyxiation. Women slouched nonchalantly against railings, broiling in leather. Every female, from babies to grannies, sported a head full of fashionable extensions. There were six-inch spiked high heels, Ray Bans, red-slashed lips, and Attitude! Man was there Attitude!

I wondered to Kaniah, "How come Jane forgot to tell us about this?"

Dar es Salaam was not a modern city. It didn't have paved streets except for the one that headed north out of the city. And that was a very fine road, indeed. You suddenly realized how fine it was once you reached the city center. It was a bit difficult to know when you were actually in the city center, though, because there were none of the anticipated landmarks of a city - like footpaths, traffic lights, and tall buildings. Only loads and loads of bewildered *wazungu* wandering around looking for the city center. They were in it, but they didn't know it.

Now, Lusaka was instantly identifiable as a city. It had all those familiar landmarks. But while I never felt physically threatened · when walking around Dar es Salaam, I did not like the feeling of Lusaka. It seemed to have taken on all the mean and ugly faces of an inner city anywhere in the world.

By Tanzanian standards, Lusaka would be considered developed. Trendy clothes were on display everywhere. Idle young men with implacably cool attitudes strutted around the bus stations. They had all the trappings of the "now" generation, from the sculptured haircuts to the fake Rolex watches. They had bought into all the illusions of wealth and progress. "What elaborate fantasies are they concocting in those carefully oiled and pampered heads, as they strike artful poses and shuffle around with their mates?" I wondered. Cultural confusion on a scale such as this had not yet invaded Tanzania, but no doubt, it was on its way. I asked myself, "Is this any different from downtown Detroit?"

My musings were briefly interrupted by an enterprising peddler who was offering to sell me aspirins. "This man," I thought, "has a very bright future." He had identified a niche market. But I advised him to find something just a little bit stronger for the traveling public.

When I gently refused his offer of aspirins, he asked if he could marry my daughter. I explained that she had already been promised to someone else. He took the rejection well and wished us a safe journey. Everyone around us was smiling.

Life was full of new discoveries. It wasn't long before I found out what was worse than being mangled to death on a bus, or trapped under a sea of sweating bodies. It was being blasted into Hades by seven hours of blaring rap music.

Sitting directly in front of us was a young man, very nattily dressed in black and wearing fashionable steel-rimmed eyeglasses. Kaniah informed me that the glasses were fake. The lenses were clear and he was only wearing them for effect. "Really? Nobody in Korogwe would have money for the likes of that!" But she was usually right about such things of fashion.

This young man had the biggest boom box I had ever laid eyes upon. He had it standing on end, on his lap, because it was so big that he couldn't hold it any other way and still sit on the seat. Now this was a very crowded bus! One of the speakers was jammed up against his ear and he had the volume turned up to the max.

He must have been stone deaf. His skull would have been shattered if he had any hearing at all. He showed no signs of life. He didn't move with the rhythm, he didn't hum or sing or tap his feet. He just sat there vacant, hour after hour. He had an endless supply of tapes. As one tape ended, he stirred himself and produced a fresh one from some diabolical trove under his seat. He even had a store of batteries. Our only relief from this unremitting barrage of noise came when he had to stop for a few minutes to recharge.

Nobody seemed to notice. Nobody was bothered. Nobody complained. Was I crazy? Was this normal? We were feeling physically sick by the time we reached Livingstone.

The worst was yet to come. We were disgorged onto the road and we looked around for signs of – I hate to say the word – transport. We didn't want to look around too much, though. At the first sign of indecision, one was instantly besieged by hordes of men yelling, "Taxi, taxi! Cheap. Special price for you." By now I knew the last part was going to be true! There was always the regular price and the *wazungu* price. Ours would be the *wazungu* one – at least three times the normal. There was no sign of a bus anywhere, but there was something standing beside a sign for Victoria Falls and I thought it might be our transport.

It was about the size of an old Morris Mini and it was already full. But that never stopped anyone in Africa. There was always room for one more. "Going to the Falls?" someone shouted. "Step right this way!"

We were getting really good at making ourselves small. This time there were no springs to contend with. We were all sitting on the floor. I mean, what was left of the floor. I had to think fast. "Should I try to hold onto my bag or my feet - because one or the other is about to be lost out the bottom of this disintegrating vehicle." I struggled to position myself so that I could straddle the gaping hole beneath me and save both. Kaniah was in kinks. Everyone else was smiling.

And the bodies kept arriving. The door was hanging off, some lucky individuals in front were perched on top of petrol cans, and the money collector was clinging onto the doorway from the outside. He couldn't fit in. But he managed to collect all the fares. He draped his long, rangy body over the twisted bodies beneath him, grabbed the grubby notes that were passed over our heads, made correct change, and retreated to his perch outside our cage.

We chugged merrily along, the vehicle swaying unsteadily from side to side, until we were stopped by a policeman on a bridge. He wanted to do a body count. "Uh, oh," I thought, "This will be the end of the line." But apparently not. We were undoubtedly within the limit because, after a cursory glance at the vehicle, we drove off. "Over the limit" must mean carrying bodies on top of the car.

Our friend in Korogwe, who had done this trip at Christmas time, had told us that we would see a small bridge connecting Victoria

Falls in Zambia with Victoria Falls in Zimbabwe. There would be customs and immigration controls on both sides. We couldn't miss it. So we collected what was left of our tattered belongings at the last stop and headed off.

"This carry-on is getting seriously old! What is wrong with us? Why can't we find the bloody bridge?" I wailed. Exasperation was getting the better of me! We had been to Niagara Falls, in the past, and Iguaçu, and we had no trouble locating the falls in those places. The problem here seemed to be that there was no obvious main road. There were only dirt tracks. And there were no crowds to follow. All our fellow taxi passengers had immediately disappeared into the bush – like illusionary puffs of smoke. Where once there had been dozens, there were now only two left standing!

We followed one dead-end that led to a cluster of dodgy-looking moneychangers. "Quick, change gear! Head back!" We took off in another direction and followed a track that led down a rocky gully, across a railway line, and up onto another track. "Surely this can't be right." But it was. The Zambian immigration post was straight ahead.

Immigration was just a doddle for us. We were tourists, *wealthy* foreigners arriving with big bucks to spend. But the locals were getting a really hard time. In 1998, Zimbabwe was a proud state with a thriving economy and everything was much cheaper than in Zambia. Since locals could pass from Zambia to Zimbabwe by foot, and smuggling was rampant, the customs men were busy checking everything for contraband. The Zambian lady behind us was abruptly told to unwrap the baby that was strapped onto her back, for inspection.

It was a sweltering hot, sunny afternoon, and we had reached a slow boil, wrapped up, as we were, in our airtight windbreakers. But all was forgiven when we got our first glimpse of Victoria Falls. Actually, I lie. Our first real glimpse of the falls was from the Zambian side. There, the falls had been transformed into a hydroelectric station. But we turned our heads, and what we saw was pure magic!

The roar of the water and the spray on our faces was wildly

exhilarating, and a perfect rainbow spanned the gorge. Rushing rapids crashed below. Amazingly, Kaniah and I were alone on the bridge, totally alone in the middle of the day with this magnificent sight. It was truly astounding. We had expected to see swarms of eager tourists everywhere. Water dripped down our faces. The spray had become a downpour and it felt fantastic.

We continued on to the Zimbabwe Immigration Post, cleared that, and felt like we had finally arrived. The gate entrance to the viewing areas of the falls was straight ahead, but first we had some serious business to attend to. We had to see a man about a room.

Our connection in Korogwe had advised us to go to the town campsite where we could rent a tented site, a chalet, or a cottage. We hoped to get a cottage. Rachel had said that there would be no need to prior book, and anyway, how could we book? One needed to forward a cash deposit to reserve a room, and how would we do that from Korogwe where there were no phone lines and where it took up to two full weeks to receive a letter from Dar? But we were hopeful. The campsite had not been full at the height of the Christmas season and we were well past that.

Our hopes were swiftly dashed. There were no rooms. There was no cottage, no chalet, and we had no sleeping bags. The couple standing in the queue in front of us had been staying in a chalet all that week and had just been told to vacate in the morning. They had rung every single hotel in Victoria Falls, but there was nothing available.

The desk clerk was not one bit helpful. He had obviously seen it all before. But I couldn't just camp out on a park bench with a thirteen-year-old child. There were those who could, and would, but I was not in that league. The clerk said that if we wanted to wait until 18:20, we might have a chance of getting something. Two parties had not yet arrived. If they became no-shows, we would be offered one of the rooms.

"Why 18:20?" I asked myself. "Why not 18:00 or 18:30?" Here was another great-unsolved mystery. But I dared not ask. I didn't want to upset this man. My child's life depended on him. So we were dutifully grateful.

Kaniah parked herself on her battered bag and I went off in search of, what? I had no idea. Maybe I could ferret out something in case those wayward travelers eventually turned up and turfed us out onto the streets. I noticed an advertisement for rent-a-tents in a shop window. But what rotten luck! It was past five o'clock and everyplace was shut up tight. So I trudged back to the campsite in a deepening gloom.

"What time is it?" "18:10." "Oh, my God," I gasped. "Here came two couples who look like they know what they're about." They had that smug look that said, "Out of our way, suckers!" We were lost.

But hold on. One of the couples had a child, a girl child who looked to be about the same age as my girl child. She spotted Kaniah, collapsed like a rag doll on her bag, and wanted to know if we were staying there too. "Oh, how we wish!" muttered a devastated Kaniah. The man and woman were busy at the desk, and, do you know what? People are really amazing. There was no problem, no problem at all. Their rental cottage had two bedrooms, a living room, a bathroom, and kitchen. We could all share. They would take one bedroom and we could have the other.

Had the desk clerk thought of that solution? Not on your life. This black Rastafarian with red dreadlocks and his South African colored girl friend had thought of it.

Kaniah and Devona, who was also thirteen, were thrilled. This was far better than anyone could have planned. The male partner in this trio, Andy, was a musician. His father was white and his mother was black Zimbabwean. He was well known in rock circles in Zimbabwe but he had moved on to Johannesburg to explore a bigger stage. Devona was his daughter, but she lived in Bulawayo with her mother and her half-sister. She was animated, articulate, and over the moon to have a new friend for a few days. It appeared that she had just met Andy's girlfriend, Venecia, who was from Capetown, but who now lived and worked in Johannesburg. Kaniah's company would help to ease a potentially tense family situation.

It was the weekend of the first multi-racial South African elections and hundreds of people had headed north and over the border for a few days, to let the dust settle. There was great uncertainty about the future for this post-apartheid society. So one mystery, anyway, had just been solved. Victoria Falls was full to the rafters with nervous South Africans.

I learned a lot about South Africa that night, while Venecia and I cooked dinner in the cottage kitchen. After settling into our rooms, we had made a fast shopping trip to the local *Spar* and I was amazed at the huge volume and variety of foods on offer. This was a different world altogether from Tanzania, and even from what we had seen in Zambia. But Venecia was not in the slightest impressed. According to her, this was like a country market when compared to what was available in South Africa. That really got me thinking.

It was fascinating to listen to Venecia talk about her country. Capetown was ninety percent colored while Johannesburg was ninety percent black and Port Elizabeth was predominantly Asian. I hadn't been aware that the races were so clearly defined in cities like that. It had been my impression that the races were more or less evenly distributed throughout the country but were segregated within those cities. That was my first important lesson in South African studies.

Venecia's surname was Dutch but she knew nothing about its origins. She was from a comfortable, racially mixed, middle-class family. She had received a good secondary school education and worked as an accounting clerk in Johannesburg. She would prefer to live in Capetown because of the blissful climate and the more secure living conditions. But all the good jobs were in Johannesburg, so she had joined a steady flow of young people heading north to the capital.

Johannesburg, according to Venecia, had become a very dangerous place. Street muggings had become so commonplace that people didn't even bother to report them anymore. Venecia's necklaces and watches had been ripped off her so many times that she had stopped wearing jewelry altogether. Street violence had become just as commonplace, with brawls, beatings, and rapes being perpetrated in broad daylight. She had the highest respect for Nelson Mandela but said, categorically, that Winnie Mandela was a witch! Venecia felt that Winnie should be run out of the country for letting Mandela down. Willie de Klerk had also been an honorable man but he had been discarded just as soon as he had served his purpose.

Venecia and Andy were feeling rather pessimistic about their futures in the new South Africa. They felt that coloreds and Asians would eventually be squeezed out of the picture altogether. While they had been second-class citizens throughout apartheid, they now saw themselves moving well down below blacks and whites in the new social order. They would love to emigrate to the United States, where they believed they would have greater professional opportunities and equal social status. But they didn't have sufficient funds to make the move, so for the present, they would remain in Johannesburg.

It had been a very exhausting day, so we were relieved and happy to retire early. Kaniah and Devona spent the evening quizzing each other on readings from the Bible – the only reading material available in the cottage. Kaniah came up woefully short. Clearly, bible studies had been very high on Devona's school program.

We were awakened at sunrise by an unmerciful crashing of dustbins in the street. Large families of baboons had invaded the campsite and were scavenging through the dustbins lined up behind all the cottages. Those baboons were as bold as brass. Obviously, they were well accustomed to rampaging through the camp, because when security men arrived in their Land Rovers to drive them away, the baboons reared up on hind legs, beat their breasts and howled in open defiance. They spat and roared their fearless challenge, then turned away and carried on blithely tipping over the bins and ripping apart plastic bags. When they were thoroughly satisfied that they had devoured everything edible, they waddled off into the surrounding bush with cool indifference.

Andy, Venecia, and Devona set off in their car to rendezvous with old friends, while Kaniah and I headed for Victoria Falls. But not before we called in to the corner "Wimpy" bar for a morning fry. We ordered the full English breakfast of sausages, rashers, fried eggs, and toast. We were not normally food-obsessed, but treats like that would not come our way again for quite some time. Once back in Korogwe, we would revert to the familiar diet of rice, beans, and *mbuzi*. So while Victoria Falls was undoubtedly toy town, a tourist haven viewed with intense disdain by real African adventurers, we were deliriously happy. *Tinseltown*, complete with its vulgar hamburger joints and boorish supermarkets, was just what we needed.

❧

It was certainly not true that, "Once you've seen one set of waterfalls, you've seen them all." Iguaçu in Brazil was spectacular. The entrance to those waterfalls was through an extensive national park and the approach road, with its lush vegetation and pungent odors, promised something wonderful ahead. Then the enchanting Hotel Cataratas came into view, with the thunder of cascading water in the distance. It was the tingling excitement and anticipation of wonders to come, that we had found so thrilling.

Nothing like that happened at Victoria Falls.

We entered the viewing area through a very discreet interpretive center and were quickly directed towards appropriate paths to follow for our excursion. Nothing prepared us for what was ahead.

Several tourists passed us by on their return leg, wearing raincoats and dripping wet. "What's with the raincoats?" laughed Kaniah. We wouldn't be caught dead in them. We followed another group, covered in identical raincoats, down a long flight of winding stone steps that got wetter and more slippery as we descended. The steps rapidly became puddles that reached up to our knees. We could hear the booming rush of water coming closer. We emerged, quite unexpectedly, into an alcove just big enough to hold a handful of people. The towering water mountain was on top of us.

The sheer power and force of that raging mountain was terrifying. Its steaming spray erupted like a volcano and beat down on us with blinding force. From every angle, a different vista hung suspended behind a veil of watery smoke. The raging Zambezi River crashed through a narrow gorge far below.

We followed the trails from lookout to lookout, each with a view

120

more breathtaking than the one that had come just before. The trails were so simple. There was nothing to distract one's attention from the magnificent falls.

By the time we reached a hidden rain forest, most of the oilskin-covered tourists had turned back, but we pressed on. Those tourists were toting expensive cameras and the ferocity of the storm would have destroyed them. Unencumbered as we were by photographic equipment, we screamed and laughed our way through the torrential rains and emerged into a nature reserve that was teeming with monkeys and baboons. David Livingstone had first sighted Victoria Falls in 1882, something akin to yesterday in the full scheme of life.

Later on that day, after recovering from the adrenalin rush of the morning's adventures, we met up with Andy and family who invited us to join them at the Elephant Hills Resort. That was the very pinnacle of tourist luxury. Andy's friend was a drummer in one of the resident steel bands, so we were admitted as his guests. It was a far cry from our Spartan campsite cottage.

Elephant Hills overlooked the Zambezi River, and only native palm, wood, and stone had been used in its construction. The entire complex blended softly into the surrounding hills. Every balcony and terrace was strategically positioned to give stunning views of the great Zambezi as it flowed lazily on towards its spectacular drop. Vast expanses of bush, populated with warthogs, monkeys, leopards, and elephants spread out from the distant boundaries of the resort.

We sat at a cool poolside bar, listening to reggae and steel drums, while Kaniah and Devona enjoyed an afternoon swim. Kaniah was booked for an early morning horse-riding safari, and we planned to follow that with a lunchtime cruise on the Zambezi. With a full day's excursions in front of us, we decided to make it an early night.

At 6:45 a.m. we were at the pick-up point. We were nothing if not punctual. After the harrowing experiences of the journey down, we had built up a paralyzing fear of "not getting on". We were soon joined by gangs of American, Australian, and European young adults. Several of those gargantuan trucks that traverse Africa for months at a time, pulled up, collected their white-water rafters, and pulled off - leaving us standing on our own. We had been the first; now we were the last.

It was long past the appointed hour and nobody had come for Kaniah. This could not be happening! Travelers could expect complications and confusion from time to time, but this was getting old, old, old!

I carefully scrutinized the tour receipt - date, time, place - all correct. So we waited and paced up and down and waited some more. By 8:00 a.m. we were still resolutely there, waiting for our pick-up. The tour office opened for business. Margaret, the ticket agent who had booked Kaniah's safari, was taken aback when she spotted us leaning against her office window.

"What happened?" she wanted to know. "Did you miss your pick-up? Were you late?"

· "No, nothing like that," we replied, trying to keep a brave face on things. "In fact, we were early."

A rushed phone call to the horse stables confirmed that, yes; there had been a slight hiccup. They had forgotten all about us. But not to worry. They could fit Kaniah in at lunchtime.

"Sorry," I said. "Remember? We are booked on a Zambezi cruise at lunchtime."

That should have sent out a red flag alert, but it didn't. We had become past masters at missing signals. So, we settled on an evening ride, from 5:00 to 7:00 p.m. Kaniah was a little put out, because the best time to ride was early morning when the animals were rising to hunt. But what could we do? Just take it on the chin and get on with it.

Margaret was apoplectic with apologies, but truthfully, it hadn't been her fault. We parted, still friends, but reminding her that we would be back shortly for the noon cruise.

And there we were, once again at the appointed time and place, outside the agent's window. Margaret was at her desk. We had our tickets ready. And we waited. At 12:00 p.m. I began to get a little anxious. This was terribly like déjà vu. So I took myself inside to confirm the arrangements.

Margaret looked up, saw me, and went pale. "Are these operators usually late?" I asked, not wanting to appear too aggressive. Margaret's face dropped. "What are you doing here?" she squealed. And again, she asked, "What happened?" "We're waiting for our pickup," I calmly replied.

She scrambled for the telephone and after a few seconds her face registered shock-horror. She looked like she wanted to run for cover. They had forgotten about us, again. That was all, they had just forgotten about us. "Are we walking under a black cloud? Should we get out of town while we are still able?" I was dumbfounded.

We were getting used to this. Nothing could touch us anymore. But Margaret was completely beside herself. "I can't believe this is happening to you," she moaned. "Why not?" we thought. We could.

The cruise had left, but they would organize something. A driver was coming round to collect us straight away.

What a bummer! That lovely little floating barge with the overhanging canopy, the glittering dining tables, and solicitous waiters had looked so appealing in the brochure. Now we were about to get *something else*. It was hard to keep smiling through it all. But, it was only a holiday and things could be worse. We knew we could count on that.

The *something else* turned out to be a motor launch for just the two of us. We climbed on board, settled down behind the driver/cook/waiter and his two cold-chests, and shot off down the dazzling Zambezi. Its cool ice-blue waters unfolded before us like a dream. Speckled little islands surfaced out of the hazy mist and we sped on past them, the wind in our faces, and the falls to our backs, and the sun glowing high in the sky.

Remi, our guide for the day, pulled up at one of the larger islands that peppered the river. He unloaded the boat and escorted us to a lovely, secluded picnic area. While he set about preparing the grill, we took off to explore the land. We were the only three humans around, but judging from the evidence of the spoor on the ground, we were among heaps of elephants, monkeys, and wild cats. Remi called out to us, as we departed, to stay within shouting distance of the picnic area.

Kaniah and I crept off, listening and watching, all senses switched on to high alert. Within minutes, we could hear the unmistakable sound of trampling underbrush. Elephants were nearby. In fact, they were no more than ten feet away. We held our breath as a mother and her calf appeared through the crackling branches, gazed languidly in our direction and lumbered off. Kaniah wanted to plod on, following the tracks of a cat, but I was not that brave. In fact, I was sure it was time to head back. Our luck had been pretty thin on the round of late. It might be running out.

Lunch was ready when we got back to the picnic table. We were totally enchanted. Remi had spread a red gingham tablecloth over the table and flecks of dappled sunlight spilled down over the glass, silver, wine, steak, salads, and bread-rolls. And we had a swarm on uninvited guests.

Monkeys were everywhere. They climbed on the roof and slid down the roof poles. They dangled from the trees and exploded from the bushes. We were under attack.

The monkeys were after our food and, man, were they brazen! While Kaniah fought valiantly to safeguard her plate by wrapping her arms around it, one of the bandits made a dive for my shoulder bag. Before I was able to catch him, he had reefed open the flap, swiped a pair of sunglasses and a pair of socks and had charged off up a tree. "Just picture the next visitors colliding with a hip-hop monkey in green sun shades and wearing white socks," squealed Kaniah, as I fell around the place laughing.

We were no match for those guys. They were slick, professional thieves. While I was trying to protect what was left of my steak, the flash of a little hand whisked the bread roll right off my plate. At the same time, the rear guard had sprung into action and another thieving scavenger sped off with the padded drinks bag. Remi tore after him in hot pursuit but the little bully reared up on his hind legs, with the bag swinging from around his neck, and let out a piercing screech. It was pandemonium! We were choking, eating, and howling all at the same time. Monkeys were everywhere. The siege went on until the table had been completely cleared. We were weak from laughing.

Kaniah's horse safari turned out to be mild by comparison. Several other riders arrived to join her group, including a middle-aged man and his wife. This ride had been flagged as one suitable for experienced riders only, because its route followed the animals to their watering holes. Riders needed to be competent enough to deal with the unexpected. "Experienced," in that sense, did not mean, "Have you ever sat on a horse?" It meant, "Can you handle a horse if you are charged by an enraged elephant?"

What kind of a fruitcake would say he could do that when he hadn't a clue? Clearly, one with a death wish, or one totally brain dead. This couple must have been afflicted in both areas, because they couldn't even get the horses to move. That put a serious damper on the expedition and it certainly limited the possibilities for adventure. Angela, the horse guide, was livid because, not only did their foolishness impair the pleasure for competent riders, but it put all of them at serious risk.

Towards the end of the ride, Angela led Kaniah and two of the more able riders up behind an elephant herd grazing contentedly at their watering hole. It was sunset, the animals were settling down for the night, and all was still. It was part of the lure and lust of Africa.

"Well," thought the pair of us, as we gathered up our bits and pieces and prepared to leave Victoria Falls. "We've had enough excitement for awhile. Let's take the train to Bulawayo."

⁊⁊

This promised to be the classic train journey. The train station at Victoria Falls was swathed in purple fuchsia and graceful, golden palms shaded the flagstone platform. Small clutches of passengers relaxed on the grass beneath flower-laden trellises. We had already purchased our tickets and took our places in an orderly queue. There was a singular absence of hysteria here. In Zimbabwe, telephones worked, people stood in queues, and trains and buses ran on time.

There was no stampede for the departure gate. Everyone held a valid ticket and a reserved seat. Everyone seemed confident that the seat would be protected.

Our compartment was straight out of the Orient Express, with its polished oak paneling, its stainless-steel sink that became a utility table when the top came down, its green leather sleepers, and its glass windows that still bore the elegant scroll of the former South Rhodesian Railways. Our cozy compartment sang with the unmistakable air of colonial opulence.

Tanzania, too, had a colonial past but forty years since independence had seen the steady erosion of roads, trains, and transport. While Nyerere's policy of *Ujamaa* had brought peace and a tribally egalitarian society, economic development had floundered. Tanzania's roads were now being built by foreign aid and its education system and medical services were crippled under inefficient and archaic administrations. Donor nations had replaced the old colonial masters.

Zimbabwe had been independent since 1980 and up until recently, when the African *big man* phenomenon exploded in the form of Robert Mugabe, they seemed to have gotten the mix between self-rule and foreign investment just about right.

While Kaniah and I were commenting on the very obvious differences between Tanzania and Zimbabwe, we were joined by our two other female cabin mates. Gloria was from Zambia and she was traveling to Bulawayo to do a bit of serious shopping. She had plans to marry shortly and move to Ghana with her new husband. Hellen was a native Zimbabwean. She was returning to Bulawayo after a family visit to Victoria Falls. Kaniah and I took the top bunks because both of our companions were very large and it took a fair degree of athletic prowess to negotiate the climb.

Our neighbors in the cabin to our right were two American couples on their first trip to Africa, and they were happy with everything they saw. They had started from Victoria Falls, so that explained that. A Danish aid worker, who had been robbed of her safety pack that day, was in the cabin to our left. She had lost all of her money and her travel documents in the theft. When she noticed my safety pack, she remarked that it was identical to the one that had been had stolen from her.

Mya had been cycling over the pedestrian bridge that led from Victoria Falls to Livingstone when she passed a group of moneychangers on the Zambian side. I had a sudden flashback to the clutch of men that we had encountered on our arrival and had fortunately avoided. She said that the ambush had happened so fast that she hadn't time to react. One of the boys in the group had darted out in front of her bike, causing her to lose her balance. An accomplice had then grabbed the safety pack from behind. Its catch was designed so that the strap opened easily when the clip was pressed down. And since she had failed to attach the pack to her belt, it had disappeared in seconds.

Now I understood why I'd seen travelers carrying similar money packs draped around their necks. Of course, with that particular approach, there was always the likelihood of losing the pack and getting a broken neck into the bargain. Instead, I borrowed Kaniah's belt, attached my pack to it and strapped it tightly around my waist.

The night was brilliantly clear. Kaniah and I pulled the top window down and leaned out to look at the stars. The air was crisp and the moon was full. All the trauma of the past few days had been forgotten.

The train began to pick up speed, and as we passed through a protected wildlife reserve, we could see the front carriages snaking around the bends, their dim compartment lights blinking in the night. The railway line was built in a deep crevice with six-foot high land banks built up on both sides. We had to pull our heads in, now and again, when overhanging branches threatened to dislocate our eyes. Gloria and Hellen were chatting away quietly beneath us. All was pleasant and mellow.

Out of the corner of my eye, I spotted the rear of three monstrous elephants standing on the bank. There is no such thing as an elephant of small proportions, but when elephants are within a hand's reach, they are positively enormous. The Americans had spotted them as well and were scrambling for a flashlight when the train suddenly hit a wall.

Kaniah was catapulted off her bunk and left hanging onto its frame, with the wind knocked out of her. But the train hadn't stopped. It lurched forward, stuttered, and crashed again. Kaniah was knocked to the floor as the train listed to a halt. People began streaming out of their carriages and into the passageway. One passenger towards the front of the carriage was shouting that we had hit an elephant.

We couldn't believe it! Conductors were racing along the tracks with flashlights, and yes; we had killed an elephant. Kaniah dissolved into tears. How could something like that have happened? How was it possible not to see an animal as big as that? We couldn't take it in. But the Americans, who had dashed off to investigate, were back. The animal was on the track and it was stone dead.

I was desperately trying to convince Kaniah to stay in the cabin. She got upset whenever I killed a cockroach in our house. She thought we should sweep it out the door, so it could fly right back in. And cockroaches were the most disgusting of creatures. What would she do when she saw a dead elephant?

All of the passengers were milling around in the corridors and some very weird vibes were floating through the air. We were all dumbfounded by the kill, and some were openly distraught. But adrenalin was flowing and excitement was mounting; it was like the fever of the hunt. We could hear the trumpeting calls of the herd in the distance. The elephants knew instinctively that one of them had been lost.

Kaniah forced her way through the crowds to the front carriage. A mass of flesh, so dark in the dark of night, lay prostrate on the tracks. People were pouring out of the carriages and nobody attempted to stop them. They began climbing onto the dead animal, laughing, joking, singing, and larking about as though they were on a trampoline. It had become party time. They had all gone stark staring mad!

One of the frenzied mob began sawing off the animal's tail. One hacked away at his ears and another at his feet. Some were after his tusks. Kaniah went berserk. This obscene mob was mutilating the dead animal's body. She leapt onto the tracks, crying and screaming with rage. She called them *maniacs* and *madmen*, men and women alike. She tried to pull them off the elephant and I was terrified that she would be hurt in the fray. But they just laughed at her. Her hysteria just added another delirious component to the already insane night. Gloria and I finally persuaded her that her efforts were useless. This madness would end only when the wildlife crew arrived to remove the mutilated carcass.

Kaniah was inconsolable. It wasn't just the death of the elephant that was so distressing; it was the mindless dementia being played out on the tracks. 'What kind of people do things like this?" she sobbed. And I had no answer. They had been normal people minutes before, people quietly going about their business, people preparing for sleep. What hidden forces had turned them into a wild and crazy mob? We felt chilled to the bone. It seemed like we were hanging onto humanity by a very fragile thread.

All hope of sleep had been abandoned. Gloria and Hellen were as baffled as we were.

"If that elephant had not been killed outright, if it had only been injured, do those people know where we would all be now? That animal would have charged the train and we would all be dead," declared Hellen. And then, I thought, "That must have been the second crash. The driver had taken no chances."

Slowly, the mania died down. The rising stench of death drove most of the people off the tracks and they filtered slowly back to their compartments. Sanity returned. A pair of cracked and damaged ivories stood in the corridor awaiting the gamesmen. It must have been a very old animal, judging by the poor condition of his tusks. Perhaps he hadn't been able to move as fast as the others and had got trapped on the track as the train came racing through.

We sat together in our compartment, talking quietly about the macabre events we had just witnessed. Gloria, a big, handsome woman about thirty years of age, with a head full of elegant hair extensions, began to relate another bizarre tale. In a casual and almost good-humored way, as a sort of commentary on the deranged behavior that we had just witnessed, she began to talk about the foolishness of men.

~~~

Gloria had married a Zimbabwean man nine years earlier and she had an eight-year- old son by him. Before her marriage, she had owned her own business in Lusaka, importing and selling second-hand cars. Her business had frequently taken her to the neighboring countries and on one such trip she had met her future husband. He was a truck driver. That was mistake number one.

They married very shortly after meeting and he joined her in the business in Lusaka. Chalk up mistake number two.

The business was thriving; they bought a house and she became pregnant. Like many of her compatriot Zambians, she had always longed to live in Zimbabwe, and because her husband was from that country, they decided to sell their house and their business and move across the border before the baby's birth. When the sales were completed, her husband went on ahead to purchase a new property and organize the move. That had been her final mistake. Gloria never heard from her husband again.

Her baby was born and she was alone in Lusaka. We listened, aghast, as she described herself waiting by the window, day after day, looking down the street, certain her errant husband would return. She had brooded over every possible explanation for his absence, and when she had run the gamut of all reasonable ones, she began to invent incredible ones. When her son was two-months-old and she had become penniless, she sent to the country for her mother. She found a job and went back to earning a living for the three of them.

For the next six years she had waited for some word from her truant husband. It seemed incomprehensible. She had waited six years for this man to return with an explanation - this man who had gone out the door with a fistful of money and had not returned. And Gloria had waited for an explanation.

Gloria had received a good secondary school education and she had completed a private college business course. She had been competent and resourceful and had established her own business. When she had married, it had been for love and for life. The hurt and humiliation of her husband's desertion had been enormous. The prying questions and malicious insinuations from family and friends became as wounding to her as her own feelings of confusion and loss.

She said that there had been no indication that her life was about to be shattered. She and her husband had been happy and had been planning their lives together. She had no idea what had happened. She didn't even know whether he was dead or alive.

Finally, after six years, she met another man. She was not in love with him, but she said that he was a good man and he wanted to marry her and take care of her son. She had discussed it with her family and they had all agreed that a new, stable relationship would make sense. All she really wanted out of life now was to be able to stop worrying. But first, she would have to find some answers and put the past to rest.

She returned to Zimbabwe on her own and asked the police to put a trace on her husband. They helped her to get the telephone numbers and addresses of families with similar names in her husband's locality. Luck was with her when she found one of her husband's uncles. She explained who she was, and what she wanted, and he was dumbstruck. He had never heard of her or her son. In African culture, uncles were considered to be second fathers, so this was a very strange development.

The uncle arranged to bring the errant husband to a meeting with Gloria in her lodgings, but when they hadn't turned up at the appointed hour, Gloria took a taxi to her husband's door. The woman who answered her knock was her husband's wife. They had been married for seven years and they had three children. She had never heard of Gloria or her son.

Gloria had arrived armed with her marriage certificate and her child's birth certificate. She said she announced to her husband's latest spouse, "I am the wife from Zambia. Now you can expect the wives from Botswana and Malawi to turn up at your door." After her husband's disappearance, she had learned that it was common practice for international truck drivers to keep wives and families in all the countries that they passed through. If they happened to run into trouble with the police and they had a local family, it made life a whole lot easier. I guessed that Zambia had been dropped from this particular driver's truck route.

Eventually, the uncle arrived at the house with the fugitive husband in tow. The uncle was furious and berated his nephew, "Upon my oath, you have wronged this woman. Have you nothing to say to her?"

And now Gloria laughed, "That foolish man just sat there with his head in his hands, and he cried. He had nothing to say. He sat there like a beaten child, and he cried."

"If you wanted to go," continued Gloria to that foolish man, "you should have told me and set me free to get on with my life. But you left with no explanation. And you left me with a son and no home. What was I to tell my son when he grew up? What kind of woman would I have been if I didn't have answers for him when he asked about his father? I don't want anything from you. God will punish you for what you have done. But if my son comes looking for you when he is older, you will welcome him!"

She went on to tell him that she wanted nothing more to do with him.

"Your wife wants me to come here and live with both of you, as your second wife. What about all the other wives who will surely track you down? What have you taken from them? And what have you left them with? But no, no, a thousand times no! I will not share a man. I am from a polygamous family and I hated it all of my life. Your wife wants me, and now you want me, because I have a son and a job. But I don't want anything to do with your wasted life. I just wanted to see your foolish face so I could finally forget you."

I was dazed. The story had been recited like some gruesome fairy tale, complete with the dastardly scoundrel and the evil stepsister. But Hellen only shook her head. None of this was news to her. "Men," she mused. "They are lazy, stupid, and foolish."

Our arrival in Bulawayo was something of an anticlimax after the turmoil of the previous night. It looked like we had arrived on a film set of a 1950's movie. Bulawayo had that cozy, sleepy feeling of small town USA.

White African ladies dressed in pastel polyesters, and their gentleman counterparts in knee socks and shorts, could still stroll unmolested along her uncluttered streets. Pale-faced ladies, with their limp blonde hair, took morning coffee in chrome-tabled coffee shops. Dashing black Zimbabwean men and their fashionably dressed female counterparts conducted official business with great competence and style. Following a violent and bloody war for independence, the two races seemed to be approaching a true meeting of the minds, all of which was about to be brutally fractured by the radical land policies of Robert Mugabe.

We happened to meet several VSO volunteers in a city-center hamburger café, and we fell into easy conversation with them. What they had to say didn't really make a lot of sense to me. They readily admitted that they hardly considered themselves to be aid workers at all. They suffered no hardship or deprivation at their posts. They were accommodated in excellent housing on a regular bus route within ten kilometers of the city center. They worked in fully functional state schools. They loved their lives in Bulawayo. Not one of them was looking forward to returning to Britain. All of them would be seeking permanent employment as teachers within the state school system when their volunteer status ended.

"Why," I wondered, "are there aid workers in places like this when Zambia and Tanzania have such crying needs?"

That was a few short years, but a lifetime ago. Those were the tranquil days, the days before Robert Mugabe decided to plunge his nation into a terrible abyss.

The return trip to Victoria Falls was mercifully uneventful. But we needed to psyche ourselves up for the final leg back to Dar es Salaam.

❧

We decided to take a day trip to Livingstone from Victoria Falls, to check out the lay of the land and leave nothing to chance for our return journey. We had learned our lessons well. We would not move hand or foot without receiving confirmed bus reservations for the next day.

Surprisingly, there was no problem at all. We easily purchased our tickets and the agent even promised to tell the bus driver to wait for us if we happened to be a little late. That was very comforting. There was no way to predict what might happen in the morning. Would we be able to get a taxi at 5:00 a.m.? Did anything move at that ungodly hour? We had seen earnest backpackers leaving the campsite at dawn but they were a different breed altogether. They marched to a different drummer and taxis didn't figure in that march. They were the true adventurers. We knew we were not in their class.

We were up, dressed, and out on the pavement - standing on the street corner ready to ambush the first taxi that came into sight. Kaniah was lamenting her first misfortune. *Wimpy's* had opened for business but the ice cream machine was not operational – yet. Did this herald the beginning of a bad luck day? Fifteen minutes later and we were still on the corner. Should we start to walk? Should we stand firm and wait? If we did start to walk, would we miss a lift?

"Hold on, Mom. Here comes a taxi," shouted Kaniah excitedly as a yellow blurb crept around the corner. We had forty-five minutes to get to the bridge, clear customs, and dash across the bridge and hope to grab another taxi on the other side. We crawled to the border post with a driver who was still half asleep, and then I leapt out of the taxi and sped through customs like a whirling dervish. I was running with what felt like the weight of the world on my back, and I wished, for the millionth time, that I could blow up those cursed bags. But after what I'd been through already trying to hold onto them, that would have seemed like an act of supreme sacrilege.

I tore on ahead of Kaniah. "Wait a minute!" I muttered. "What's wrong with this picture? She's the young one. She should be out in front." But I was cheering her on. "Hurry up! Run! If we miss this bus we may never get out of Livingstone!" That got her moving. She found her second wind and we shot across the bridge together.

A taxi was fast approaching from the Intercontinental Hotel on the Zambian side. According to the billboard overhead, "When you have arrived at the International Hotel, you know you have arrived." Try figuring that one out while you are hurtling along the road at breakneck sped.

The taxi was already full - with a load of men who magically disappeared when the driver stopped to pick us up. I guessed that we were fare paying and they were not. We had ten minutes left to the witching hour.

Our man at the wheel was Rambo. We clipped corners on two wheels, we crashed down back alleys and in and out of craters that could swallow a bus, and we narrowly escaped skinning alive a man who was pulling one of those massive handcarts that are seen all over Africa. I would have expected to see a pair of oxen harnessed to that hideous thing. Instead, it was a poor unfortunate man with the muscles on his back, arms, and legs bulging.

The bus had not yet departed but the mob milling around it told its own story. Forget the, "I'll tell the driver to wait for you," bit that we had heard the day before. The only reason the bus was still there was that the mob wouldn't let the driver on. They had tickets but there was no room. We pressed forward, slipped under the driver's arms, and up onto the steps. Oh, were we getting good!

There were loads of seats in the back of the bus, but they were all stacked high with luggage, boxes, crates, and bags of every description. "What the blazes is going on here?" I mumbled. "We have tickets and those seats are ours." I was in no mood to compromise. We were getting out of town and we were not doing it on our feet – not all the way to Lusaka.

"Does anyone own this stuff?" I asked the seated and unconcerned assembly of passengers. They were all staring blankly out of the windows. We were invisible. Nobody moved a muscle. Nobody even looked in our direction. We did not exist. Finally, some brave soul from the office appeared and roared down the bus, "Get all those things off the seats. Now!"

Nobody saw anything. Nobody heard anything. So we did it ourselves. The boxes came off the seats and onto the floor. And we were in. Then came the brave warriors from the pavement. They had won the war but their victory would be standing room only, all the way to Lusaka.

Our Rambo had morphed into a kama kazi driver. "Brothers and sisters," he bellowed from on top of his mutilated and foam-challenged seat. "Let us say a prayer before we set out on our journey. If we do not experience any inconvenience along the way, we may reach Lusaka."

"Merciful God! If we get out of this alive, I shall be a walking saint. I will give my last precious child to the Church. I will - - Jesus Christ!" We had taken off like a rocket! Our driver was deranged! Skin and hair was flying in all directions. Once again, Kaniah and I were jammed into the last row across the back. Was this some kind of diabolical retribution for the sins of the American South? Was there some lunatic scheme afoot to compress all light-skinned travelers into sardines?

Our driver paid no attention to the road. His head was spinning around like a carousel. He laughed and joked with the passengers spread out on the floor, under the seats, between the seats, and under and over the boxes. They were having a whale of a time. Nobody seemed to notice the terrible screeching that was coming from the innards of that tank. Our driver was invincible. He had called upon the powers of the Almighty and nothing could stop him now. Nothing except, maybe, a little inconvenience.

Big trouble was lurking in the dark recesses of that machine. I could feel it. I sensed impending disaster every time our driver started playing with the controls. Suddenly we crashed to a screaming halt, but he revved the engine furiously and we lunged ahead. My head crashed against the side of the bus. We were on the road again. The bus sputtered and spat but our hero would not give up. We sped down the cavernous track and tore into some town, who knows what town, but a town with a bus stand. We had made our grand entrance in a hail of stones and a cloud of dust. We were ordered off the bus. That damned inconvenience had struck and we needed help.

We spent the next hour trying to escape the noonday sun. Only mad dogs and Englishmen sat out in that and we were neither. A vicious-looking prophet of doom stalked the bus stand, berating his fellow Africans for their hatred of one another. He spotted Kaniah and me and headed our way. No doubt about it, we did stick out in the crowd. We were cornered. He decided to philosophize with us, telling us that he was an educated man and all these other people were "ignorant, all ignorant". Africa was doomed. I wasn't so sure about that but I, personally, had been feeling the cold hand of doom on my shoulder ever since we started on this insane odyssey.

My child was a wonder. She must have been convinced that her mother was a maniac for taking her on this flight into madness, yet she was still speaking to me. She was even unconcernedly eating some dreadful grunge that was being served out of a hole in the wall. I was indeed a woman blessed.

We were ushered back onto our chariot and was our driver even a little bit chastened? Not on your life! He had been given a new lease on life. Now we were really going to show the world what we were made of. We were quite literally hitting the roof. He gave no quarter to speed bumps. He gunned down everything in his way. That is, until a mountain appeared on the road from out of nowhere, and he couldn't slow down - even if he had the mind to. This time the whole bus was screaming! Babies were being smashed against the rear of seats, my knees were belted up against iron bars that were sticking out from under the seat, and one, only one, irate passenger was storming his way up to the front to confront the driver. He was roaring. My God! The driver looked offended. What had he done wrong?

The speed was reduced, marginally, and we all reached Lusaka alive.

❧

We repeated the whole tedious procedure of booking into a hotel and tracking down buses and tickets for the next day, and spent a quiet night gathering our resources for the final leg of our journey. We had succeeded in getting seats on a coach, so we were hopeful. We arrived at the station in the markets area with a full hour to spare.

As always, the station was jam-packed and people were spilling out into the yard.

The cramped waiting room was hot and sticky, so we stepped outside for a breath of air. That was not good. A wild, club-wielding vagrant was staggering along in our direction, taking vicious swipes at anyone unfortunate enough to be in his path. His face and clothes were covered in blood. He was either drunk as a skunk or stoned, or both. We melted back into the sweltering waiting room. "Better to suffocate with heat than be battered to death," we reasoned.

The passenger queue was already forming and we joined it behind several elegant ladies. It was early morning but they all looked like they were going to a wedding, or a cocktail party at the very least. One was wearing a pink taffeta fishtail number with spreading wings. It clung to her body like a second skin. Another was in a tomato-red, backless rayon creation all edged with black lace. Acetates don't breathe very well so these ladies were sizzling. They were quite wearing themselves out, furiously fanning their dripping faces with newspaper and then wiping their sweat-beaded necks.

A commotion suddenly erupted at the bus entrance and the baton-wielding madman barged through, ranting and raving and heading our way. We tried to flee but he bore down on us, banging himself up against a terrified Kaniah and demanding all of her money. Nobody wanted to be clubbed to death, so the people standing in the queue had scattered, leaving the two of us pinned up against the wall.

I vowed, there and then, never again to travel with a waist pack. They were lethal things. They had caused us nothing but grief, ever since we had started on this journey. They were like magnets to every thief preying the world's streets and stations. Put such a pack on a woman traveling without a male companion, and the situation became a disaster. Backpackers had it right; one pack strapped firmly, front and back, with valuables carried on the person. Leave the cosmetics at home.

A young man who had been sitting opposite the queue, and who had witnessed the attack, ran off to get help. He returned with a guard. The lunatic vagrant was bundled out the front door, but we could still hear him raving incoherently as he stumbled up the street, on the prowl for another hapless victim.

The coach back to Kapiri Mposhi was a wreck, like all the others, but the driver was sane. Because I was not now frantically praying for dear life, I could look out at the featureless countryside, mile after mile of flat and barren bush. There had been an early drought that year and the maize fields were parched and brown. The fields were deserted. That inexplicable fascination that Jane had shown for the green hills of Tanzania came racing back into stark relief. Travel was, indeed, an education.

We transferred from the bus depot to the train station in a beaten-up pick-up truck, and one of our traveling companions turned out to be Rhameen, the Good Samaritan from the early morning's bus station drama. We were to get to know Rhameen quite well over the next forty-eight hours.

Kapiri Mposhi railway station was frantic. Like the main station in Dar es Salaam, it was massive. The Chinese thought big when they built it. But even considering its enormous size, it was still not big enough to cope with the huge crowds that were pouring into it. I would, honestly, describe Africa as a mass movement of people. Every bus and train station was crammed, day and night, with thousands of people on the move.

These people were not tourists. They were people with head loads and babies on their backs, people carrying baskets, and chickens, and charcoal, and maize. They were people traveling incredible distances with what appeared to be their daily wares. These people were all heading for Tanzania. Why? Tanzania was a poor country. Was the grass always greener on the other side? The more I saw, the more questions I had. I was perpetually confused. But ever so slowly, by watching and listening, some of the answers were beginning to emerge.

Gone were the days of orderly queues. We were jolted back to the reality of the mob scene; and it was getting distinctly old. Pushed, shoved, squeezed, jostled, pummeled, punched, stepped-on, trampled, smashed; you name it. It was all happening in Kapiri Moshi with a vengeance.

"First Class?" There was a window up there, somewhere, about a mile away and the whole world was in front of it. Kaniah and I didn't actually hold tickets, as such. We had booked our return seats the day we had arrived, but since I hadn't any Zambian *kwachas* with me at the time, the ticket agent said it would be fine for me to pay on the night of departure. I had been having vague misgivings over that, from time to time, but I had made a determined effort not to think about it. There was nothing I could do. And, I had made sure that the agent had written our names down in the book. Plus, she had said that she would remember us. That was two weeks ago and she must have seen thousands of travelers in the meantime. But, "*hamna shida*," said I to myself. "Think positive."

There were two ticket windows in the terminal. One was for first class and the other was for second and third classes. There were thousands of people. If they kept on pushing at the rate they were going, they would all smash right through a wall. Nobody was getting anywhere but they kept on pushing. I began to feel a riot brewing. So did some other people, the ones in the background holding the whips.

Suddenly, a small number of soldiers pounced on the terminal, cracking leather whips in the air and herding waves of people into corrals. It was like Dodge City. People with head loads and babies on their backs began running in all directions, obeying the snapping whips and forming orderly queues that had been but a mad hallucination just moments before. Miraculously, Kaniah and I found ourselves standing right in front of a smiling ticket agent.

This was amazing. It was the same girl we had met on arrival and, what's more, she actually remembered us. She smiled broadly, looking like she hadn't a care in the world, and she pleasantly told us to come back later. She didn't have *the book*. I smiled too, just as broadly, and said, just as pleasantly, "I would feel so much better if you would take my money now." She didn't move a muscle, but she kept on smiling. Good sign! So, I persisted. "I would really love to have my tickets in my hand."

Well, that could be a problem. *The book* was in another room and she would have to go and get it. Why was *the book* in another room when it had the seat reservations in it and she was selling the seat tickets? I knew what questions to avoid, so I didn't ask. I just kept on smiling and asking her to please take my money.

"O.K." If it meant that much to me, she would go and get *the book*.

Now there was only one ticket seller for thousands of people. Our agent had departed through a rear door. I saw her go. We waited and waited, and waited some more. People started to get restless and that impatient pushing was beginning all over again.

I thought I heard someone rapping on the door that our lady friend had just exited. The only other ticket agent was swamped, and he heard nothing. But I was certain someone was banging on that door, so I called to the swamped agent. He looked up, startled, and approached the door. He couldn't open it. He was locked in and our agent was locked out. She and *the book* with *our names* in it.

"The key! Who has the key?" Everyone was shouting, the swamped agent, the would-be passengers, and the soldiers with the whips. And no one was selling tickets. Everyone was looking for the key.

Maybe those soldiers with cracking whips eventually found it. I don't know, but our agent mercifully reappeared, still smiling, then she took my money and disdainfully tossed it into a cardboard box on the floor. It was overflowing with tattered and crumpled notes. I felt a bit miffed. Throwing money on the floor? What was that all about? But the unsmiling soldiers were now standing guard. I took my precious tickets, smiled and left. We were on our way.

Rhameen, on the other hand, hadn't been quite so lucky. He hadn't put his name in *the book*. But he did know the ropes, and he knew "who to see about a horse". For a few thousand *kwachas* extra, he was able to purchase a second class ticket with no trouble at all. But other friends that we had made on that ill-fated trip to Bulawayo had hit rock bottom. Their tickets were third class, standing. Thirty-six hours of standing, all the way to Dar es Salaam.

❦

Rhameen was very tall, very thin, and stunningly handsome. He had jade green eyes with black lashes, and straight black hair. My first impression was that he had to be Indian. But his complexion was very pale and I had never seen an Indian with such magnetic green eyes. Plus, his features were sharply chiseled, very aquiline.

I was very observant. There were those who would say that I had a bad habit of scrutinizing people, although I did try not to stare. In Africa, staring was one of the all-time favorite past times and considered not even the slightest bit rude. But old values die hard, so I tried not to stare. Also, I didn't want people staring back. That could cause all kinds of discomfort. Nonetheless, I was trying desperately to figure out where this young man came from.

We had retreated from the mayhem of the open terminal to the first class shelter. We had a four-hour wait until departure time. Rhameen appeared, offered us some fresh oranges and squatted down beside us on his leather travel bag. I asked him where he came from and where he was going. I liked to establish basic facts right from the start.

Rhameen was twenty-four years old and an Afghan refugee. "Although," he said, "I know I look like an old man." While that was certainly not the case, he did look more than twenty-four. He was, in fact, younger than one of my daughters and she would have looked like his kid sister. But after hearing his painfully sad story, I put it all down to the trials of life.

Rhameen was a Muslim who had fled his country because it was being torn apart by fratricidal slaughter. When the Russian Army had withdrawn from Afghanistan at the conclusion of their bloody war, the Mujahidin, a fanatical Muslim sect, quickly rose to power. In common with so many fundamentalist thinkers, they refused to share power. The Shiite and the Sunni Muslims found themselves excluded. The people of Afghanistan had driven out the foreign invader only to find themselves sinking into in a new and more brutal civil war.

Rhameen was the youngest child of a large wealthy family. When he was fourteen years of age, his father, who was a doctor, had been killed in a snow avalanche. His father had been able to support several wives and fifteen children. Rhameen recalled that they had been a very happy family, and even in the current circumstances, with his family scattered all over the globe, they tried to stay in touch.

The family had owned three large farms, several country and town homes, and an automobile import business in Kabul. Rhameen voiced a mantra that he would repeat over and over again during the telling of his story. "I loved my life and I loved my country. Maybe I loved them too well."

He had been a university student when the internal conflict had started. There were fifty students in his second-year agricultural science class. Within a few weeks of the onset of the civil unrest, the number had dropped to twenty students, then ten, and finally he was the only student left. All of his classmates had either fled the country or had been drafted into the army. Finally, his professor came to him one day to say farewell. He too was fleeing, and he urged Rhameen to do the same. "Run, while you still can." But Rhameen was the youngest son, and although all of his brothers and sisters and their families had fled, his grandmother was still alive and living in Kabul. His own mother would not leave Afghanistan without her, and Rhameen would not leave his mother to struggle on alone.

He was subsequently drafted into the army and spent two years tramping through the hostile bush "with no food, no uniform, no ammunition, and no reason to fight." Upon the death of his grandmother, he decided to desert. He paid ten thousand US dollars to people traffickers to smuggle his mother out of Afghanistan and on to relatives in Los Angeles. His family homes and businesses had all been confiscated. Priceless Persian rugs and heirlooms that had been in the family for hundreds of years were all gone.

Then, with his mother safely out of the country, he decided to approach a corrupt government official and request an official passport. He would have had to complete five years of army service to qualify for one legally. As a deserter, he only qualified to be shot.

"That corrupt official took me to the airport with one bag," he said. "That's all I was allowed to take. He handed me my passport and walked with me through immigration. I boarded the plane and I watched him watching me. I lifted off into the sky, not knowing where that plane would take me. He left the airport a happy man - and eight thousand dollars richer. I left as a fleeing refugee."

Rhameen had abandoned everything he had ever loved. Again he repeated his mantra, "Maybe I loved my life too much." He spent the next three months as a fugitive in India. The thirty thousand dollars he had been allowed to take with him began to disappear rapidly. He had to bribe people for food, pay bribes for a bed, pay bribes for the right to be a despised refugee. "I hated India," he said vehemently. "They had no time for me, or people like me. They wanted only my money. When I would have no more, they would kick me out."

He applied for admission to The United States, Germany, and England, but he was refused everywhere. Afghanistan was no longer at war with Russia, so he was not a refugee in any political sense that mattered. His last chance was to enter Zambia, where one of his sisters and her husband were living. "In Zambia, you can buy anything, even a visa if you have the money," he continued. "I got a three-month visa and I have been extending it ever since. The officials come to my house in the middle of the night and demand more money. I have no choice but to pay."

I asked him if he could become a Zambian citizen and perhaps regularize his situation, but his answer was emphatic. "I don't want to. I have one useless passport; I don't want another. I will keep trying to go to The United States or Germany." And all through his long, sad, painful story, he continued to smile with those beautiful green eyes.

Rhameen worked for his brother-in-law in a gemstone mine outside of Lusaka, and he was heading for Dar to arrange for the shipment of a consignment of stones. There seemed to be little or no joy in his life. As we trundled along on our train journey, we bought the usual oranges and bananas and coca cola, and Rhameen's life story unwound a little more with each stop.

"I am a Muslim but I am not a good Muslim," he admitted. "Good Muslims pray five times a day but they shoot people like dogs for walking in the street with their girlfriends, or for dressing in jeans. They shout, 'Allah akbar,' but they are bush people who have never read the Quaran. They don't know anything about the laws of Muhammad. 'We are the good Muslims. Obey us or die,' is all that they know."

I asked him about his life in Lusaka. "What do you do when you are not working? Do you have friends? How is your life there?"

"I don't have a life," was his answer. "I work. I go to the mine. I am like an old man, but I must be in the house by 7:00 p.m. or my sister will tell me that I am not a good Muslim. I live under her roof. I must not disgrace her. But I am Muslim, and Muslims do not enjoy life."

He went on smiling while he told us his sad, sad story. And Rhameen just about broke our hearts.

☙❧

Our traveling companions on this journey home were two sisters who ran a business in a village outside of Kapiri Mposhi. They sold things. That was their business. When I asked them what sorts of things they sold, they answered, "Anything we can buy cheap in Dar es Salaam." Shortly after we had crossed the Tanzanian border, immigration and customs officials boarded the train to inspect our documents. They gave a cursory glance at my papers, stamped them, and moved swiftly along to the sisters. This was their intended quarry. The interrogation took place right in front of Kaniah and me.

☙❧

The officials were very interested in finding out how many Tanzanian shillings the girls were carrying and where they had bought them. The girls did not speak Swahili and the customs men were fully aware of that, but they persisted, nonetheless, with their interrogation in Swahili. They reprimanded the girls soundly for breaking the law; they had brought Tanzanian shillings into the country without the appropriate documentation.

But it was all a farce. There were no currency controls anymore

145

and we all knew it, the officers, the ladies, Kaniah, and me. But while the main man remained officious and indignant and vented his righteous anger on one of the sisters, his accomplice accepted a generous donation from the second sister. Then, like magic, the official stamp came down on their papers and the officers swiftly departed.

The sisters, called Marie and Rosa, plied this rail line twice a month and had been doing that, every month, for two years. They knew all the customs people on both sides of the border. Every two weeks the same scene was played out - the indignation, the lecture, and then the pay-off. They all knew their lines and they played them well.

"So tell us," I asked, "exactly what will you be bringing back with you this time?"

Apparently, everything in Dar was cheaper than in Zambia. They would buy bales of second-hand clothing imported from Europe. These were the *used* items that people had donated to charity shops and which had not sold in Europe. It was also the clothing that had been dropped into recycling bins. The ladies bought a few bales marked Men's, Women's, and Children's. Then they brought them back home, sorted them out, priced them, and sold them on.

Shoes had become a big item in Zambia. While Tanzanians clung loyally to the Chinese rubber thongs, Zambians were into shoes in a big way. High-top trainers, with those aberrations of huge tongues, were high on the *must have* list for affluent Zambians. The ladies could sell as many pairs as they could find. And plastic buckets, cups, saucers, and jugs were always in demand - just another environmental nightmare in the making.

Marie and Rosa would rent an entire first class train compartment for their return journey, and fill it with their purchases. This was not a cheap proposition. A single one- way, first class ticket cost forty US dollars. Multiply that by four, add in a week's lodgings in Dar, then count up all the *baksheesh* paid out along the way and conclude - there must be an almighty profit in plastic and acetates all over Africa.

These ladies did not carry suitcases or sports bags. They carried all their belongings in plastic bags. They spent the thirty-eight hour journey dining from plastic containers filled with cooked rice and meat, and they offered us some of everything they had. They had even brought along their own plastic jugs of fresh water for drinking, and some for washing. They were two very large ladies, a sure badge of prosperity all over Africa. They stripped down to the skin, morning and evening, and unabashedly groomed themselves in the comfort of our compartment. They washed and oiled themselves from head to toe while carrying on a steady stream of fascinating conversation.

Marie seemed to be the CEO of the firm and we discovered that she had two young daughters, aged ten and seven. Those *foolish* men of Gloria's yesteryear had never even entered into Marie's picture.

The conversation veered off from business and into education, and Marie asked if I would be able to recommend a good international boarding school for her girls. She was not happy with the educational standards and the general climate of life in Zambia. She thought that her girls would be much better off in Tanzania.

Now, that was a change! Most of the wealthy families in Tanzania were into sending their offspring to schools in Kenya. "Do Kenyans send their children farther north to Uganda? Is the grass always greener the farther north you go?" I began to wonder.

I knew of several boarding schools that were favored by the expatriate communities, but they were horrifically expensive. The fees alone would run to eight or nine thousand pounds sterling, per child, per year.

Our two lady friends sat beside us and smiled, totally unfazed. "We have the money. That is not a problem," they replied. These ladies were street traders. They traveled with their belongings in plastic bags, and they were super rich. They could buy and sell us all, the naive *wazungu*. As we approached the city of Dar es Salaam, Marie and Rosa changed into their business dresses, braided their hair, swapped their rubber thongs for high-heeled shoes, and prepared to disembark. They looked, for all the world, like African queens. The station porters spotted them from the platform and began running alongside the carriage, all smiles, and ready to welcome the rich business ladies from Zambia.

❦

African women left me speechless. They were the backbone of the continent. They were the child-bearers and the child-rearers, the farmers and the laborers. They were the brains and the brawn of Africa.

Chapter Five
A PARCEL OF ROGUES

Sheena looked like a brunette version of the original Dolly Parton. She had her glistening baby-doll face, her wide-eyed smile, and her high-pitched voice. She smiled innocently while she devoured you. She was a five-foot tall brunette bombshell.

I met Sheena and her husband in the car park of the Agip Hotel one day when I had gone to Dar es Salaam to collect project supplies. A co-worker, Brian, and I had just finished lunch and were about to climb into our vehicle, when Sheena flagged us down.

"Well, hello there, Brian," she gushed. "Haven't seen you in such a long time. Where have you been keeping yourself?" Brian was employed on another Ireland Aid program, but Sheena and her husband, Tom, were real expatriates. I was soon to learn that a "true expatriate" was a horse of a different color altogether.

"So you're with Ireland Aid too," cooed Sheena, drawing me cozily into her charmed circle. "Well, how very exciting. You live up north, do you? We haven't been up that way yet but we simply must do the safari circuit soon. We're just waiting for the migrating season, you know. We hear you can see millions of animals but only if you go at the right time. But we do love Dar. In fact, we think Africa itself is just about the best kept secret in the world." Then Kaniah, who had been trawling through the used bookstands on the footpath, made her appearance and Sheena changed into top gear.

"Is this your daughter with you?" enquired Sheena, all aglow. "Oh, Kaniah, how very lovely to meet you." She immediately started to enquire about Kaniah's schooling arrangements, as Kaniah was obviously not a familiar face around Dar.

"You don't mean to say that you go to school in Korogwe!" sputtered an alarmed Sheena, staring at the plucky Kaniah and scrutinizing her face. Then she turned on me. "Good gracious, you really must look into the International School for her. Country schools are just not suitable. My daughter, Jessica, is thirteen as well, and she just adores the International School. It's exactly what a school should be. Not at all like secondary schools back in Ireland. They have no idea how to deal with children, back there. Not a clue! Here, they listen to what kids have to say. And parents have no rights in Irish schools. I was on the parents' committee at Jessica's old school and it was a sham. A complete sham! We had no say in anything." I was beginning to have visions of an annual general meeting in the local parish hall, with an acid-tongued principal facing down this indignant and interfering mother.

"And as for learning that Irish," she rattled on. "What a complete waste of time that is. Just like Swahili down here. They should all be learning English. English is the language of the world. Everyone needs to speak English."

My doctor friends from Lushoto would have had some very interesting things to say about that. Like, what about the unifying force of a native language? What about the cultural roots of a language? What about language as the soul of a people? I put these points to Sheena when I managed to stem her flow of outrage.

"Rubbish!" responded Sheena. "English should be the first language in all of Africa. Look at the Indians in this country. They recognize this and they are the only people in Africa making money!" Before I had a chance to defend my preposterous notions, she had bounced on to another matter of parallel importance.

"We live on the compound," she interjected, all in a rush. Presumably, I was meant to know what and where that was. It clearly needed no explanation because none was offered. But I had never heard of the compound; it sounded like some sort of military camp.

"You really must come visit us when you're next in town. Jessica is in a talent show at school. She's singing one of those Madonna songs. What's it called, Tom? *Spanish Eyes?* She really has a wonderful voice. My older daughter is coming out from Dublin next week. She'd love to teach here. She speaks Russian. She'd love the International School. Such marvelous facilities."

Tom hadn't uttered a single syllable yet. "We come here to the Agip for a few drinks now and again. It makes such a nice change from the compound. Well, cheery-bye, see you soon. Don't forget to call."

Tom nodded to us and toddled off behind his beaming wife, just like Madame Bucket and the hapless Richard!

Kaniah hadn't had any real *wazungu* contact since our arrival, nearly a year before that peculiar meeting. She had lots of African friends in Korogwe, but communication became a little stilted when all they had to talk about were the *mahindi* fields, the rice patties, and the local gossip. So she was excited, but nervous, about the prospects of meeting some girls of her own age with similar interests, if only to talk about music groups. I contacted Sheena and arranged to visit *the compound* on our next trip to Dar.

❧

Sheena and family lived on the expatriate strip along Oyster Bay. We turned onto Kenyatta Drive and followed the tree-lined road past stately diplomatic residences, all ringed with wrought iron gates and armed security guards. I couldn't imagine farming my daughters out next door in that neighborhood! We passed rows and rows of fashionable restaurants, all elegance and charm, with their candlelit tables and glittering fountains. Gentle waters lapped up along the shores of the bay.

Sheena greeted us at the door. She had invited her friends from the International School for this evening's soiree, to make the acquaintance of a new expatriate family in town. They were the Chapmans, who had recently arrived from Canada. Sheena had muted into a look-a-like Elizabeth Taylor for the night, dressed in a black taffeta creation that was pinched in so tightly at the waist that her ample bosom spilled proudly over the top. The front of the dress reached only to her dimpled knees, but then it tapered down the back like a long shirttail. Kaniah and I felt terribly underdressed.

Lu Chapman followed me into the sitting room. She was listing at a 75-degree angle. A fraying straw hat sat cocked sideways on her frizzy blonde hair, and she wore flared trousers and a yellowing tee shirt. Her horn-rimmed glasses were tilted askew. She looked like a towering beanpole; she was so thin that she threatened to crack on contact. Kaniah and I began to feel a little more confident about our dress sense, following Lu's bewildering appearance.

Lu slumped into a chair with her long, skinny legs splayed out in front of her. She looked like a refugee from a thrift shop, or perhaps somebody who had got strung-out in the 60s and never quite clambered back.

"I've had the most awful two days of my life," began Lu, as she examined a long strand of hair. "I can't begin to tell you how awful. I have this painful yeast infection and I've been treating it myself. I use this recipe I have at home? I really don't trust doctors. Not since my great-uncle died of a nosebleed that was really a hemorrhage? Anyway, I've been sick all the way over from Vancouver. When we got to Dar, Bob said he was taking me to the most expensive club in town? So I had to get all dressed up. We got a cab and there we were in the restaurant and I had to get up and run to the fountain. I got really sick. I mean, I vomited into the fountain? So you know, I really don't feel very well right now."

After that broadside of an introduction, Lu collected her wits about her and rambled on. "I'm a teacher myself? I've been teaching for fifteen years. I'm really a Special Ed. teacher, you know, kids who have problems? Most teachers don't know anything about kids." It seemed to me that teachers were getting a bad time everywhere. "My own kids are bright," continued an unstoppable Lu. "Here, I have all their records. See? Two years ahead in everything. That's the McGinn tests? I had them done specially before I left Canada. And the class reports? They're all there." Lu thrust the reports at me, the teacher trainer.

"They really look great," I agreed. I was determined to be the epitome of diplomacy on this rare visit with polite society. "Are your children with you now?" I asked.

"Oh, no. It's just me and Bob. He's my boyfriend. We're from Port Hardy – well not really, I should say Port Alice? He's from Port Hardy. I'm from Port Alice. My husband, Fran – he's a teacher too? He's Chloe's teacher right now. She's thirteen. We'll be coming down to live with Bob in a few months."

Jaysus, was I slow-witted or was everyone in the room as confused as I was?

"What about Fran?" asked Sheena. Great, I was not alone with this puzzle.

"Oh, I'm leaving my oldest boy with him. He's decided he doesn't want to come to Africa. It's probably better that way. We don't get along."

"Who doesn't get along?" I was desperately trying to untangle this web. "Your husband or your son?"

"My son," snapped an irritated Lu. "We split up a few months ago. Actually, we were rebuilding this old house we had bought in Port Alice? And you know, I had done all these great stained glass windows for it?" Lu spoke in question marks. "I'm a glass artiste. Well, I'm really a teacher but I am an artiste too? Anyway, Bob – he's the husband of my friend, Pat? Well, Pat's not really a friend. More an acquaintance? We met at this new-age center. I have out-of-body experiences? I mean, I can transcend – come into your bedroom at night if I want to?"

"Ah-hah!" thought I. "So this is what we've have been missing, shut up there in Korogwe, all alone, when we could have been having the likes of Lu for company." Lu continued to ramble on, lost in her own transcendental world. "So Bob came to fix the electric problem we were having in our new house. We hit it off right away. Like a live current, you know? Ha, Ha!"

"So, what are you doing in Dar?" I asked. "What happened to Port Alice?" Slowly, take it slowly!

"I just told you! Putting my kids in school," she snapped again. Well, just how dense could I be?

"Are you coming to work here?" Now Sheena was looking bewildered.

"Well, yes, of course. Well, maybe! Actually, I'm a teacher. I told you that. So, I'll probably get a job at that International School. But I'm really coming here to be with Bob."

"Oh, Bob's working here!" We were finally getting somewhere.

"Well, of course. He's the mill manager at a mine out by Lake Victoria."

"My God. Lake Victoria is days from here." It was back to me - my turn to be bewildered. "How will your kids go to school in Dar?"

"Oh, the company is giving us a wonderful house here in Dar. Bob can fly back to visit us every three weeks."

"How many children do you have?" I persisted. It sounded like a football squad.

"Three. Greg is the oldest. He's staying in Port Hardy with his dad. Chloe and Stanley are coming with me."

I began to wonder if Greg might be the bright spark in this group.

"You'll find living in Africa a big change from Canada," I offered, and immediately bit my tongue. What about her new-age spiritual excursions?

"Not me. I'm a world traveler. I spent six months once backpacking through Greece. And I speak German. I worked in a factory in Germany. I even got married there."

"Your husband is German?" squeaked Sheena. Here was another unorthodox ingredient in the pot!

"No, no. That was my first husband. Fran is just plain Port Hardy. Ha. Ha!"

"So, when is all this going to happen?" Another guest, Jan, had slipped into the room and was immediately caught up in this web of confusion. Lu's sense of time was more than a little disconcerting. Past, present, and future tenses were all an amorphous blob, and Jan was gamely trying to sift through it.

"I have so much to do," muttered Lu as her eyes glazed over. She was now chewing on the spiky ends of her brittle hair and staring off into space. "I need to go back and get my things ready to ship down here. I'm not bringing much? The company will have to do all that, you know? But I warned them that I will need to have an extra room built onto the house for my studio? I'm a glass artiste. I think I'll have some art shows here – maybe start my own little business? I might sell hologram watches too. I brought a whole suitcase full down with me, you know, to sort of test the waters? But they were taken from me at the airport. They're in customs now. I'll probably just have to pay some little thing to get them out. I haven't told Bob about that yet."

I wouldn't count on that *little thing* too much. More than likely, those hologram watches were on the streets of Dar es Salaam at that very moment, making some Tanzanian street dealer very happy.

"And the carpets! Now there is a real joke." Lu had refocused and was tearing along into a fresh tirade. "I can't have them! I told the company, I need three-inch thick carpets. I will get foot stress on these hard floors."

Lu paused to take a breath. Sitting beside her was a very pretty woman, very typically American, called Jan. She had blonde frosted hair cut in the skater's bob. And she wore a long-sleeved blue and white striped starched cotton shirt and a long navy blue cotton twill skirt. She looked like she had just stepped off the campus of Pennsylvania State University.

Well, actually, it was Montana Tech, as it turned out. Jan was a teacher. Africa was just bursting at the seams with teachers. She had a master's degree in education and she wanted to work. Her husband's company called her a *trailing* wife and they said that she couldn't get a work visa for Tanzania. She was highly offended.

"I don't see how they can say that. I'm a professional too. And I don't see why I have to give up my career just because I had to come and live here." Jan was not just offended; she was incensed.

"Did you know you wouldn't be able to work when your husband took the job?" I asked. That little detail seemed pretty important to me.

"Oh, that's what they said, but I didn't believe it. I've been enquiring about possibilities at the International School and I think I can work something out."

"What do you teach?" I asked. I was beginning to sound like an investigative reporter.

"I was teaching part-time business studies in a community college in Billings, but I'd really like to teach primary school," she informed me. Why hadn't I seen that coming? She'd like to teach primary school, just like that. Like, anyone can mind the store! And, furthermore, she had some specific requirements in mind.

"I'd really like to teach my own children because I'm sure I'm a better teacher than any of the ones they have at that school. Sarah's teacher is a total mess. I had to go to the head mistress about her, today. Do you know that her teacher had sent Sarah home with homework that she couldn't do and Sarah spent the whole night crying over it? James and I both went in to see that teacher today and you would not believe what she told us. She said that Sarah had done the exact same work in school with no trouble at all and she couldn't understand why we were so upset."

"So, what do you think is the problem?" I figured, maybe I had missed something.

"Well, the teacher was lying, of course." There was clearly no doubt in Jan's mind where the problem lay. "She took out some papers to prove her point, but I told her – I know what I know and Sarah couldn't do that homework assignment even though I kept working with her all night."

"Maybe she was just too tired and needed a break," I suggested. "Everything will probably click into place with her today." I knew I was skating on thin ice. There was an old adage that said something like, "Never come between an enraged mother and her child's teacher." "Nonsense," scoffed Jan, dismissing me like a pesky insect. "Sarah's very bright. She wouldn't be having such problems if that teacher could teach."

There was a lull in the proceedings when Lu stirred and struggled up to stretch her long legs.

· "I had a little accident a few months ago," she said as her legs creaked into place. "I fell off a horse and broke my hip? I really don't know how it happened. I was just walking around the riding arena and I slid right off! God, was that painful! I was in agony lying there. But then I hypnotized myself? I can do that – have you heard of self-induced hypnotism? Anyway, after a while I really didn't feel the pain. Then they took me off to the hospital and doctors could not believe my pain tolerance. I mean, you should have seen me – strung up and encased like a mummy. I was in hospital for three weeks? I have a metal clip in my hip now and I get stiff when I sit too long."

That explained the leaning tower effect on her gait and, no doubt, she had been on a mind-bending astro flight at the time of her fall. All the jagged pieces that made up Lu were now beginning to fit nicely into place.

She began to root around in her shoulder bag for a photo of just plain Bob. There he was, built like a bulldozer, short and squat and powerful. Lu towered over him. He looked to be a man of about fifty with huge biceps, and there he stood, in all his glory, clutching a guitar and wearing a red Willie Nelson bandana. "Jeez, Louise," I mumbled. "Are they for real?"

During another short lull, it transpired that Jan was not happy with her housing situation either. She hadn't mentioned carpet stress yet, but the red tiles on her foyer floor were an absolute heartache. She had her house-girl buff them every day with that monstrous machine she had bought but the ochre color still kept coming off on their shoes, and then, for heaven's sake, it got tracked into the sitting room and you know, they just don't know how to care for carpets in Africa. There it was! I was right. I knew those demon carpets would eventually raise their ugly little heads!

Plus, she had looked high and low for black furniture. You wouldn't think that would be such a problem, now, would you? But you'd better believe it. There was no black furniture to be had in Dar. And she just loved black. She had even thrown a black and white wedding. Her mother nearly had a fit. Who ever heard of wearing black sashes at a wedding? But, then, this Jan was a real tearaway!

Lou, with an "o" sat defiantly pouring scorn on all of Jan's woes. Lou, with an "o", was six-feet tall and she was as broad as she was tall. She was British, her husband was British, and her children were British - notwithstanding the fact that her husband had an American mother, an American passport, worked for an American company, and banked American dollars. He was British. All his children were born in America, Wyoming to be exact, and they all carried American passports; but they too were British.

Lou had just withdrawn her children from the International School, causing screaming alarm in Sheena's cozy world. They taught an American-based curriculum at that school and Lou had no time – no time at all – for American education or educators. They were substandard - second-rate all the way.

I was beginning to sense a rabid lynch mob breathing down my neck. I had no doubt that Irish educators would fare no better, in her estimation, than the reviled Americans.

Consequently, Lou had gone on to hire home tutors for all her children, and, competent woman that she was, she had even designed her own curriculum. Her husband's company was picking up the bill.

Lou was wearing a shapeless gauze tent, she was bare-footed and her stringy blonde hair could have used a good wash. She disdained all expatriates who didn't speak *Kiswahili*. Even those who tried, but faltered, suffered her unbridled contempt. Only Lou had truly mastered the language. Lou, and her brilliant children.

Penelope, who was eleven, had been the first of her children to be withdrawn from school. Penelope was gifted. She had been told this in her previous school in California. (Apparently, the assessment system was far superior to the educational system there.) But when Penelope had started school in Dar, she nearly suffered a nervous breakdown. They had to send a bodyguard to school with her every day, and that shadow would sit behind her, all day every day, so fearful was Penelope that she was about to be attacked. It was not clear to me who might be doing the attacking, or why, but Lou looked so fierce that I considered it best not to ask. I'm sure it was patently clear to everyone else and only a dunce like myself would have needed an explanation. And besides, my *Kiswahili* wasn't up to scratch either!

Phoebe, the next child in descending order, wasn't quite as brilliant as Penelope. She learned at her own pace. The teacher needed to know how to challenge Phoebe, how to spark her interest.

They had been trying to make Phoebe learn her multiplication facts at that silly International School. Well, Phoebe just had no interest in learning facts. And anyway, what were calculators for? So, Phoebe was now getting her Renaissance education at home with the hired governess and the private tutors. The family had visited a home-study center when they had last visited London, and they had brought back tons of reading material. Lou wanted them to start reading *Romeo and Juliet* and *Hamlet* in the original, in fourth class, just as she had done.

Her third child, Jason, was a four-year-old prodigy and there was no good reason why he couldn't be allowed to enter first class at the International School. He was certainly ready and it went without saying that he was exceptionally bright. But the rigid little headmaster at that silly little school wouldn't have it. All those petty rules about age, and readiness, and social maturity. So, he too, was now enrolled in their little red schoolhouse.

Ferocious howling erupted from the rear of the house. The screen door flew open and four-year-old Jason came brawling in - punching and scratching Penelope who was hopelessly trying to restrain him. He had the face of a cherub. He had translucent skin and huge blue eyes - all framed with curling black lashes and a mop of ash-blonde hair. His milky-white face had turned purple with temper, and his vivid blue eyes were on fire.

"You fathead! You stupid fathead! I hate you!" he screeched, as he lay rolling on the floor, kicking anything and anyone within reach. This raging dynamo was the socially mature candidate for formal school.

"Oh, poor Jason, cooed Penelope. "Now it's OK, Jason." Penelope lifted him from the floor and continued to pet and coo, while poor little Jason reefed her hair and spat into her face. Poor *Penelope*! As well as being brilliant, she had obviously become Jason's surrogate mother. Lou sat scowling into her gin and tonic - the third one since we had arrived and she had already been there an hour before us. Penelope tried soothing the little tyrant and coaxing him back into the garden.

Sheena was shaken. Her genteel tea party was falling apart.

Jan was bristling. The indignity of it all - being forced to witness such a disgusting display of gaucheness. Lu without the "o" was tripping off into her own world – quite oblivious to everything going on around her.

"What makes people like Lou so bitter," I wondered, as I looked around the room at that curious collection of women? Tanzania was not a penal colony and they had not been condemned to hard labor.

People gravitated to places like Africa, and the East, and South America for so many reasons. Some were missionaries, driven by an inexplicable religious zeal; some were young, idealistic volunteers who were giving two years' service to mankind and searching for a little adventure along the way. Some were retired professionals, men and women who had finished their working lives at home but who still had the energy and desire to serve, and valuable experience to impart. And some were expatriates who arrived in places like Africa to further their careers. They were well paid, lived in exceptionally grand circumstances, had access to private school education for their children, and still, many of them were intensely unhappy.

Those women, who had given up their own careers in order to follow their husbands, seemed to find the adjustment unbearably difficult. But our formidable Lou had not been working outside the home in her former life. She had been a full-time homemaker. Yet, she seemed to carry with her an inbred, but reverse sense of superiority – like, "I'm so superior I can be as scruffy and objectionable as I like and still be superior." She haughtily dismissed the expatriate "soft life" stuff with scorn, but there she was, sitting right in the middle of it. Some very complex social dynamics were exploding all around us, in Sheena's living room, on that glorious summer's evening.

Sanity was eventually restored to the proceedings with the feeding of the masses. The children were occupied in the garden, but Jason kept plaguing the older girls who wanted no part of him. They were trying to hold a disco beneath a set of Chinese lanterns strung among the trees. But Lou insisted that Jason had to be included in everything, so Penelope was dancing with him. "God help the poor child," I thought. She seemed to be destined for a future of hovering on the sidelines, ready to jump in and extricate her meddling mother, or her tornado of a brother, from a lifetime of sticky situations. The sooner she returned to the real world, the better.

"Sheena must be planning to retire here," I mused, as I listened to her saga about forwarding a container full of foodstuffs from a Dublin wholesaler to Dar es Salaam. She proudly displayed cases of corn flakes, pastry mixes, food seasonings, dried sauces, soups, custards, trifles, bread mixes, and pastas. She might as well have been preparing for Armageddon. It was beyond bizarre; it was impossible to take in!

She had a glorious home. There could be nothing in her former Rathmines to compare with it. We were seated in a dining room the size of a football pitch. The front bay window looked out onto a tropical garden. Twelve-foot high walls shielded it from the passing traffic. The dining table was a mile long. Sheena kept a little brass bell in the middle of the table. As each course concluded, she tinkled the bell and the *mpishi* entered through swinging doors. He then proceeded to clear away the debris and serve the next course. "Where," I asked myself, "did she learn all of this?" It was as though she had been to the manor born, and she had not been in Africa a wet or dry year yet!

"Omari, please, do not use instant coffee when we have guests," moaned a petulant Sheena, as she shook her perfectly coiffed head in dismay. Sheena was holding court. "I tell him this all the time, but he just refuses to listen. They can be so, so stubborn. They just won't learn. But I keep him because it's not easy to find a cook who is experienced in cooking *mzungu* food."

I was seated at the table beside a little bumblebee of a woman who was the Mutt to Lou's Jeff. Clare was only four-feet ten inches tall and she had a head of red curls. It looked like a 1980s Afro gone mad. She was twenty-seven years old and had recently celebrated her tenth wedding anniversary. She had no children. Her husband was a shovel operator at that infamous mine out west.

Clare looked like a hillbilly from the Ozarks. She wore a black satin bomber jacket with gold lettering on the back and baggy blue overalls. She was strung out like a trapped animal, nervously chain-smoking and guzzling coca cola. This was her first experience in living "foreign" - and she found herself in Dar es Salaam, discussing international education and African cuisine with astro travelers and degreed – but deranged - educators. She had heard of Lu, back home in Canada, and I began to wonder if there could be anyone in Port Hardy who hadn't. But they had never met. They hadn't moved in the same circles.

Clare had been miserably unhappy since her arrival in Dar es Salaam. Her husband, Danny, had been in Tanzania for six months on his own while she had remained in Canada, trying to settle up their home affairs. "We lived in a really nice trailer park back home in Port Hardy," she told me. "We owned a double-wide trailer house with a small garden and we'd just bought *a Jimmy 4X4*." That was a particularly good type of all-terrain vehicle. "We had it put up on blocks at my Dad's house when we left, because we couldn't bear to part with it." Clare didn't have a driving license and she didn't know how to drive, but Danny loved that vehicle.

She had not wanted to move to Tanzania; it had been all Danny's idea. She missed her family - and most of all, she missed going to the mountains, camping out, and fishing with her Dad. Frowning into her coke, she told me that Danny had changed. She hardly knew him at all now. All he wanted to talk about was his work, and he didn't want to talk to her. He was only interested in the mine.

Danny had been promoted to shovel supervisor since he had come to Africa, and Clare thought that the promotion had gone to his head. He had just told her that she should go back home to Canada because she didn't fit in with his new life. She didn't dress right, she didn't talk right, and she should cut her hair and look more glamorous. Clare suspected that he had found a local girlfriend while she was still in Canada, and she was sick with worry. Danny was her whole world, Danny and his *Jimmy 4x4*. She could not even begin to imagine life without him. She didn't know what she should do. She couldn't talk to any of these women. They would probably think that Danny was right.

"What do you do with yourself while Danny is away all week?" I asked, picturing Clare barricaded into her lonely apartment. There she sat, all hunched over, her shoulders drawn up so tight that her neck had disappeared. Her frizzy red head hung dejectedly on her plump chest. She was the picture of unremitting misery.

"I sleep most of the day," she replied. "But then I can't sleep at night and I'm afraid of all the weird sounds in the street and I'm even afraid of the security guards. I don't know what they're saying. I can't go out to shop. I don't know where to go or what to buy. I can't buy those slabs of meat I see on stalls on the streets. They're covered with flies and dirt and I can't even tell what animal it is - or was. I wish I could get some *Miracle Whip*. I can't make potato salad without *Miracle Whip*. I wait for Danny to come home on weekends but then he gets mad at me for not being able to talk to people. How am I supposed to talk Swahili? He's been here six months already and he has lots of people at work to help him. I don't understand how he can like it here. He told me it was a paradise. He said that I would love the sunshine and hot weather. But he didn't say anything about the dirt and the horrible smells. I really hate being here."

"Maybe you could get a tutor to come to your house and help you to learn Swahili," I suggested. "If you could find a woman tutor that you liked, she would be company for you as well. She could help you to shop and you'd get to know the city. You'd be happier if you were busy during the day. And you'd have something to talk about with Danny."

God, I felt so sorry for her. "What a creep that guy, Danny, must be," I thought. "Bringing her down here to a strange place with a strange language and no friends and then throwing it up to her that she doesn't fit in. Macho Man. That's what he must be."

And, as it turned out, super mom, Jan, wasn't so bad after all. She'd overheard our conversation and offered to go around to Clare's house the next day and take her shopping. Clare looked so grateful. She couldn't stop thanking Jan. I wasn't going to be much help to her, away up there in the north. I hoped Jan would stick with her. Clare desperately needed a friend.

A beach party was organized for the following Sunday, and Kaniah and I decided to go. It was a hoot. Those expatriates certainly knew how to live life in style. They had brought along beach umbrellas, boogie boards, beach balls, coolers, and hibachis. They had beach chairs and beach mats. They had wicker baskets and wine. They had transistor radios and surfboards. And it was all accompanied by a bubbling air of camaraderie, excitement, and nervous enthusiasm.

Old African hands served up words of wisdom and advice to the newly arrived. The men became involved in a serious game of beach volleyball while their ladies compared shopping notes. "I found a great place to get brown sugar," and, "Have you found the *duka* on India Street that sells those curtain hooks you were looking for?" Or, "Did you know that you can get Kerrygold in Marangu now?" and, "Have you tried that bakery on Old Bagamoyo – it's really excellent." Bahari Beach had become an oasis of quiet contentment.

The kids had detached themselves from adult company and were behaving quite normally, once their parents were out of the way. Clare had cut her hair and Jan had persuaded her to ditch the farmer's overalls in favor of a long flowing skirt. The errant Danny must have been happier because Clare certainly looked happier. I also met Danny that day, and he was not at all what I had expected. In fact, he was a real charmer. "Perhaps," I thought, "it's a case of street angel, house devil."

This dizzying expatriate life-style certainly did strange things to people. Clare and Danny were two ordinary people who had been catapulted into a celluloid world. All of a sudden, Clare was associating with people from the big house but she still wished to be back in her own small garden. She would try to make the best of it, for Danny's sake, but she would continue to cross off each tedious day on her calendar and yearn for her first trip back home. On the other hand, Danny had left his old life a few thousand miles and a lifetime behind. He had taken to his new life the way a duck takes to water. He was already planning his next move to Australia, or South America, or anywhere else his company might want to send him. .

A new couple had recently arrived on the expatriate scene and they were unwittingly providing part of the afternoon's entertainment. This guy, with the very wonderful name of Shelden, had been kicking around Africa for a good many years. He had once had a wife in Zambia, but the first time he had taken her back to the United States for a holiday, she had scuttled off with all his credit cards and had proceeded to run them up to the limit. Then she had high-tailed it back to Zambia without him, never to be seen again.

Shelden had moved on to Tanzania. There he encountered a stunning eighteen-year- old beauty at a local disco. Shelden was a forty-three-year-old engineer who didn't know whether he was divorced or not since he hadn't laid eyes on his former wife since their Floridian debacle. But undeterred by trivial legalities, Shelden decided to marry Sifra.

Shelden and Sifra were united in an elaborate church ceremony, on St. Valentine's Day, six weeks after their first meeting. And the presiding minister gave a *straight-to-the-heart* homily stressing the noble virtue of marital fidelity. Seemingly, at the youthful age of eighteen, the bride, too, had a vivid past. She had been living with an ageing European company director when she first met Shelden. The minister was not ignorant of the facts.

Ever the cockeyed optimist, Shelden took Sifra back to Disney World for their honeymoon. They returned to Dar es Salaam with a trunk filled with soft toys. Hundreds of teddy bears and baby-dolls now lined their bedroom walls. Shelden was so thrilled Sifra, too, had not run out on him, he bought her a Peugeot 205 convertible - the only automobile of its kind in Dar es Salaam. Sifra could be seen, day and night, bombing around the city with her canvas top down and her best girlfriend sitting by her side.

Sifra had also become a popular figure at the army and police barracks. She had a well-known weakness for men in uniforms. While Shelden was toiling away at the mine, Sifra was on the town. The whole world knew about the not-so-secret life of Sifra Clay; all except Shelden. He kept his head down and paid all the bills. He supported his mother-in-law, his grandmother-in-law, his sisters and brothers-in-law, Sifra's nieces, nephews, second wives of brothers-in-law, and half the remaining population of Dar. He must have known what was going on but he was mad about he girl, and she was playing him along for all he was worth. It seemed that poor old Shelden would never learn.

We'd had Dolly Parton and Elizabeth Taylor and now we were presented with Jane Fonda. April was a dead-ringer for the aerobic wonder, with similar height, hair, and physique. She was pencil-thin and so, too, were her husband and their two small children. April had been working as a columnist for a small-town newspaper near Melbourne, Australia before embarking for Africa. Her husband was a civil engineer with a road construction team near Dar es Salaam. They were in Tanzania on a two-year assignment, but the smart money said that they would split up long before that.

April and Nathan had two adorable children. Little Alfie was one of those children you could just run away with. He was gentle, sweet, and loving. Kelsey had the guarded look of someone harboring a terrible secret. She was old beyond her years. They were both malnourished. Kelsey's knees and elbows were like razor blades jutting out from her stick-like little body. April was a fitness freak who counted calories fanatically, and she was slowly starving her children in the process.

April ran five miles every morning along the seafront before sending her children off to school. They brought carrot sticks and a piece of fruit for lunch and they were not permitted to eat anything else until dinner. That meal was, invariably, something like a leaf or two of lettuce or cabbage, a few slices of tomato, and perhaps a sausage, or a slice of grilled meat. Bread and pastries were banned, except on very special occasions, like birthdays, when April baked chocolate chip cookies.

She was fixated on weight and she abhorred fat people. They were moral degenerates. Overweight was a conspicuous mark of sloth, self-indulgence, and stupidity. Obesity was a condition quite beyond anyone's comprehension.

She was scathing in her condemnation of the unfit. "Lean and mean" was the motto by which she lived. So she spent hours at the local gym, lifting weights and studying physiology books. Since she planned to open a fitness gym when she returned to Australia, she had begun some pre-service training at the International School, conducting aerobics classes for bored and flabby expatriate housewives.

She and Nathan were like two lovebirds, the picture of wedded bliss as they jogged contentedly along Bahari Beach, pacing each other with a steady and familiar rhythm. But the gossip mill said that April was deep into an affair with the trainer of a local soccer team and Nathan would be the last to know.

⌀∽⌀)

Mark was British Lou's British husband. He was tall, taller than six-foot tall Lou, with graying hair and an aristocratic bearing. Mark's father had been an officer with the British Diplomatic Corps, so Mark had spent his early years in Kenya and Swaziland and he had become part of the British boarding school contingent at a very young age. "Ah, hah," thought I, as the scales began to fall from my eyes. It was becoming increasingly clear from whence their convoluted superiority streak had sprung. North Americans and Australians were mere former colonists and, therefore, several notches beneath them in every way.

Mark had organized an expatriate rugby team, and on this occasion, the boys, resplendent in black and red jerseys, were tearing around in the scorching sand, under a mid-day sun, tackling and trying. They were bound to expire from heat stroke or heart attacks.

Bob, Lu's Port Hardy bulldog, was in the middle of the fray, with thighs like tree trunks, a red bandana wrapped around his forehead, and a bulging beer-belly preceding him down the field. A lanky, narrow-shouldered young Argentinean, who had been conscripted onto the team, was flat on his back under the squad and it looked like it would take the second rising of Lazarus to get him up.

Berndt Gutman was an accountant with a large German dairy farm near the town of Morogoro. The owners of that property had been in Tanzania for four generations, ever since the early days of German East Africa. They raised quality beef cattle, dairy cows, and pigs, and they kept vast orchards of apples, mangoes, and bananas. The farm had its own packaging plant where they prepared smoked ham, bacon, sausage, and roast beef for delivery to the retail markets in Dar and as far south as Lusaka. They also supplied the large restaurants, hotels, and safari parks throughout Tanzania. As one of the very few producers of cheese and fruit preserves in the entire country, their business was booming.

Berndt's wife, Marie, was a rock of common sense. They were expatriates on a two-year contract from Germany, and Marie was conducting a school correspondence course at home for her two children, aged thirteen and eleven. She readily admitted that it was hard going and she was sorely tempted to give the whole thing up as a bad job. "It's hard enough being mother to two growing adolescents without trying to be their teacher as well," was her candid observation.

I'd often felt the same frustrations myself. Kaniah was a reasonably uncomplicated youngster, but we had nearly come to blows several times. Familiar roles got terribly confused within such "pot-boiling" situations. While I always had endless patience with someone else's child, I expected my own to grasp new concepts before I even taught them. The mother/teacher/daughter/student relationship was a very unnatural one. The objective and detached instructor suddenly morphed into the concerned and anxious parent. For both child and parent, it was a schizophrenic experience.

Catherine and Harry Manley were the "elder statesmen" in this eclectic expatriate mix. Both were white Tanzanians who were approaching retirement age. Catherine had arrived in Tanzania with her parents as a young child. Her father had been an adventurer of no fixed abode and no fixed occupation, and he had spent most of his young life managing tea and sisal plantations throughout the south of the country.

Catherine had spent her childhood days running and playing in storybook fashion - days that were filled with sunshine and carefree indulgence. But at the age of twelve, her parents had abruptly shipped her off to boarding school in England. She had hated every minute of her forced exile.

England was a cold and foreign land populated with cold and foreign people. She never adjusted to the English winters, the bleak school dormitories, the damp school beds and the dripping windows. She loathed the stern, harsh voices of the uncaring matrons. As an African, she was always on the outside, looking in, and she longed for her family's house-girls who were more like second mothers than hired help. Since her family was not wealthy, and her father was engaged as a "local hire" rather than as an expatriate, frequent trips back home to Africa were impossible. But as soon as she had completed her secondary education, she returned to Tanzania, where she promptly met and married Harry Manley.

Harry had been born in Arusha, where his father was the manager of a British bank. He had grown up speaking Swahili and he had gone off to Kenya, instead of England, for his secondary school education. He had been working with the tea plantations in Mbeya when he met Catherine at an Anglican Church festival in Zanzibar. Their two children, John and Pat, were born in Tanzania, and when the children were about to enter primary school, the entire family emigrated to Canada. There would be no cruel boarding school experiences for that new generation of white Africans.

When Harry arrived in Vancouver, he found a job in the personnel department of a large Canadian mining operation. Eventually, that company merged with a multinational conglomerate that was expanding its operations to Tanzania. As a fluent Swahili speaker with an intimate knowledge of the Tanzanian culture and people, Harry became the obvious choice to fill the critical position of personnel manager. He quickly became an indispensable link between the Tanzanian government and company officials. Not only was he the only Swahili speaker in the company hierarchy, he was also a popular figure with nationals and expatriates alike.

Catherine became another valuable asset to the company, albeit an unpaid one, as the surrogate mother to a growing army of trailing wives. She could offer them a soft shoulder to cry on and simple words of advice when nothing around them seemed to be making any sense.

The couple's daughter Pat, who had been training to become a teacher in Canada, returned to live with her parents in Tanzania. And it was there that she met one of Catherine's first-cousins, Alan. Catherine was less than pleased when Pat and Alan decided to marry, as she could see another uncomfortable family complication coming down the road. Alan was rooted in his family, and in Tanzania. Alan's mother was a stern family matriarch. Alan would never be allowed to leave. Pat's future would now be wedded, not alone to Alan, but to his entire family, and to Africa.

⟨∽⟩

So many people in the expatriate community seemed to be unhappy and unstable. "What is it, initially, that sets them adrift?" I often wondered. "Is it Africa? Is it the lingering tribal culture and the vast unknown? Is it the loss of the familiar, however dull and pedestrian that may be? Or did the unhappy ones abscond from home because they were already messed up? Did they escape to Africa, hoping to leave their troubles behind, only to find the same problems waiting to ambush them under a new guise? And were they intent on blaming Africa for that too?"

⟨∽⟩

I met another one of those confused expatriates, along with his wife and three small children, as we were leaving mass in Moshi one Sunday morning. We greeted one another on the church steps and discovered that we were staying at the same hostel. So, we arranged to meet for lunch. Don and Sharon were not Catholics; in fact they didn't belong to any church. But Sharon was searching for a faith and Don was going along to keep her company.

This couple had grown up together in a small reservation town in South Dakota, called Eagle Butte. Don had been in the American Army, and as a young officer, he had been stationed for a tour of duty in Turkey. At the time that we met, both he and his wife were well into their forties and their three children were aged five, three, and a year and a half. It soon transpired that they had three older sons, aged twenty-three, twenty-two, and twenty-one. This was clearly not the All-American family - the one with a boy, a girl and a dog – all appropriately spaced out. My curiosity became instantly aroused.

"I really think I might some day become a Roman Catholic," began Sharon, as we relaxed in the hostel garden. "It just seems right to me," she continued. "I was at the Lutheran Church a few weeks ago and at the Pentecostal Church before that, but I have a strong inclination towards the Roman Catholic faith. When I was a child in South Dakota, I had good friends who were Catholics; so I know quite a bit about the faith already. I even have a set of rosary beads that were given to me by a classmate - and a martyr's relic. I've always treasured them. Catholicism just makes a lot of sense to me. My family was Free Mason. That's not really a religion, of course; it's more a set of does and don'ts - and one of the don'ts was the Catholic Church. But I never really understood why. I still don't."

Sharon had done a lot of research and was on a quest for the one true faith. She was articulate and thoughtful. But she was obsessed. Don, on the other hand, seemed to have lost all interest in religion. That seemed hardly surprising since everything we talked about, no matter how remote or even mundane, seemed to return inevitably to the subject of religion. Don had searched enough. He was on a break.

Over the course of lunch, Sharon started to relate their life's story. It was even more gripping than the one that I had heard from Gloria on that fateful train from Bulawayo.

⌀

When Sharon and Don first moved to Turkey, the three eldest boys were very young. The couple had never been part of any church or religion, and they began to fear that their lives were drifting along without any clear direction. They worried constantly about the future for their boys. They could see potential dangers on all sides, from illegal drugs and alcohol to a prevailing free sex culture, and they desperately wanted to find a safe anchor for all of them. Members of The Church of Latter Day Saints, commonly known as The Mormons, were actively prostelizing on their army base, and Don and Sharon found themselves instantly drawn to the wholesome quality of that family-centered worship. It was exactly what they had been searching for.

"We joined the Mormon Church and our lives were transformed. We had never been happier. The whole family took part. It was a constant round of prayer meetings, family days, teen nights, children's days, mothers' groups, and men's leadership sessions. We were encouraged to make friends outside the church and bring them to worship with us, to share in our happiness. Believe me when I tell you that there were no two more enthusiastic evangelists than Don and me. We wanted to share all this newly found love and fellowship with the world. We were bursting with fulfillment."

When they returned to the United States and Don was discharged from the service, they settled down to civilian life in Abilene, Texas. Their lives continued to revolve around their church and Don began to rise very quickly within the church hierarchy. Their good fortune seemed boundless and their family income took a quantum leap forward. The Mormon Church was very influential in local government so Don's practice, which had moved into substance abuse counseling, started to boom. With the goodwill of his church at his back, he managed to secure all the health education contracts in his county. The Johnsons became the quintessential All-American family - a devoted couple with three handsome sons, a fine suburban home, two cars in the garage, and a string of platinum credit cards in their pockets. It was during this period of good health and prosperity that their three younger children were born.

"The Mormon faith teaches that creating new souls for the church is the true path to heaven," related Don. "We love our young children, but the truth is that we had them for the church."

By that time, both Don and Sharon had begun to question some of the more "unreasonable" teachings of their religion. They questioned the belief that the land of promise, America, had been given to them, the chosen, "for their inheritance". And even more alarmingly, "That they (the chosen) were white, and exceeding fair and beautiful." "Where does that leave us?" they wanted to know. They were from a reservation town, and although they looked white, they were part Indian. Was the "wrath of God," referred to in the Book of Mormon, delivered upon the Indians? Were American Indians among the *smitten people*?

In their first rush of enthusiasm, and with profound gratitude for the warm and loving welcome they had received, they had accepted everything. They had doubted nothing. They had been more than content to exist as part of the loving circle. But Don had reached the stage where he was being groomed to ascend to the position of bishop and he had a lot of questions he wanted answered first. But no answers were forthcoming. In fact, the more he challenged the teachings of their religion, the greater was the resistance that he met.

Although their faith had become very shaky indeed, they continued to practice as active church members. The alternative was too hideous to contemplate. To retreat to their prior existence as non-believers was a fate they did not want to even consider. However, during their first pilgrimage to Salt Lake City for the registration of their family names into the genealogy records, the final fissure occurred. The whole ritual was cloaked in such dark secrecy that Don's commonsense approach to life demanded explanations. He was told to be patient; more and more truths would be revealed as he continued to climb the ladder of leadership. Don and Sharon returned to Abilene convinced that they were involved with a sect.

The church's youth group leaders began to interrogate their older sons. "What are your parents saying about the church at home? What are they discussing? What are they planning to do?" Don and Sharon were reduced to whispering in bed at night so that the boys would not overhear them.

Their open questioning of church doctrine within church assemblies proved to be very unpopular, and even their closest friends began to shun them. Finally, when they became convinced that they were being socially ostracized, they decided to make a clean break. They resigned their church membership. Immediately, all of Don's counseling work dried up. He lost his contracts with the school board and the entire family became non-persons in the town.

Don and Sharon had been dashed from the heights of religious zeal to the depths of deep despair. They sold their home, their cars, and their belongings. The oldest boys had already enlisted in the armed forces, so the couple left town in a beat-up Chevy, with their three babies and whatever they could pack into the trunk of their car. They headed back to their reservation town in South Dakota.

It seemed to me that this couple had spent their entire married life on a search. After a short period of self-assessment amidst familiar surroundings, they eventually found their way to Africa. They needed time and space to re-gather their resources and rebuild their lives. They had divested themselves of all their personal belongings and had begun working as volunteers, as they were essentially simple and very good people. The most astounding aspect of the whole story was that Sharon had not yet given up hope of finding the one true path.

Africa was not a bad place to begin to recharge. There were precious few distractions and no shortage of time to think. Maybe, in the case of Sharon and Don, there was too much time. All their intense soul-searching seemed to have brought them very little personal peace so far. I wished them well. They truly deserved it.

⌒∿⌒

Not all expatriates that we met fell into the "mixed-up" category. A lot of them were very normal and well-balanced people, like the people working in and near the town of Tanga. Some were Scandinavians who were employed on a colossal hydroelectric aid project in Hale. Notwithstanding major questions surrounding the wisdom of the project itself, which was turning into a potential white elephant, the expatriate workers were the most laid-back and reasonable people one could hope to meet. They seemed to be thoroughly enjoying their African experience, and they had a very levelheaded approach to it all.

They didn't see themselves as setting the world on fire or doing anything truly great. They were just doing their jobs. Most of them had lived and worked in developing countries before, so perhaps that was the clue to their successful adjustment. Basically, they viewed their time abroad as a pleasant interlude in which they could experience new cultures and have more time to spend with their children. If the children had to lose a little school time, or even repeat a school year when they returned home, it would be a small price to pay. They would have gained a worldview that was worth a great deal more.

There was also a sizable community of people in the Tanga Region who could not be described as expatriates, but who were, nonetheless, *wazungu*. They did not work for large international companies and they did not enjoy all the perks that came with that life style. Many had arrived in Tanzania as volunteers and for a variety of reasons, they had decided to stay. Some had married Tanzanians, some had married white Africans, and some had simply fallen in love with the way of life and never left.

They had all established their own businesses. One was a consultant in animal breeding, one was a computer technician, several were doctors, and several operated successful export/import businesses. Education was the one problem they had in common.

Twenty-three children were attending a private international school founded and maintained solely by these parents. The school received nothing in the form of funding from the state or from foreign agencies. The national school system was failing the country's children so abysmally that parents who could pay for an international education were opting to establish their own institutions.

The traditional and long established international boarding schools were exorbitantly expensive and only diplomats, or those who worked for large multinational companies, and certain Zambian business ladies could afford them. So the Tanga parents had launched a brave effort on their own. They worked through individual correspondence study courses for primary education and used the international baccalaureate program for secondary school. They hired their own teachers, raised their own finances, and did their own quality control. It seemed to be working well. But time alone would tell if the community had the stamina and the necessary commitment to keep it going.

❧

Although normal people, such as these, were not nearly as entertaining as the eccentric ones, they were much less stressful to have as friends.

Chapter Six
THE MAASAI

Stefan and Irmtraud lived on a mission estate located on the edge Tanzania's most northern frontier. Wasso was their closest town and it sat on the fringe of the Serengeti Plains about fifty kilometers south of the Kenyan border.

Stefan was one of two Austrian doctors working at the Catholic Diocese of Arusha's mission hospital for Maasai. An Austrian priest had founded the hospital in the early 1960s. Over the next twenty-five years, he worked at that isolated outpost alone. Although he succeeded in training a number of local men and women to become competent paramedics, he remained the only qualified doctor during all that time. Shortly before he died in 1988, an assistant doctor was sent out from Austria to help him. Stefan, our new friend, became the head doctor's new assistant.

We first met Stefan and his wife, Irmtraud, at the Danish Language Training Institute in Arusha, when we were all learning Swahili. We soon became close friends. But because a month of total language immersion was a fairly stressful experience, even for adults, Kaniah, Irmtraud, and I began to visit the local food and crafts markets for a break. We often came upon young Maasai men walking along the roadside with their cattle and Maasai women selling their beads and baskets in the town center. Kaniah quickly became enthralled with those elegant, beautiful people, and she decided to find out everything she could about them. So she began to haunt the institute's small library. The book, *Maasai, by* Teolit Ole Sailoti, himself a Maasai, soon became her daily companion.

We all managed to complete our grueling language courses in reasonable fashion and, after the very short period of four weeks, we were about to launch ourselves upon the Tanzanian people. It was a frightening prospect, not alone for ourselves but for the brave people who were about to receive us.

In a final parting from the institute, Stefan and Irmtraud invited Kaniah and me to visit their mission hospital whenever we could manage a trip farther north. They gave us the contact number of The Flying Doctor Medical Service, the only air transport that operated in and out of Maasai territory. They said that the Flying Doctors would be happy to take us to see them.

⌒⌒⌒

Kaniah and I eventually succeeded, after countless battles with the temperamental telephone services of Korogwe, to arrange transport from Arusha to Wasso with Stefan's Flying Medical Services. It was an independent aviation service consisting of two pilots and one airplane. Those pilots traversed a circuitous route that connected the Tanzanian towns of Arusha and Wasso with Kenya's capital city, Nairobi, and they regularly made emergency landings at outlying villages and stations along the way.

We arrived in Arusha by hired automobile and located the private landing strip on the north end of the town. A single windsock flapped forlornly in the breeze. Half-a-dozen aircraft sat on the tarmac. They looked like tinker toys. "What do you think happens when a raging windstorm suddenly sweeps across these plains?" I asked Kaniah. "What do you reckon holds these little toys down?"

Our departure time was set for somewhere around the noon mark, so we thought it might be prudent to check things out right away. The maintenance man was busily sweeping the floor   He appeared to be the only official person around, so, using our newly acquired Swahili language skills, we enquired about the time schedule. "Yes," he said, confidently. "The Flying Doctors will be in soon. Just have a seat and wait." That's what he said. At least, that's what we hoped he had said.

Our own driver was in a hurry to be off. He wanted to return to Korogwe that night and it was a six-hour journey at the best of times. Night-driving was never an option; the roads were unlit, bad patches emerged from out of nowhere, and breakdowns brought their own woes. So, Hamza left. Two hours later, the maintenance man returned to inform us that the medical plane would not be coming in after all. A water buffalo had attacked a Maasai out on the Serengeti and the doctors had gone to attend him. Consequently, the doctors and their airplane would not be returning to Arusha until the next morning.

The bar's proprietor graciously offered to order a taxi for us, and that which arrived turned out to be the classiest piece of transport we had seen anywhere in Africa. It was built very close to the ground; in fact, it seemed to be scraping the ground. A little lace tray doily covered the dashboard, the doors were all securely attached to their hinges, and the driver solicitously dusted off the seat springs before we got in. The drive back into town was far smoother than the trip we had endured earlier in our up-market Land Cruiser. We took all of these factors into account and decided that we were being blessed by the very best of good omens.

After we had checked into the local "Y", we went off to wander around town for a few hours. We enjoyed a rare ice cream cone and bought several strands of beautiful Maasai beads. When we returned to our lodgings, we discovered that a television set had been rigged up in the residents' lounge and the entire male population of Arusha seemed to be packed in there. They were viewing the Soccer World Cup. We retired early.

Nobody really knew what time to expect the airplane next day. We had been told to ring the airport bar early in the morning but the "Y" didn't have a telephone and the post office didn't open until 8:00 a.m. I decided that we should leave town a lot earlier than that. We were up and out and at the airstrip by 8:00 a.m. Subliminal panic about missed connections had already begun to set in.

I didn't mind being hours early and I hated being late. So we passed the time watching stylishly turned-out tourists boarding private aircraft for chartered flights to the Serengeti. "What a strange and pampered way to see the world," we thought. There they were, all decked-out in khaki suits, wide brimmed hats, and sturdy walking boots, with private planes, private airstrips, luxurious field camps, and private game drives. That would guarantee that they'd never have to whiff or taste the dirt. But, on second thought, they had probably paid out small fortunes for this *once in a lifetime* experience. So we conceded that, right enough, they were entitled to get what they paid for.

At long last, we caught sight of our plane coming in - distinguishable only by the fading red-cross painted across its doors. Our pilot, Steve, was a very young man with an American accent. He had been born and raised in Tanzania but had gone to college and flight training school in America. His parents were American missionaries who were currently on a house-building project in Uganda. The family owned a permanent home in Colorado Springs and Steve intended to visit there for three months following this return trip to Wasso.

Steve was a one-man band. He did everything himself. He checked out the water supply and all the gauges, and then he took on fuel and did all the other jobs that pilots do before taking off. Finally, he loaded the hospital's medical supplies and stacked half a dozen trays of fresh eggs beside his seat. I felt immeasurably better after seeing that. "He must be one sensational flier," I thought, "if he can be trusted to deliver a stack of open egg trays, safely, to a mission hospital 500 kilometers away."

Our airplane was a *no frills* twin-engine model, with four passenger seats. It would be carrying two Maasai, plus Kaniah and me.

We climbed aboard, strapped ourselves in, the propellers began to rip, and we bumped off along the runway. The whole performance hardly seemed real. There was no screeching of engines and no sudden backward thrust. It was no more complicated than driving a car. Not being a flying enthusiast, I had been a little nervous about this small craft adventure. But it was a breeze. Absolutely painless.

We flew south and then circled north, and, suddenly, the powdery peaks of Kilimanjaro and Mount Meru came into view. Because we were flying at low altitude, we could clearly see the circular *bomas* of Maasai hamlets below us. Then, just as we were approaching the sacred mountain of *Oldoinyo le Engai*, a blanket of thick dark clouds obscured our view. Steve promised to fly over the crater again on the return leg, and with luck, the clouds would have lifted. We would then be able to see into the heart of this live and sacred volcano.

❧

The Maasai people were one of the most fascinating and unique cultures in all of Africa. Proud young *morani*, swathed in cloaks of blood red, glided silently over the vast plains. Their tall, willowy figures drifted quietly along with their cattle - at peace with themselves and the world. Haughty and regal in bearing, these were the Maasai of the Serengeti.

The urban Maasai, on the other hand, were a vain lot. They colored their hair with the grease of an animal mixed with the red *muram* of the earth. They then braided long animal extensions into their own hair and completed the picture with looped earlobes and intricately woven beaded jewels. They wore white plastic sandals and rode black Indian bicycles, and they sat patiently by the roadsides waiting to pose for a tourist camera. And waiting to "sell their souls" for ten *shilingi* at a time.

Farther south towards the Morogoro District, the *morani's* fashion of dress changed dramatically. These southern cousins were far more flamboyant. Their preferred colors of dress ran the gamut from dazzling white splashes on electric blue to purple plum - and sometimes even to a wild orange. For a long time, I was convinced that these southern Maasai were no more than latter-day frauds posing in outlandish costumes for the unsuspecting tourist and collecting stacks of *wazungu shilingi* along the way. But I was assured, by people in the know, that they were indeed the real McCoy, the genuine article, albeit from a different region. Nonetheless, to my mind, there was definitely more than a touch of the rhinestone cowboy about them!

❧

Oldoinyo le Engai, according to local legend, was "The Mountain of God", a lone candle under whose flaming soul the Maasai people lived and prayed for cattle and for children. The rumbling thunder and lightening flames at its core were living testimony to the presence and power of *Engai*. It was to this brooding mountain that the Maasai people brought their white sacrificial lambs and it was from this mountain that *Engai* sent his life-giving rains.

❧

At the beginning of time, *Engai* gave life to three children; and he presented each one of them with a special gift. He gave his eldest child an arrow with which to hunt. The second child received a hoe to dig the land, and the third child received a stick to herd his cattle. The third child, a son named *Natero Kop*, became the father of all Maasai.

Thus, since the beginning of time, *Natero Kop* and his descendants became the proud keepers of all the cattle in the land. In the shadow of *Mount Engai*, the Maasai observed smoldering sunrises and fiery sunsets and their sacred cattle grazed lazily on the golden savannah. Those timeless herders of *Engai's* greatest gifts let time drift by, unconcerned and untouched by passing strangers in their magical flying machines.

Engai had two distinct natures. *The Black God of Thunder and Rain* was a benevolent spirit who sent grass, cattle, children, and prosperity to his people. In Maasai prayer, children and cattle were intertwined. If a Maasai were blessed with children, he needed cattle to feed them; and if he had cattle, he needed children to tend them.

Engai displayed his avenging nature in the *Red God of Lightening*.

182

When his people offended him by breaking tribal taboos or by desecrating his sacred mountain, *Engai* sent drought, despair, and death. So, it was to him, the avenging spirit of *Engai*, that the Maasai brought their ritual offerings of unblemished lambs.

⟨᠎᠎᠎᠎᠎᠎᠎᠎᠎᠎᠎᠎᠎᠎᠎᠎᠎⟩

Archaeologists believed that the Maasai originated in North Africa and gradually migrated south along the Nile, defeating all the other tribes they encountered along the way. Their fierce and warlike nature made them formidable foes and, consequently, the growing numbers of European explorers and Arabic slave traders initially left them very much to themselves. By the end of the nineteenth century, the Maasai had reached and settled vast areas of land that extended from Northern Kenya to the slopes of Kilimanjaro - and westward to the Maasai Steppe.

The Maasai dominated all other native cultures in East Africa for hundreds of years but their power began to decline when Europeans, aided by powerful territorial armies, began to arrive in even greater numbers. The insatiable European "land grab" of continental Africa had begun, and those intensive European settlements marked the "beginning of the end" for Maasai tribal dominance.

A series of natural disasters, compounded by deadly communicable diseases, nearly wiped out the Maasai race during the late nineteenth century. Widespread famine followed a severe drought, and then a voracious strain of *Rinderpeste* infected the surviving herds. Finally, the deadly scourge of smallpox, introduced by immigrant Europeans, dealt the Maasai people a lethal blow. Eventually, they became so severely weakened by hunger and disease that they became prey to neighboring tribes, tribes who had been the keepers of long and vengeful memories.

Germany was the first European nation to acquire the land that extends from today's city of Mombassa, on the east coast, west to the great Serengeti Plains. But during that shameful period of colonial expansion, Britain also laid claim to Maasai land, territory that lay to the south and east of Germany's acquisition. The very dubious treaties of 1904, 1911, and 1912, signed between the British colonial governor, Sir Charles Eliot and the Maasai people, served to open the way to the systematic appropriation of more huge swathes of Maasai land, appropriations that compared, in scale and greed, to the plunder of native American territories a continent away. Widespread European settlement soon followed.

The colony of German East Africa eventually became a British protectorate following World War I, and the Maasai people were again pushed back, this time to a much smaller area, one that straddles present day northwestern Tanzania and southwestern Kenya.

Under a British colonial policy of deliberate isolation, the newly shrunken Maasai territory became a closed district. No one, not even a native African from another tribe, was allowed to enter without written permission from the British colonial governor. In terms of health care, education, and development, the Maasai were officially ignored; they were left to survive as best they could without assistance of any kind. It was not until the dawn of independence, in 1964, that the Maasai people became recognized as integral partners in a new nation. However, official recognition did very little to improve the living conditions of the people, and parity of esteem was not even on the agenda.

☙

There were only two seasons in Maasailand and those seasons ordered the daily pattern of life. The rainy season started in November and ended in May. Then the dry season began. The months of July and August were bitterly cold.

All of Maasailand bloomed with the coming of the rains. Gazelle, buffalo, and wildebeest flooded the plains, and storks and flamingoes descended upon dried-up lakes. A green velvet carpet spread out over the parched brown earth. Maasai warriors moved their herds to open country, storing up body mass for the lean days ahead. There, they endured harsh days and long nights of biting cold. They built thorn-tree fences to protect their herds; they cleared drifting sands from dried-up wells, and they slaughtered occasional animals for tribal celebrations.

❧

Legendary cattle raids filled with bold and daring feats, raids that made the warrior life so thrilling and glamorous, were all in the past. Cattle raids were now forbidden by law. Today's warrior was relegated to retrieving stolen or lost cattle, wearing white plastic shoes, and he could often be seen riding a black Indian bike.

❧

A Maasai warrior with fewer than fifty head of beef was considered to be a very poor man, indeed. And each *moran* knew his animals well. He knew them individually, by sound, color, and markings. One slit on the ear represented the totem to which the owner belonged and the other represented his clan. Therefore, if a cow or a bull became lost or stolen, his owner could track him down and easily identify him.

Although his warring days were now over, the Maasai warrior retained an impressive arsenal of weapons. He used a double-edged knife, normally sheathed in a red leather sleeve, for slashing and cutting down trees, and a short, blunt club protected him from predatory attacks during his lonely nocturnal vigils. He carried a long, pointed stick with sharp projectiles jutting out on both sides and the traditional iron-headed spear for hunting game. While a Maasai seldom slaughtered his own cattle for food, he did hunt wild game. He never deliberately hunted a lion, but if his herd were threatened, he would kill. As King of the Beasts, the lion was the only animal that merited a Maasai celebratory feast.

The rainy season was a busy time for Maasai women. They were the house builders as well as the homemakers. While their men folk traveled many miles away in search of new grazing grounds, the women attended to the needs of the home. New houses were built and old ones repaired. New garments were sewn and old ones mended.

The women stuffed leaking walls and roofs with grass and tender leaves, and sealed them with fresh cow dung. They scraped wild animal skins clean and stretched them out on timber looms; then they softened skins with animal fat and decorated them with glass beads. They made dozens of family *calabashes* from vegetable gourds that they dried in the scorching sun.

Good quality calabashes were vital to the family's health because the women used them to store cow's milk. After every use, the calabashes were washed and sterilized with burning embers from a wild olive tree. When the spent embers were removed, the insides of the calabashes were cleansed with a cow's tail brush.

Reams of unbleached cotton cloth were dyed with vegetable oils and sewn into soft, flowing garments. The women and children were also responsible for milking their domestic cows twice a day and for collecting water and firewood. After a long day of backbreaking chores, they relaxed around their home fires, stringing beads and making jewelry.

While the rainy season was filled with hard work and an abundance of food, the dry season brought only hardship and sorrow. *Morani* moved their hungry herds onto higher land. In the perennial search for grass and water, they were constantly on the move. Cattle often weakened and died and hunger stalked the land. Those at the far reaches of the Serengeti buried their dead and waited for the first seasonal rains of renewal.

⟨~9⟩

We were five people cocooned inside a fragile flying machine and locked within our own private worlds. I mulled over all these things as a watched a young *moran* move quietly over the plains, disturbing nothing, blaspheming nothing. He was at one with nature, faithfully guiding his herd to new feeding grounds and listening to the songs of lonesome cowbells - lost in a titanic vault of time.

The intermittent crackle of the plane's radio and the soft hum of her engine were the only reminders that we were linked to anything beyond that space. Dappled sunlight broke through the clouds and cast great shadows over the land below. The vast expanse of lonely savannah that unfolded below us was the secret weapon that gripped adventurers from afar, and held them captive for life.

I could see a crude red dirt track rising and falling with the land. Possibly, it was the track that Stefan used. He traveled that same route to Arusha at least once a month, to pick up hospital and home supplies – driving mile after mile alone, with the sounds and the smells and the pulse of the Maasai Mara.

❧

There was no airstrip in Wasso. We dropped down on the open plains and lurched to a sudden stop. Cocoa brown meadows stretched out before us and touched the far horizon. An old, beaten-up Land Rover waited at the landing strip, ready to deliver medical supplies, eggs, and passengers to the mission hospital.

Stefan and Irmtraud met us in the front garden of their new home. The garden was ablaze with color, displaying carefully tended beds of blood-red anthurium, orange birds of paradise, hot-pink dianthus, and soft yellow cymbidium. Meadows of wild baby's breath bathed the rear of the house in a soft white mist. The gently swaying meadows drifted down towards a dense forest, home to a collection of exotic wild birds.

Their timber-frame house was compact and comfortable. A quirky assortment of locally-made tables and chairs, deftly carved and highly varnished, sat welcomingly beside an open fire. Wide windows let in the cool night air. A large fenced-in vegetable garden was in full bloom and Stefan was in the process of building an oaken smoke house. Though Stefan hated shooting animals and would never do it for sport, game hunting was the only practical way for them to procure meat. The nine-hour drive to Arusha could only be undertaken once a month and, since they didn't have a freezer, bringing back large supplies of fresh meat was out of the question.

Stefan and Irmtraud were very nearly self-sufficient. They raised their own fresh vegetables, hunted and preserved their own meat, made cheese and yoghurt from cow's milk, and Irmtraud even baked her own brown bread in a wood-burning stove

The Maasai Mission Hospital served a huge catchment area, essentially the entire Serengeti Plains, and it was a very impressive facility. It had seventy beds, a laboratory, an X-Ray room, a pharmacy, and a well-equipped operating theater. Stefan offered us one of the hospital's three guest rooms for the duration of our visit. Pilots who had to overnight during emergency missions, and visiting surgeons who attended twice a year to perform elective surgery, were their most frequent guests.

However, because the Maasai people practiced their own native medicine, they often chose to use the mission hospital only as a last resort and frequently arrived at the hospital doors only after all else had failed. All too often, it was too late and the patient died. That created the unfortunate impression, among many Maasai, that entering a hospital could only lead to certain death.

❧

Wasso Hospital was in the Liliondo District of Ngorongoro Region and it served about 30,000 Maasai. Since the tribe did not recognize national borders, the Maasai people traveled back and forth between Tanzania and Kenya quite freely. If the population of a particular family group became so large that the land could no longer sustain them and their cattle, they split into smaller groups and went off in search of new pastures.

Traditionally, the Masaai did not cultivate land. They lived on wild game, cow's milk, and cow's blood. The *moran* drew blood from a vein in the animal's neck and then plugged the vein with mud. The women then mixed the fresh blood with cow's milk and they all drank. That powerful potion provided the family's basic nourishment. To supplement their diet, the warriors hunted gazelle, buffalo, and other wild game. Although some Maasai had begun to keep small maize plots for private use, farming was still relegated to the sphere of ignoble pursuits.

The only source of Maasai wealth was in their cattle and, according to popular beliefs, the Maasai were very wealthy people. But this wealth was far from disposable. They never ate cow meat and they would consent to the sale of an animal only in times of extreme hardship.

The Maasai had an incredible stamina for walking. One day, while Kaniah and I were engaged in a fairly timid attempt at bird watching on the riverbank that passed behind Stefan's house, a Maasai elder and his young son arrived to water their pack of six burros. Each animal was carrying several saddlebags, and each bag held ten kilos of salt and sugar. They had just returned with their load from the other side of the border in Kenya. They had walked a distance of 100 kilometers in three days.

The Maasai were an open and friendly people. Their native language was *Kimaasai* but the younger children learned Kiswahili at school. Formal schooling was difficult because of the shifting nature of their nomadic lives. Education problems were exacerbated by the fact that the least qualified teachers were often sent to these isolated settlements, without books, materials, or training - and with very little understanding or appreciation of Maasai culture.

The Maasai children very soon became discouraged. Due to huge inadequacies in the entire education system, the children often failed to make any real progress in language or numeracy and the inevitable consequences followed. Parents began to question the value of wasting valuable time on a pointless exercise and the children dropped out. Thus, the catalogue of ills that will forever fall upon a people deprived of basic education continued to fester.

6⟡9)

During our brief stay at Wasso, local Maasai frequently stopped us on the road and greeted us with smiles and questions. They knew that we were visiting the doctor and they were very curious. They wanted to find out all about us. They found it hard to understand why we would come in an airplane, far away from our own homes, without a purpose. If we weren't doctors, and if we didn't have animals, then what were we doing there?

"Where are you from?" they asked. "Do you have animals where you come from? What do you do if you don't have animals? Are you near water? Are you a doctor? Are you helping the doctor? Will you come back again?"

❦

Early one morning, as we were walking along the road by the river, we came upon a handsome young *moran* who was driving a herd of fifty-seven cattle in front of him. He knew every one of them by name. They were all beautiful specimens, all fat and healthy and a far cry from the rangy cattle we were accustomed to seeing around Korogwe. The young man spoke excellent Swahili and he proceeded to tell us that the cattle were all his. I found it hard to believe that he could really be the owner since he didn't look to be more than sixteen or seventeen years old. But then I remembered Stefan telling us that older Maasai normally retired from active cattle raising once they passed their prime – at a mere 35 or 40 years of age. They then handed full ownership of their herds over to the next generation. That certainly gave me pause to think. "It wouldn't happen like that at home," I thought. "Land is what makes a man a man, and he'll hold onto it until he has one foot in the grave!"

I had just been saying as much to Kaniah, talking about how very wise they were, these Maasai. "Just imagine what amazing trust! Imagine handing all of your worldly possessions over to a youngster and then sitting back and trusting him to go out there and handle it like a man. It's like telling him to go out there and start taking care of *you*."

But quite suddenly, that handsome young Maasai brought me back down to earth with a bang, because he went on to say that he was preparing to take his entire herd to Kenya and sell them. We were stunned. "What about cattle being the bedrock of Maasai society?" I queried. "What about all your cultural taboos? What about the fury of *Engai*? What about his avenging spirit? What about..." We were thunder struck. "What about everything we've read and heard? Is it all just poppy-cock?"

We asked him what he intended to do with all the money that he would get. He said that he wanted to buy a car.

"My Lord. What will you do with a car?" I asked, shocked and more than a little outraged at the idea of this magnificent young Maasai being so corrupted by our material world. "But cars break down all the time and they fall apart," I persisted. "With all your cattle gone, you will be left with nothing. What will you do then?"

He was not even a little impressed. In fact, he just laughed and proceeded to show us his watch, another newly acquired possession. "Good Lord, what possible use can you have for a watch out here, light years away from the world of timepieces and timetables?" I was dazed. This magnificent young man was in the process of destroying all my idealized notions about his steadfast people with every single word that he spoke. But obviously, "use" was not one of those words. "Possession" was.

Just as we were beginning to recover from those two lightening shocks, he threw another cat among the pigeons. He asked us to take his picture. It was our turn to laugh. We had been warned, by well-informed foreigners, that true Maasai absolutely hated to be photographed. They believed that the camera could rob them of their souls. But this brash young man had approached *us,* and had asked *us* to take *his* picture. No doubt about it, he was certainly breaking the mould. A watch, a car, no cows, and now photographs!

Maasai *morani* were the very essence of vanity, and with good cause! Our new friend was tall and slim with finely chiseled features and an exquisitely small, rounded head. His hair was eloquently braided and colored red, and he wore a white beaded pendant on his forehead. He carelessly flung his scarlet cloak across his shoulders, leaned casually on his decorated spear, and looked directly into the camera. This was, indeed, a very proud young man, and I couldn't imagine him asking anyone at all for parity of esteem. We promised to send a copy of the photo to him, through Irmtraud. "Perhaps," I thought, "he will stick it up on a doily-covered dashboard whenever he manages to sell all his precious cows and buy that flashy new car."

❧

Two days later, we joined Stefan and Margaret, a community health officer, on their weekly rounds to outlying areas. We were off to bathe the children.

Margaret was a young Maasai who spoke Swahili and was in training to become a registered nurse. We were heading for an open field about 20 kilometers north of the hospital and very close to the Kenyan border. Fifty Maasai children would be patiently waiting for us under the spread of a giant baobab tree.

The Maasai children were severely afflicted with scabies and open sores covered their skin. Swarms of flies buzzed around their heads, hands, and feet. The only permanent source of water was many miles from their settlements. Small, occasional streams dried up whenever the rains failed. Consequently, neither adults nor children had acquired the habit of bathing regularly, and scabies had become a chronic problem.

We had brought along three fifty-gallon drums of water, several basins, and loads of soap, rubber gloves, and salve. The children ranged in age from very small babies to young adolescents. As soon as we arrived, the older children gathered up their soap and water and took themselves off to splash and laugh and enjoy their baths behind a screen of bushes. Stefan was on duty at the outpatients' clinic that day, so after he had left, Margaret, Kaniah and I set about bathing the little ones. The young infants fussed and cried and loudly resisted the cold water on their tortured skins. Their eyes were heavily crusted and their lips were dried and cracked. Mothers mingled with their children, undressing and redressing them and then helping to apply the soothing salve. Margaret commented that

192

the children were very well dressed that day. Their dresses were much cleaner than had been the case on previous visits.

When the older children finally emerged, fresh and newly bathed, they became fascinated with Kaniah's hair. It was long and thick and the color of copper. It hung right down to her waist. She was wearing it securely tied back in a ponytail but the girls began to pull and tug at it until it eventually fell free. Then they began stroking it the way one would stroke an animal. They thought it was an extension, like the ones that *morani* wore, and they wanted to examine it. They continued to pull and tug until Kaniah howled in protest. They could not believe that the hair was all her own. Maasai girls had no hair at all. Their heads were all clean-shaven and their elegant scalps glistened brightly in the morning sun.

But overall, the children did not look healthy. Along with their dreadful skin problems, their teeth were also in shocking condition; they were all discolored and jagged and had huge gaps on top and bottom. The common wisdom about spectacular Maasai wealth seemed to be nothing but a far-fetched fairy tale at that particular moment in time.

We continued on with the washings until late afternoon. When Stefan arrived to take us back to the hospital, he asked Margaret to find out from the mothers what they had learned that day.

"We have learned that we must wash the children to get rid of the sickness. And we will wash them now even if we do not have soap. But we will try to get soap."

They wanted to offer the doctor a gift. Stefan said that he didn't need a gift; he was happy to help them. But, still, they insisted. They needed to give him something. So Stefan said that they could sing for him on his next visit. They were delighted. They would be ready to sing when he returned.

As we approached the end of our brief visit to the Serengeti, Stefan asked Kaniah if she would like to return for a longer period and help with his outreach program. He would teach her how to do immunizations and she could continue with the bathing and health education, since her Swahili was far better than his. Furthermore, the young Maasai girls had really taken a shine to her. She was their own age and she was not afraid of them. She was thrilled, really over the moon. So it was settled. She would return for a month, later in the year, and perhaps one of her sisters would be able to return with her.

We were the only passengers on the return journey to Arusha. A few weeks before our visit to Wasso, one of the Saudi princes had arrived in a giant Hercules aircraft on that very airstrip, for a game drive. The crew and servants had unloaded Land Rovers, sleeping and dining tents, all their own food supplies, and special living quarters for the prince's several wives. His large entourage of servants had established camp around the airstrip for a week's hunting and dining. Official fees for such private hunting expeditions were substantial, and the Tanzanian government was happy to issue special licenses in return for badly needed hard cash. The next stop on that particular hunting safari was to be in Alaska, to shoot caribou and moose. Something told me that the hunting of Alaskan grizzlies would never be in season, not even for royal families.

The day of our departure was calm and cool. The hospital Land Rover stood solemnly beside the grassy airstrip, like a solitary sentry, as we waved good-bye to our hosts and friends and climbed into the clear blue sky. It had been a time of tranquil walks and quiet reflection; almost like a spiritual retreat from the restless world of Korogwe.

The volcanic mountaintop of *Oldoinyo le Engai* came into view and we were about to pass directly over it. Blankets of flaky ash formed a snowy white lake at its crest and deep ridges of boiling hot lava flowed over its crust. The Maasai people held a healthy fear of force of nature and a clear understanding of the fragility of man. They paid daily homage to the hidden forces that they could not control.

Quite nonchalantly, Steve asked Kaniah if she would like to fly the plane. Kaniah looked stunned, and then she laughed. I was bewildered. "Can he be serious?" He was. Kaniah quickly recovered her wits, proceeded to climb over the gears, and settled herself into the co-pilot's seat.

Steve began to explain the functions of all the controls, and then he showed Kaniah how to push the joystick forward to raise the aircraft and backward to let it fall. I could not believe my eyes. To my horror, a recent disaster in Russia, where an Aeroflot commercial flight had crashed killing all on board, came flooding into my mind. An official enquiry revealed that the fifteen-year-old son of the pilot had been sitting at the controls.

The peaks of two mountains loomed ahead and we were en route to passing right between them. I couldn't look. "He must be stark staring mad," was my only thought. Instead, Steve was as cool as ice, keeping his eyes on and directing Kaniah's every move. Her eyes were riveted straight ahead. Miraculously, we passed through the range and onto a clear flight path. Kaniah had been at the controls for twenty minutes when we approached the landing strip in Arusha and Steve took over. I had just lost ten years of my life.

Chapter Seven
KOROGWE REVISITED

Before departing from Korogwe for home leave, I discovered that the excellent little pre-school that VSO worker Ann had established had completely run out of writing and drawing paper. And, because of the unfortunate circumstances surrounding Ann's resignation, the modest funding that she had so skillfully negotiated with her agency, had completely dried up. So on Christmas morning in Dublin, as I watched all of our brilliantly colored gift-wrappings and ribbons going into the bin, I decided to salvage the lot. It wouldn't take much effort to smooth out and refold the paper. Most of it was almost like new. And since the pre-school never had colored pictures or posters for its bare walls, discarded Christmas cards could be cut up and remodeled by the teachers and children.

Then the girls and I decided to raid the attic and collect all the outgrown toys and clothing stored away up there. I eventually returned to Dar es Salaam with two huge suitcases stuffed with wrappings and ribbons, pencils, play-doh, crayons, cuddly toys, and Kaniah's outgrown clothes. But there was one big problem with ventures like this; recycling could easily become an obsession. Today's conscientious recycler was in danger of becoming tomorrow's recycling nut.

The calamitous ten kilometers of cracked and scorched earth that ran into Korogwe from the neighboring hamlet of Segera had undergone a splendiferous transformation during my absence. Ten years of interminable road works had finally reached completion. A band of steely gray hardtop now slithered across the sun-baked landscape, snaking its way through soft green sisal plantations and fragrant citrus groves. Gone were the jungle tunnels of yesterday. But I could see one glaring disadvantage in this remarkable transformation. It would be brutally hot on the bare feet of the villagers.

The old roundabout on the approach to town had been cleared of garbage and rubble and was now surrounded by a stone-packed drain. The new *Keep Lefti*, the new road, and the new bridge bravely lifted the sad, sagging face of Korogwe. But for some mysterious reason, the old road, now leveled and graded but nonetheless, still dirt, continued on through the last few meters of Manundu. Perhaps it was a touch of nostalgia, though I doubted that. More than likely, the project had simply run out of tar and stone, once again!

The Taj Mahal Bar, the Paris Guest House, the Daytona Beach and the Miami Hotel were all long-standing establishments in Korogwe. But as we continued on our drive through town, we encountered a fine, new enterprise located just across from the new bridge. It was a typically low, concrete, one-room building that sported a fresh coat of paint and it carried the noble title, *The Onassis Grocery*. Entrepreneurs thought big in Korogwe. The specialty of this particular establishment, displayed in three-foot high fluorescent yellow lettering against a background of electric blue, screamed out, "Fresh cane juice sold by the bucket."

As we continued along the main drag, I noticed that the *Total* petrol station had erected a dainty Japanese bridge over a delicate bed of stones. A cluster of shapely little bonsai trees surrounded the miniature bridge. "Wherever did they find them?" I wondered. The backdrop to this very artistic feature was a little incongruous, with row upon row of drooping banana trees and dried-up *mahindi* fields stretching for miles around. It was, nonetheless, different, and it made a welcome change from the rusting hulks of crashed and abandoned motor vehicles that normally littered the roadside.

Farther into the center of Manundu, we came upon two stalwart women who were making a brave attempt to hack their way through tons of weeds, broken concrete blocks, and mountains of garbage. They were trying to clear a small patch of land for planting. "Fair play to them," I thought, "but a few dozen broad backs working beside them wouldn't go amiss." The refuse-clogged storm drains had been emptied and the town was really beginning to come into shape.

❧

The clear powerful voices, the drums and shakers, and the startling high-pitched ululating of the female singers at Sunday mass were as mesmerizing as ever. Babies and toddlers crawled around my feet and stared quietly at the strange *mzungu.*

If this were a church in Ireland, babies and toddlers would be crying and fidgeting, or crawling over church pews. Anxious parents would be shifting them from mother to father and back again, all in vain attempts to pacify them. Soothers and bottles would be produced, noisy keys jangled, and coaxing sounds whispered. All over Africa, toddlers looked after toddlers while their mothers sat back coolly unconcerned. Babies and toddlers looked after themselves.

A special ceremony was taking place in Kilole Church on that first Sunday after my return. Initially, I had presumed that it was the sacrament of The Holy Eucharist. Young girls, aged eight or nine and ranging on up to adulthood, lined up outside the church. They were all clad in white. The dresses were elaborate visions of taffeta and lace and the lead girl, who appeared to be about eighteen-years-old, was the picture of a bride. She was swathed in multiple layers of ruffled organza. A mass of white plastic flowers covered her hair and a white net veil drifted down over her face. "It could be a wedding," I thought, "or maybe even several weddings at the one time."

But then, a curious collection of young boys appeared at the rear of the procession. Their form of dress was much more eclectic than that of their female companions. The lead boy was a fair-skinned Asian, which was most unusual in this congregation. It was normally one hundred percent black Tanzanian. The leader wore a bright red blazer, long green tartan trousers, and black patent leather shoes.

He also wore black-rimmed eyeglasses. I had never before seen a child in Korogwe wearing spectacles. Cool dudes from the village sometimes appeared in dark shades brought back from the capital, but eyeglasses were not even in the picture. All the other boys were dressed in an assortment of shirts and ties with a tempting variety of length, color, and condition. This was indeed a rare and splendid display of style.

The procession began. The girls led the way. A soft, melodic hymn drifted out from the congregation. The procession moved slowly and gently towards the church entrance. As the lead girl stepped into the church, the pious tempo suddenly changed. Drums and shakers thundered and the reverent procession broke into a rollicking African stomp. A wild, piercing ululation filled the air as a crescendo of exultant voices peaked. The church erupted into a celebration of joy.

The rapturous procession reached the altar and, as suddenly as it had begun, the jubilation ceased. The original processional participants stood in close formation before the altar. They were quickly joined by a wide array of women carrying infants. "Could this, perhaps, be a churching?" I wondered. Churching was a traditional Catholic blessing bestowed on women following childbirth. The practice had largely died out in the developed world, but it still held an honored position throughout Africa.

Just as I began to establish that particular idea in my head, a large delegation of men joined the ladies. The front of the church was now crammed with people and they were overflowing down the middle aisle. A parish usher started reading out a roll of names and people began to pop up from their seats all over the church. I was, by then, totally confused. We had been in church for over an hour and mass had not yet begun. This bore all the hallmarks of becoming another marathon religious session.

I then concluded that it had to be an amalgamation of sacraments, sodalities, and blessings, with the visiting dignitary from Arusha officiating. So I began to plot a discreet exit. However, before I was able to make my escape, a woman in the crowd pushed her way through, with a chair, and graciously offered it to me. I was mortified. I didn't want to accept it and become the only person in the overspill who was seated, but I was afraid I would cause offence if I refused. Life in Africa was a bewildering litany of confusing moments.

So I sat on the offered chair, slowly dissolving in heat and embarrassment. I was also suffocating. People were standing all around me, cutting off any chance of a breeze. My head felt light. After a further half hour of growing confusion, I quietly excused myself and headed for the door. I had been in the church for two full hours and mass had not yet started. Africans possessed the most extraordinary powers of endurance. I was no match for them. Not by a long shot!

☙❧

My reclaimed vegetable garden had reverted to its original state during my absence. Several months of dry weather had baked the ground hard and I needed to wait for the new rains in order to begin planting again. But there were one or two consolations. The *paupau* tree that had been a mere slip before my departure had flourished and bloomed. It was now twelve-feet tall with the trunk of an elephant. It was laden down with fruit, after only three months' growth. Also, the indeterminate climbers that I had planted as camouflage across the rear security fence were now two inches thick. I broke off one of the fat, green pods to investigate. To my amazement, when I peeled back the tough skin, I found a *loofah* inside. "I could begin a roaring export trade from my vegetable garden to The Body Shop," I thought. "Or, this could be just the perfect new enterprise for Beatrice." It required no investment at all. The seeds obligingly dropped to the ground; and the *loofahs* would never rot, need special ingredients, or get smallpox.

I had returned to Korogwe with a new supply of vegetable seeds for Juma, Beatrice, and myself. As well as the already successful crops of tomatoes, kale, and cabbage, we could now try broccoli and rhubarb. I could almost taste the exquisite tartness of a rhubarb pie already. But Beatrice and I would have to do a cookery refresher course first, because Beatrice had lost her touch. I had been living on a diet of watery soup made with a few potatoes, an onion, and some dried-up peas since my return. Sadly, we were back to square one.

I was anxious to find out how Beatrice's bakery business had progressed over the Christmas period. I had paid a visit to a smashing new hotel in the village, built and run by an enterprising *Chagga*, the week before I had left. The days of the Traveller's Inn, with its rubbery chicken and rice, were now numbered. The new *duka mwenywe* had many influential friends in high places, as did most *Chaggas*. So the thrice-daily buses which plied the road from Dar to Arusha and back, now stopped outside his door instead of at the bus stand. This meant that he could serve at least one hundred hot lunches every day and his five hotel bedrooms were permanently filled. Everybody was happy with the new arrangements - the hotel owner, the bus drivers who received their cut for accommodating him, and the passengers who could now purchase a decent meal. But there were uneasy rumblings among the traders at the bus stand. Trouble was brewing. It could come barreling down that road at any time.

The new hotel seemed the perfect place for Beatrice to sell her wares. I had enquired from the owner if he would be interested in buying a daily supply of fresh muffins for his customers, absolutely first class – made with fresh eggs and Blue Band margarine. These were unknown ingredients in Korogwe, maybe even in Tanzania. Tanzanian pastries were always as dry as sawdust because they were made without butter and eggs. Beatrice could supply the eggs from her own chickens, now free from *ndui*, and I would supply the *Blue Band* and flour. She could bake them in my oven and deliver them to the hotel on her way home from work. I had presented the owner with a sample to test. He was a man with an impressive girth and a refined taste for the good life. He had licked his fingers and happily agreed to my proposition.

Once again, Beatrice was elated. She arrived at the hotel the following afternoon and negotiated an agreed rate with the proprietor. He would sell the muffins for fifty *shilingi* each, and she would get forty-five.

The arrangement had lasted one week. The hotel owner told her that the passengers did not want to buy them, which was a monstrous lie. Bus passengers succumbed to the most loathsome of food offerings because they had no choice. They would devour anything even remotely edible on their epic cross-country journeys.

In fact, the real obstacle in the way of Beatrice's fledgling business had been the spiteful hotel cook who had refused to work while the muffins were on sale. Bitter jealousy like this raged on everywhere. So, shot-down by the deadly sin of envy, another budding business bit the dust. "Is it any wonder that people lose heart?" I asked myself.

Our own project team members had also begun to feel the sting of jealous tongues. They were an extraordinarily hard-working, enthusiastic, and committed group of ten people. The young men were in their mid-twenties, the women in their thirties and the eldest advisor was a sprightly gentleman of sixty-five. Their list of accomplishments, within two short years, was truly astounding. They had progressed from being very unskilled secondary school mathematics tutors to highly professional and competent teacher trainers. They had also begun to think and write creatively, had become computer literate, and were developing to a stage where they could hope to become a national resource - a professional teacher training team.

When our mathematics project had been tottering along in its infancy, very little attention had been paid to it, either by the local community or by the academic community in the capital. Projects like ours had come and gone over the years and one more wasn't about to create much of a stir. However, with every successful step that we took, public awareness had grown. Increasingly fractious questions were now being raised.

"How had team members been chosen and what had been the criteria for choosing them?" The answers were clear and straightforward. From the outset, this had been a Tanzanian-proposed, Tanzanian-led, and Tanzanian-developed project. Only the two technical advisors and the development funds had been foreign.

The project's team members had all been regular staff members of the host institution, at the outset, and they all still worked at their original positions. Only their responsibilities and workload had increased. They had received no additional pay. The project had delivered a series of on-site training workshops, and had sponsored graduate study abroad for project leaders. Consequently, as a result of the project training and their own hard work, all the members had acquired new skills, expertise, and self-confidence.

"But what else are they getting from the project?" the skeptics continued to ask. "What other benefits are involved?" And the bottom line was this: "What extra allowances are they being paid?" The ever-churning rumor mill said that they were being paid a king's ransom. "Nobody does anything for nothing," they said. That was the way the aid industry worked. Gaining a foothold on the lucrative "aid" ladder was the vital first step to financial success.

⚜

Kaniah's school friend, Vero, had attained the unattainable and had gone off to a state secondary school in *Bungu*. Those late night English sessions outside our house had really worked. Vero was ecstatic. Especially now that there was another new baby in the house.

The entire Nkigi family paid me a visit shortly after my return and I was flabbergasted to see the size of the new infant. It was the fattest baby I had seen in all of Africa, a regular butterball. She was even heavier than Lucy, who was now two and a half and as tiny as ever. This baby was spectacularly fat, but everyone was bursting with pride, truly enchanted with their beautiful, fat baby.

Paulina, Kaniah's other school pal, had also passed her exams but her mother had decided that she was needed on the *shamba* in Lushoto. And Paulina hadn't protested. She said that she preferred to stay home; she wanted lots of children and a man with a good *shamba*.

I scrupulously attended to my daily chloroquine and palludrine regime. Two weeks before I had left on leave, I had come down with a nasty dose of malaria - passing from sweating bullets to freezing cold. My head had felt like it was tied with steel belts and my whole body was wracked with pain - at the base of my neck, across my forehead and inside my skull. I had no medicinal cure on hand but, thank God, Hazel kept a small supply of Falsidar at the mission hospital. But even after taking the prescribed six tablets, I still felt wretched. I was vomiting and shivering up to two weeks later. There was no sure way of avoiding malaria, even with prophylactics, but I knew that if I did take the medication regularly, at least I wouldn't die.

I was soon reunited with the foreign community at the Scandinavian Club in Hale and learned that Hazel and Richard were expecting their third baby. They related a truly ghastly story about an experience they had just been through, and one that could influence their decision to remain in Tanzania for the rest of their working lives.

They had all been fast asleep one evening when Hazel was jolted awake by little Grace's hysterical cries. She was screaming, *"Wadudu, wadudu"*, which in Swahili means, "Bugs, bugs." Hazel leapt across the room in the dark to the baby's cot as Richard frantically tried to light the kerosene lamp. Armies of ants had invaded the house and were crawling all over Grace and her cot. Millions of them covered the walls, the floor, the bed, and table and they were heading straight for their second daughter, Jessica. Richard raced to snatch up the sleeping child, but within the few seconds that it took to reach her, the phalanx of ants had attacked both him and Hazel. The besieged parents fled the house with their screaming children and headed straight for the mission hospital. By now the bugs had attacked the eyes, ears, mouths, noses, and hairs of the entire family. It was like a maniacal scene from Alfred Hitchcock. If they had been able to plunge themselves and the children into a bath of water, or jumped under a towering shower, they would have had some hope of relief. But they were left with only the pitifully weak splashes of water from a plastic hand bucket. In the end, they had to pick the bugs off the bodies of their writhing, screaming, kicking children, one by one, while they tried to beat the beastly parasites off themselves.

"How does anyone ever recover from such a diabolical assault?" I asked Hazel. I knew that I would have been scarred for life. However, seeing Grace playing at the pool, happily collecting fallen mangoes, I was once again confounded by the resilience of some children. Nonetheless, I think the light went out for Hazel and Africa that awful night.

❧

Lashings of fist-sized raindrops trapped me in my office on the feast of *Id*, the important Muslim holiday that marked the end of *Ramadan* and a month of daylight fasting. I had done my six laps around the soccer pitch earlier that morning, relishing the unusually cool air that had followed a heavy downpour. The males of the Muslim community were still at their mosque and their plaintive chants poured out over the village. But the day's nasty weather threatened to put an end to the traditional *walking out* parade, where men and boys struck artful poses in their long flowing white robes while their women sparkled brightly in new *kangas* and head veils.

❧

There had been a serious escalation of banditry on the roads surrounding Korogwe and the appearance of pistols and knives, previously all but unknown in these parts, was becoming chillingly commonplace. The term "banditry", when used to describe brutal hijackings, druggings, and vicious pistol-whippings, seemed highly inappropriate. The most recent such incidents involved two young Canadian aid workers from Arusha and a visiting Israeli businessman. The three foreigners had all ended up in Korogwe District Hospital on the same night.

The Canadians had been traveling south along the main Arusha to Dar road in their project vehicle, a Land Cruiser very similar to our own. I had recently read some scathing commentaries made by journalists and travel writers alluding to the use of such vehicles by foreign aid workers. When compared to traveling by *shanks mare*, bicycle, or even motorbike, a Land Cruiser was, indeed, a luxury item. But the ones I had seen being used by aid workers were empty shells. They operated without seats, radios, or air-conditioning and were only used to transport project personnel and supplies safely from one site to another.

The Canadian couple had been traveling on one of the best roads in Tanzania when a car that had been following them for several kilometers suddenly cut them off. Four armed men jumped out and ordered the Canadians onto the ground. The bandits then dragged the *wazungu* into the rear of the Land Cruiser and sped off into the vast sisal fields. When they were several kilometers into the plantation, they stopped the vehicle and dragged the Canadians out. The attackers then forced their victims to drink a local potion of poison and drugs. When the victims sputtered and spat and tried not to swallow it, the bandits put guns to their heads and ordered them to drink or be shot. As they crouched on the ground, bound by their hands and feet, they were taunted with, "Do you want to live or die?" They drank the poison and immediately passed out.

Sometime near dawn, the young man regained consciousness and, shivering and groggy, he struggled out of his bonds. All of his documents, his money, and his vehicle were gone. He then discovered that his female companion was missing. As he thrashed around blindly in the dark calling her name, he stumbled over her comatose body lying close to the main road. Bit by bit, he managed to drag her onto the road while periodically falling in and out of consciousness himself. Plantation workers arriving for the morning shift came upon the two young people lying together, cold and unconscious, and sped off with them to the district hospital. Coincidentally, another *mzungu* had been brought in that same night, and he too had been found unconscious by the roadside, and he too was suffering from severe head injuries.

A district policeman arrived at our project manager's house the next day, to ask if he would go to the hospital and try to communicate with the Canadians. They were both still incoherent. It took two full days for the couple to become lucid enough to tell their stories, and after spending two more days recovering at the home of Frank and Monica Gaynor, they were sent to Dar es Salaam for further treatment.

The third gentleman never regained consciousness. Since there were no facilities in Korogwe to treat him, local medics transferred him to a larger and better hospital in Moshi. We discovered later that he had been an Israeli businessman who had been ambushed on the same road, beaten severely, and left for dead in a ditch. Luckily, caring field workers, and not hungry wild animals, had found his battered body.

Banditry on a grand scale had arrived in our town. That was not an entirely surprising development. Tons of guns and ammunition were flooding the African continent in the wake of conflicts in Rwanda, Somalia, and Mozambique. And coupled with the free flow of arms and munitions, there was a growing tendency for border guards to look the other way. Cash compensation could easily cloud their vision. I decided that I needed to be just a little more vigilant about venturing outside of town in the future.

Local newspaper journalists were fond of making caustic comments about rich aid workers who whizzed past African pedestrians in their fancy aid vehicles. But cavalier asides, such as those, only served to foster the false impression that road travel in Africa was a frivolous past time. In fact, there were very real dangers everywhere. A full scale, *High Noon* type shootout took place on the main street of our town, shortly after those particularly horrendous hijackings.

Gerald, my trusted but ineffectual *askari*, arrived at my house at about sunset, set out his bows and arrows and settled down for the night. Darkness had already descended, and when I went out to the garden to take in my clothes from the line, Gerald began relating a bizarre story that I found very hard to follow. Gerald had a natural tendency to embellish and dramatize everything, and in all his excitement, he began to relate an extraordinary tale told with lightening speed. So while I was able to grasp that something out of the ordinary had happened in town that day, I was still very skeptical about all the gory details. I later discovered that all of Gerard's basic facts had been correct.

A car, now known to have been stolen on that increasingly notorious Arusha to Dar motorway, had pulled into one of the Indian-owned *dukas* on the main road. Three men armed with *submachine* guns, now known to have been automatic rifles, had entered the *duka* and demanded all the money. It was not a large business so I wondered why they had chosen it instead of one of the busy hotels or petrol stations nearby. I then learned that all the petrol stations had armed guards planted inconspicuously on the premises, to counteract the alarming rise in armed robbery. The local criminal element had, obviously, been *clued in*.

Furthermore, robberies such as this one were never opportunist. This particular *duka* had been chosen for a very good reason. Most people on steady incomes purchased their foodstuffs on credit. When they received their monthly wages, they paid their bills. Government salaries had been late that month, arriving mid-week, so customers were still clearing their accumulated debts. The bandits had struck at 5:00 p.m. on a Friday evening, too late for the owners to make a bank deposit. Since there were no late-deposit facilities at the bank, the cash was still in the shop.

Gerald's version of the raid went like this. Two armed bandits had entered the Indian *duka* when an off-duty policeman followed them in. He tackled the one who was armed and wrestled the gun from him. He then turned the gun on the intruders, hitting both of them with three shots. One of the wounded thieves fled the shop and was pursued down the road by a screaming mob. A police Land Rover came speeding towards the scene and the bandit, sensing his chances of survival might be better with the police than with the mob, headed for the van. By that time he was unarmed and bleeding. The police opened fire and emptied thirty rounds of ammunition into him while at the same time killing the hotel van driver who had been sitting in his vehicle watching the action. Two local children were also injured. The second injured bandit was taken to the district hospital while the third villain escaped at high speed through the town.

The official version differed slightly and it went like this. As the armed men entered the shop, an on-duty policeman opened fire, killing one bandit outright. Another *bandit returned fire*, hitting and injuring several children who were innocently viewing the excitement. That bandit was then cut down, but not before *he*, the bandit, had hit and killed the driver of the hotel van that was parked outside. In the midst of this hail of bullets *from the bandit*, the third villain had escaped at high speed through the town. He had not yet been apprehended, but the wounded bandit was in the district hospital.

It was doubtful if he would ever get out. There was no medicine and less will to save him. So, with a subtle shift of emphasis, we had arrived at a convenient shift of blame!

This alarming drift into mob justice and police vengeance was becoming increasingly common throughout the country. Just recently, a marauding crowd in Old Korogwe had beheaded a young man whom they had caught stealing a chicken. In another incident, a local policeman had shot and killed a youth whom he had suspected of stealing copper wire from the telephone lines. Wild rumors were spreading throughout the community that the Tanga region was on the cusp of introducing Islamic law. Under Islamic justice, there would be "an eye for an eye and a tooth for a tooth;" and offending organs would be cut off.

The one local casualty of the *duka* attack was buried right after the tragic events and his funeral arrangements began to fuel some deeply rooted and long-simmering racial resentment. Only two members of the very considerable Asian community attended the internment services. Consequently, the black population interpreted this apparent cold disregard for the grieving family as gross insensitivity. After all, an Indian *duka* had been under attack and black Tanzanians had gone to the rescue.

The whole issue of race relations was becoming a ticking time-bomb, not alone in Tanzania but in many other African countries where a sizeable Asian presence existed. The African/Asian relationship was a delicate one at the best of times. In Tanzania, Asians represented a major force in many business and commercial ventures. Therefore, it seemed that prudence alone should dictate their closer integration into the wider community - self-preservation being the first rule of survival. But, alas, in Africa, the obvious seldom seemed to apply.

෧෨)

One evening after work, Frank Gaynor and I chanced upon several of the local town personages at the Mountain View Inn, where we had all retreated to escape the deadening heat of an extremely hot day. What transpired during that evening's casual conversation managed to throw more light on the complex issues of race relations and political integrity than anything else I had learned so far.

Our college had closed down a full month early due to lack of funds. The school term should have run from the first of August through the 29th of November. In fact, it ran from the 29th of August through the 31st of October, accounting for a total of eight weeks of tuition. We were due to reopen on the 9th of January, but because the national financial situation had not improved at all during the intervening months, the first-year students had not returned until the 13th of February, with a loss of another four weeks in the school calendar. The second-, and final-year students had not returned at all. Instead, they were instructed to look for teaching practice at local schools, and find lodgings with local families and friends.

In normal times, students received sufficient rations of beans, *mahindi*, and flour to sustain them during their practice teaching, and furthermore, those provisions were meant to be given as gifts to the receiving community. But since the college was now flat broke, the students had nothing to bring with them and they would have to rely on the generosity of their host families for their room and board. The hosts were very poor people with hardly enough provisions to feed themselves.

Such a development was nothing short of catastrophic. The final-year students, who were due to leave as fully qualified primary school teachers from June, would have received a total of nine weeks training that year. It would be the same story in every one of the forty teacher training colleges throughout Tanzania. There would be no possibility for students to repeat a year, or make up for lost time, because the situation was never expected to improve - not the next year, nor the next, nor the next.

The government had just called for Tanzania's first multi-party general election and planned to hold the poll some time around October or November. But the exact month or date had not yet been divulged. Since independence in 1964, Tanzania had been governed as a one-party state, with *Chama Cha Mapinduzi (CCM)* in undisputed control. Therefore, multi-party elections should have heralded clear progress along the democratic path. However, there was still no evidence that any one of the current opposition parties was prepared to even contest the election. That political issue, along with strained race relations and the crisis in education, started a stormy debate at our Mountain View retreat.

⌐∾๑)

"All of those so called opposition parties are full of former CCM leaders and members of parliament. Do they know anything about operating in a free market economy? Are their aims any different from the ones we already have?" asked one of the local luminaries. "No, no, and no again!" was the angry reply.

"Who then will be the likely successor to President Mwinyi?" I asked.

"Whoever it is will have the stamp of approval of *Mzee*," he replied. "He is the one who really holds the power. As long as this is so, there will be no change." *Mzee* was the "wise one," the former and first president of the Republic of Tanzania, Julius Nyrere.

Frank mentioned that he had just read a World Heath Organization report that had identified Tanzania as the second poorest country in Africa. The esteemed gentlemen in our company expressed shocked disbelief. Not one of them accepted the statistics that Frank went on to present. And they were all prominent community leaders.

"Abject poverty such as this is not evident anywhere in Tanzania," they contended. "When or where have you ever seen a Tanzanian child starving? Have we ever asked the world community for food aid? In fact, we export surplus food to our starving neighbors." While they all agreed that Tanzania was slipping down an economic abyss, they flatly rejected the idea that they had already plunged to those depths. "Water is not available in some parts of the country, when the rains are poor. This is true. And electricity does not exist in many parts of the country, but most people cook outside with firewood so they have no need for electricity."

By cutting down the last remaining forests, the Tanzanian people were actively contributing to widespread continental desertification. The fact that rapid desertification would inevitably lead to national economic ruin was too far in the future to consider. It appeared that, for these men, poverty would only be gauged by current levels of starvation. And there was no mass starvation in Tanzania.

They did concede that health care was tragically poor, especially in the area of medicines available to treat malaria. "And what about the Aids epidemic?" asked Frank. "Isn't that the unknown and potentially volatile factor in all of this?"

Although some statistics indicated that one-third of the population in towns on the Tanzanian/Ugandan border were HIV positive, these prominent Korogwe gentlemen hotly disputed the figures. "Statistics from other areas suggest that there is no severe Aids crisis in Tanzania as a whole. Such inflammatory reports do nothing to protect the good name of Tanzania," they protested.

Then the discussion moved on to our own particular problem with education. "While nine weeks of education do not constitute a viable school year, the ministry is in the process of developing an Educational Master Plan to take Tanzania through the first part of the twenty-first century. Things will get better, you will see, but we need more development funds and more successful projects like yours," offered one of the town's council leaders. And I shook my head in despair. Development funds! The panacea for the developing world.

Then slowly and cryptically, an even more startling and angry discussion began to surface, one concerning personal fraud and hidden wealth.

"At least sixty percent of the wealth of our country is undeclared and the great bulk of that is in the hands of Asians and their black Tanzanian minders." This uncompromising outburst came from one of the most senior members of the town's development council. And with this bold statement out in the open, every other man rushed in to concur.

They also disclosed, late into the night, that contrary to their previous pronouncements, there was, indeed, a new and revolutionary opposition party growing throughout the country. One with radical new ideas. But it had been banned by the government and it would not be allowed to contest the upcoming election. It was known as *Uzamau* – The Indigenous People.

The *Uzamau* party advocated a complete reorganization of Tanzanian society so that black Tanzanians could take back control of the country's economic power. The process for advancing this change had not yet been clearly defined, but it could mean confining Asian communities to certain large urban centers while transferring control of the vast rural areas to local people.

Such divisive social and economic ideas were dangerous and could possibly resurrect the haunting scepter of Idi Amin's Asian purge in Uganda. So the government had quickly stepped in. They branded *Uzamau* as a racist party and roundly condemned it. But official condemnation did nothing to eradicate the widespread belief that Asians were the architects of Tanzania's economic decline.

To facilitate daily business transactions, the Tanzanian Treasury Department had recently issued new large denomination currency notes. Previously, the largest denomination in circulation had been the one thousand *shilingi* note. When a kilo of sugar could cost up to five hundred *shilingi*, ordinary people needed to carry heavy sacks of useless currency around with them. The new denominations were, therefore, widely welcomed by the business community.

"Has anyone here been able to find a ten thousand *shilingi* note in Korogwe, this week?" asked one of the most vocal contributors to our discussions. I hadn't given it any thought up until then but, if fact,

I hadn't. Neither had any of the others. Then our very angry social commentator focused on another component of this phenomenon. "There is not a single ten thousand *shilingi* note available in Korogwe, not in any of the petrol stations nor in any of the banks. And that's the way it is in Mombo and Segera and all the way up to the Kenyan border."

"Asians have hoarded them," came the blunt allegation from another gentleman. "Now they can take their small stacks of *shilingi* to the banks and change them for dollars. They don't need to bring ugly brown suitcases like before. It makes it nice and convenient - so much easier to export their hard cash out of Tanzania for safekeeping in Canada, England, and Switzerland. Do you think they leave their money in the bank in Korogwe? Hah! Their real homes are not in this country. They only make their money here."

Whether or not this allegation was one hundred percent true, one hundred percent false or somewhere in between, the fact remained that an increasing number of Tanzanians were willing to believe it. They believed that Asian merchants and their black Tanzanian cohorts were plundering Tanzania. But they carried particularly strong venom for their Tanzanian compatriots, those unscrupulous scoundrels who were willing to facilitate the looting of their own country for personal gain. This brooding, angry discontent festered away beneath the calm surface of Tanzanian life, looking for release. And it had the Asian community, along with their Tanzanian minders, in its sights.

A terrible gloom hung over our assembly of sages that night. Nobody could see any hope for change. They all believed that the impending election could only lead to further squandering of badly needed development funds in order to oil corrupt party machines.

My next question seemed a logical progression from what I had heard so far, but it only served to unnerve the learned gentlemen even more. "Isn't there any possibility for people like yourselves to organize an effective opposition?" I asked.

I had thought about this many times before. All of the men present that night, and every second Tanzanian I had met within the professional classes, had studied abroad. One of the school administrators had spent four years studying psychology in Cuba and another had completed a doctorate in sociology in Bulgaria. The English tutor had done advanced studies in education in Zimbabwe, at least four more held graduate degrees from England, several had studied psychology up to doctorate level in Germany and at that very moment, our program was supporting one fellow on a three-year course in Dublin and three students in Leeds. Every year, an exodus of students headed off for Europe or the United States on foreign aid fellowship grants. "What happens to all that talent when they return home?" I continued. "Shouldn't they be the ones to introduce new ideas, new ways of thinking, and new avenues for development? Shouldn't they be able to marshal enough support from within the disillusioned and the disenchanted to launch a viable opposition?"

Sadly, those wise old men only shook their heads and mumbled unintelligible comments. I had done the unthinkable. I had pointed a finger in their direction. Those gentlemen, and the vast army of women who really kept the country running, should have been the creative forces for change. But, once again, I had to admit that the obvious was not always possible. Those men needed their jobs. The party bosses controlled their jobs. The risk was too great. They were not revolutionaries; they were unhappy realists. They knew how far they could go with dissent; but action demanded risk. And they hadn't quite reached their nadir yet.

In a faint attempt to mollify their own disquiet concerning the uncertain direction of their country, they went on to exhume an old chestnut. It was not the first time that I had heard the old refrain: "But at least we have had peace for forty-five years." Tanzania was surrounded by nations in turmoil: Rwanda, Burundi, Zaire, Mozambique, Malawi, and Zambia. Tanzania alone had escaped the savage wars of tribal hatred.

"But is it also possible that this much honored peace has drugged the population into a state of lethargy, a sort of immobility?" I asked. "Perhaps, yes," agreed one of the gentlemen. "But do we want to call down upon ourselves all the pain and suffering that national struggle would bring? Are we not better off just muddling along as we are?" After throwing around these ideas for several hours, we arrived at only one conclusion. It would take much greater minds than ours to chart the future course for Tanzania.

❦

Some of those greater minds were openly engaged in public debate about the future of East Africa. One leading Tanzanian newspaper, "The Guardian" had carried two articles that highlighted the widespread abuse of state funds. One stated that the Minister for Home Affairs was facing imprisonment, rising out of charges and counter-charges involving 916 million Tanzanian shillings. Another article covered the Minister for Finance's fears for the fate of future donor funds, following the revelation that over $35 million US dollars were found to be missing from expected import duties. Substantial amounts of development aid funds to Tanzania had been frozen, pending Tanzania's ability to demonstrate a serious shift towards "accountability and transparency."

A new and excellent newspaper, launched in Nairobi to encourage regional cooperation among the East African states, carried an article written by the head of the Center for Accountability and Debt Relief in London. Karl Ziegler had said:

"The sources of corrupting cash are mainly corporate bribery, drugs, extortion, plundering of natural resources, aid and developmental lending. The first four begin life as totally illegal, ending up as legitimate investments after careful laundering. Aid and developmental loans start out as well-meaning, legitimate funding, much of which is diverted by ruling elites. In Lord Peter Bauer's memorable phrase, 'Aid is a phenomenon whereby poor people in rich countries are taxed to support the lifestyles of rich people in poor countries.' In the shadowy land of grand corruption, it is often the poorer nations – or rather their small cliques of rulers – who are economically dominant. This new corrupt internationalism, though largely created by criminals, is likewise fed by some of the world's leading companies in pursuit of markets.

It also stems, in part, from an intellectual corruption manifested by those who sanction aid and loans from richer countries, from the international financial institutions and other organizations, which believe that throwing money at problems is the best way to solve them. Over the last 50 years, more than 300 billion US dollars have been transferred by the World Bank alone from the First World to the Third. Too often the effect has been exactly the opposite of the intention. Poorer nations have become aid junkies, craving more, achieving less, their aid debts increasing beyond any hope of repayment while their elites have seized much of the aid and the resources."

Another journalist from the same edition, Robert Rweyemamu, made an impassioned plea for the opposition parties of Tanzania, twelve at the moment, to unite and offer a viable alternative to the people.

"What the public expects of the newborn political groups is for the young leaders and old timers to see the crying need for a devoted and selfless struggle to prevent a revival of the so-called one-party democracy, to bury their differences and to capitalize on their common ground. A way must be found by the more senior and experienced leaders of the opposition to bring about a committed dialogue with the aim of at least presenting one presidential candidate in October. Leaders must abandon their petty selfish ambitions for State House when they have no specific policies to sell to the electorate and no clear ideologies to fill the vacuum left by the doomed *Ujamaa*. Indeed our politicians need to establish their credibility and integrity. They should know that the people of Tanzania have been cheated for far too long and now desire nothing less than high-quality leadership, effective management, technical proficiency and moral discipline."

October came and went, as did the multi-party election, and absolutely nothing changed. The opposition parties mounted a fractured and feeble challenge. Amidst a barrage of strident claims about corruption and fraud, *CCM* rode back to power. They had won a landslide victory.

I traveled to the town of Tanga just before the summer break in a state of high expectation. I was about to take the first drafts of our Kiswahili primary mathematics books to the printer.

Elegant high walled houses stretched out along Tanga's coastline. Romantic dhows with their tall, triangular sails drifted by, dreamily gliding off to the rich fishing grounds of the Indian Ocean. It was hard to believe that some of the strangest battles of the First World War had been fought on the golden sands of this former German colony, a remote, tropical place where Great Britain's African Rifles had faced the army of the German Emperor. That was all just history now. A fractured Europe went on to pile wrong upon wrong and lay the groundwork for a new and even more devastating war. Meanwhile, Tanga, then part of the newly constructed British colony of Tanganyika, slipped effortlessly back to its slumbering ways.

On the road to Tanga we passed one of the most productive orange grove plantations in the Tanga Region. It was the village of *Michungwi*, "of the oranges," in Swahili. Most of the new villages created through Julius Nyrere's philosophy of self-reliance and *Ujamaa*, had been named for the produce of their region. Hence we also had the village of *N'gombe*, meaning cows, and another village named *Mboga*, meaning vegetables.

The profusion of orange and tangerine trees in the region of *Michungwi* was staggering. The roadside became a mountain of fruit, every year, with the coming of the harvest. Little boys, burly men, and wizened elders ran along the roadside besieging passing cars and long-distance buses, waving plastic bags filled with sweet, green oranges. Hand-to-hand was their only means of distribution. Some of it was shipped to Dar es Salaam where it collided with more mountains of fruit coming up from the Morogoro region. Consequently, tons of delicious fruit simply rotted on the roadsides. The population of Dar alone could not consume such vast quantities.

The critical problems were, once again, those of transportation and distribution. Either the food rotted in Michungwi or Dar es Salaam, but one way or the other, the people who produced it never reaped the benefits of their labor.

A simple canning operation, established in Michungwi, could

solve part of the problem. With the necessary training and stewardship in place, the local community could turn their annual waste into an employment and income-generating scheme. While they would also need vehicles for transportation and exportation abroad, that kind of assistance would be well within the scope of several foreign aid programs. "Another good idea for the Irish Minister for Foreign Affairs," I mused, as I continued on my way to Tanga.

❧

I had a very strange and oddly disturbing encounter in Tanga that same day. As Juma and I were pulling away from the post office, a frantic young man came racing after our van, desperately calling for us to stop. He was very well dressed in navy blue trousers and a blue shirt with four gold bars on the shoulders. When we pulled over and stopped, he began to bombard us with a flood of French hysteria peppered with the odd snatch of fragmented English. He didn't speak Swahili and my French had been lying dormant for twenty years. But I persuaded him to slow down, and between his French/English and my English/French, I managed to piece together the following story.

He was a Rwandan refugee from the Ngara Refugee Camp. He said that he had been a pilot for the Rwandan national airline before the terrible wave of genocide had erupted in his country. He had flown long-distance flights to Europe, and during the course of his work he had met, and later married, an Irish woman. They had two children. He knew that I was Irish from the insignia on the vehicle door. He was stopping over in Tanga with two of his colleagues, who were also pilots.

Then came the troubling part of his tale. He said that he had met President Mary Robinson the previous October when she had visited Ngara on her presidential tour. That part of the story seemed reasonable enough, but he went on to say that President Robinson had given him five hundred pounds to send his wife and children on to Nairobi. "Does the President of Ireland travel around with stashes of cash in her purse, ready to offer it freely to needy people along the way?" I asked myself. However, these were strange times and refugees did not lead normal lives, so I was ready to give him the benefit of my very big doubts. Allowing for the communication gulf lying between us, I conceded that perhaps someone in the presidential party, or one of the aid agencies had stepped in to assist this man and his Irish wife and their children.

I then tried to find out what exactly he was doing in Tanga, which was a long, long way from Ngara. What was his immediate problem? How could I help? The answers were confused and convoluted and I began to wonder if this could, in fact, be another elaborate scam. Did I have the tag "sucker" emblazoned across my forehead? "What is he doing in his airline uniform, all laundered and pressed, months after he first became a refugee? How come that uniform looks very fresh indeed?" I was growing more and more skeptical by the minute.

While I was busy tossing those questions around in my head, he was busy assuring me that he was not looking for money; he was not poor. Here was his problem. He was driving a very good vehicle, a Pajero, and the vehicle belonged to his wife. He wanted to cross the border into Kenya but he did not want to bring the vehicle with him. He didn't explain why. He wanted to know if I could keep the vehicle for him in a safe place.

That suddenly got my full attention. Crossing the border with a vehicle would require extensive documentation and valid exit visas. I had been through that process several times myself and it was no walk on the beach. "Can it be that he has no documentation? Is the vehicle stolen?" Oh my God! Run!

What was I to do? I didn't want to disbelieve him. What if he really was a genuine Rwandan refugee and needed my help? "Do you have a valid passport and papers for the car?" I asked. He said that he didn't have a passport, but he could cross the border with a UNHCR pass. At least, I thought that's what he said. "What has happened to his passport? Surely, a pilot would have to own a valid one." My mind was racing. And I was really, really worried about that car.

I told him that I did not live in Tanga, but at least a hundred kilometers inland, and I suggested that he should go to Dar es Salaam and contact the Irish Embassy there. If his story was genuine, and he did have Irish connections, they would surely be anxious to help him. But he was in a highly agitated state and insisted that he needed to get into Kenya quickly. He didn't have time to go to Dar es Salaam.

A million questions raced through my mind. "Why did he come all the way to the coast when he could have crossed into Nairobi at Arusha?" I needed time to think but he was pleading with me to help him. So I told him that I had to run some errands in town and that I would return for him within the hour. I would decide what to do, in the meantime. Juma, our driver, was looking very worried. He did not like the look of the whole situation, not one little bit!

After I had completed my business, I decided that I would take the young pilot along to talk with some of my friends and see what they could make of his story. I returned to our meeting place and waited there for a full hour, but he never resurfaced. "Perhaps he misunderstood. Maybe he got the time wrong," I said to Juma. I kept tossing these possibilities around, as we waited, but Juma was getting very jumpy and he wanted to be on his way. So we left. But the whole sorry episode continued to prey on my mind for weeks. I tried to imagine the confusion and anxiety of someone caught up in that predicament, if indeed it had been genuine.

When I related the story to my friends in Korogwe, they concluded that since there were so many expatriates living in the Tanga region, someone would surely have come to his rescue. That was, assuming he was, indeed, a refugee in need. If not, then I should consider myself well out of the whole mess. Nonetheless, I couldn't stop worrying what had happened to him.

My answer came sooner than I had expected. Late at night about a month later, during one of my brief spells out of Korogwe, a knock came to Frank and Monica's door. My Rwandan friend had made his way from Tanga to Korogwe, on foot, and had asked directions at the bus stand to the house of the Irish Mama. Since I was out of town, Gerald, my watchman, had brought him down to Frank's house.

Frank became as disturbed by the woeful tale as I had been. But now it had become even worse. Apparently, the police had arrived shortly after our brief encounter and had hauled him off to jail, where he had spent the next four weeks. Strangely enough, although they had taken all of his money, they had not confiscated the Pajero. But when they eventually released him from jail, they instructed him to get out of town immediately. He had only reached the neighboring town of Muheza when he ran out of petrol. He had no choice but to walk the rest of the sixty kilometers to Korogwe. Frank gave him the money he needed to return to Muheza, where he had abandoned his Pajero, collect and refuel it, and drive all the way back to the Arusha/Nairobi border. Dar es Salaam and the Irish Embassy had disappeared off the radar. And the Irish wife and children? Who knows? These were strange times. It was the last we ever heard of him.

⟨❦⟩

Low-lying clouds obscured the village. It was only a half-hour drive by car from Korogwe but it might easily have been on another planet.

A daily bus from Korogwe followed a narrow, winding dirt track up a thousand meters into the Usambaras. Most bus passengers chose to sit on the roof of the bus with the chickens and livestock, strategically positioned to jump in case the chugging and clanging tank toppled over the cliffs. The air was cool and clear and clusters of shabby little huts fringed the mountain ridges. These people were the *Wasambaa* and they were predominantly of the Muslim faith.

It was most unusual to find such a large Islamic community living in the highlands. They had originally been lowland dwellers, scattered along the old Arabic trading routes to Tanga and the Indian Ocean, but tribal warfare and later, colonization, had sent them fleeing to the mountains.

The dirt road ended at the approach to the village and from there onwards, it was a vertical climb. Deep gullies carved out by heavy mountain rains cut through what should have been a path but was now, in fact, an obstacle course of peaks and valleys, rocks, boulders, and gravel pits. Huts were dropped everywhere and anywhere; ramshackled and deserted ones collapsed alongside rapidly decaying newer versions. A thatched roof normally suggested some type of plaiting with grass or leaves. But there was no thatch in that village. Palm fronds were spread out over naked log beams. Fraying sisal strings held the tenuous roofs together. Bony and miserable-looking cows, goats, and chickens grazed communally on the roadside. Worn and weathered mothers, young and old, gathered in doorways with babes at their breasts while toddlers squirmed at their feet. Old men squatted on their hunkers, propped up against mud walls. A desperate stench of abandonment saturated the air, vomiting up a harrowing vista of desolation and despair.

This was the site of one of our poorest project schools. Four of our student teachers had been lodging with local families over the past month in order to complete their block-teaching practice. The fact that they had managed to arrange any type of housing in this village was nothing short of miraculous. Not one of the huts looked sufficiently large or stable enough to house a guest. But in reciprocation for their hospitality, the project had offered to train four of the village primary school teachers at our center, simultaneously. This arrangement had brought a ray of light to a very depressed community, one that had not received assistance of any kind from education officers for five years.

The Department of Education had built the original primary school campus in 1975. It had comprised seven classrooms; all were furnished with double-seated desks and benches, and there were several fully-furnished staff houses. Only five of the classrooms were still standing; two rooms had collapsed completely, all of the concrete floors had disintegrated, and the corrugated iron roofs had been spirited away. Two broken and mauled desks leaned against the back wall of the standard seven classroom. Nothing else remained of the original school furniture. "What happened to all the rest?" we enquired. "It went into the village huts to be sold," came the straightforward reply.

The school had an official enrollment of two hundred fifty pupils, but less than half that number attended at any one time. We noticed clutches of school-aged children idling the time away all over the village, lying under trees, or sitting in the dirt scratching pictures in the sand. They were sickly and underfed. Swollen bellies and jagged limbs poked out from their limp bodies.

One of our college tutors had told us that mountain land was very rich - so rich, in fact, that hill people didn't even need to apply animal dung to fertilize their maize. They also raised large quantities of beans and cassava, and had orange and mango trees in abundance. The highlands always received ample rain, even when the rest of the region was dry. There should have been no shortage of food and certainly no want. "So why are the children so ragged and under-nourished, and the why do the young mothers look so haggard?" we asked. Nothing we saw made any sense.

The answer was simple, and predictable. Women sowed and raised the crops. Women also harvested the crops. But men sold the crops and spent all the money on drink.

When would we, the *wazungu*, ever learn? Even after years of experience, we still expected life in Africa to follow pre-ordained patterns. This was a Muslim village. Therefore, it automatically followed that alcohol was not a problem. But, just like in the western world, rules were made to be broken. Up there in the mountains, hidden away from the eyes of the rest of the world, the village was Muslim in name but not in practice.

There was no social outlet in the village - no community center and no physical evidence of a mosque. Then, as we rambled around the village and greeted women and men lounging in doorways, all curiously watching the strangers, we came upon something extraordinary that nearly took the sight from my eyes. It was a small, thatched hut with the word, *Ukimwi*, scrawled above it. There, in what we had taken to be a black hole of despair, was a small hospice for Aids. It was the first acknowledgement of, or compassion for, sufferers of the disease that we had seen in the entire region. We may have been teachers but we had a whole lot left to learn.

In one of the surviving classrooms that we visited, a young

second-year student teacher from our college was demonstrating a mathematics lesson for standard one. Twenty-five students squatted solemnly on the dirt ground, behind large boulders that served as their desks. Each child held a stack of ten sticks cut from bamboo shoots, and a new mathematics book, written, illustrated and printed by our project members.

The books were very simple and unembellished, but they were written in Swahili and they talked about mathematical situations familiar to the children's every day lives. They were also the first books that many of the children had ever held.

The student teacher had prepared her lesson well. She had constructed number cards from cardboard boxes and had attached soda bottle tops to illustrate the numbers. A set of these colorful cards lined the mud-spattered walls. The lesson progressed remarkably well, with the students using more bottle tops, which they had collected as their homework, to form number sets on the dirt floor. Then they walked a number line, also scratched into the dirt floor, to demonstrate mathematical operations. They combined and took away bamboo sticks to act out mathematical problems and then calculated their written sums on the pitted chalkboard. Finally, they referred to their valuable project textbooks for further explanation and enrichment. The dreaded note-taking and deadening silence of the past were lost in a hive of activity.

Everyone was delighted, from the teacher, to the students to the visitors. Real teaching and real learning was taking place, despite the appalling physical condition of the school.

The head teacher proudly told us that, because of the help that they were getting from this Ireland Aid project, the villagers had decided to make enough desks for one of the classrooms and have them ready for the new term. The children would then have the proper tools with which to work. They wanted to protect the new books and prevent them from being destroyed by mud, so they would also build secure storage cabinets. August was only five months away, but they were determined to have the desks completed on time.

Our contribution had been small; lots of staff training and technical advice, combined with large doses of encouragement, and some funds. But the potential for success was immense; the mathematics primary school project had ushered in a spirit of hope for that long-forgotten village.

⌘

At a very high-powered education meeting held in Dar es Salaam, hosted by a leading European donor country, endless discussions centered upon the dreadful lack of suitable classrooms, supplies, and books in Tanzania's primary schools. But the crucial factor, the critical link in the educational chain, the teacher, was scarcely mentioned.

As we had seen in our ten project schools, real learning could take place under a tree, if teachers were motivated, trained, and skilled. All the desks and books in the world would not make a dent in Tanzania's educational crisis unless the ministry and the donors put their money into teaching teachers to teach. Unfortunately, that was not a popular message. There was very little personal profit or hard currency attached it.

⌘

The day following that mountainside trip, we found out that the wife of one of our college tutors had suddenly died. She had given birth to a baby girl the week before, with no apparent complications. They had seven other children, including two sets of twins. At 9:00 a.m. that morning, Sebastian's wife had begun to suffer severe headaches and sharp pains in the back of her neck. Her condition rapidly deteriorated. Our project driver, Juma, dashed off to collect her from her home, but she died before reaching the hospital. Nobody knew the cause of death, but everybody presumed it had been cerebral malaria.

Maryam had given birth in the hospital but she had returned home immediately to look after the rest of the children. She had received no medical after-care and, consequently, her blood level had dropped dramatically. When bitten by the parasitic anopheles mosquito under such weakened conditions, sudden death was often inevitable.

Everyone believed that she had died from malaria.

Sebastian was now left alone with seven children and an infant. I asked my neighbor how he would cope, and she said that he would surely remarry immediately. It was the only way he could care for his children. As a college tutor, his status in the community was high, so he would have no difficulty in finding a new wife.

Our team members went along to his house on the day of Maryam's burial. All the college staff sat with Sebastian under a tree, quietly talking to him and offering their sympathy and support. They hadn't much else to give. They had organized a collection and passed on the proceeds. Sebastian would need all the assistance he could get, with eight young children to support.

❧

Another St. Patrick's Day had arrived and we decided to keep the faith in Korogwe, considering our gross misadventure the previous year. The Korogwe celebrations, however, turned out to be both unorthodox and unprecedented and they bordered on the truly phantasmagorical.

There was a long history behind this particular story. Our aid project was all about improving primary school methodology. But we were working with student-teachers who had to undergo the same trials of bush living as the rest of the population. These included constant electricity blackouts, water shortages, and unhygienic sanitary conditions.

The training college had a seventy percent female population, flush toilets, and no incinerator. We had been in Korogwe a few short months when the scale of the sanitation problem became odiously clear. After the first protracted dry spell, the downwind from the college lavatories threatened the entire campus population with asphyxiation. Consequently, the project undertook to build four pit latrines and two incinerators, even though the building of such structures had no direct link with primary school mathematics. But it had everything to do with the general health of the students and consequently, their ability to learn. So we embarked on the construction of the facilities and that, we thought, was the end of that.

But we hadn't counted on the outstanding entrepreneurial skills of our wily college principal. The college sports master had approached Frank a few weeks before St. Patrick's Day, with a novel proposal. At first, Frank had been dumbfounded to hear that the college had such a person as a sports master on its staff. Apparently, he had been masquerading as the English professor for the previous two years. In any event, he announced to Frank that he was interested in organizing a sports day for the students and, as it would take place sometime close to Ireland's national holiday; perhaps the Irish Primary Mathematics Project would like to sponsor the awards.

"Most certainly," declared a stunned Frank. "Absolutely! With great pleasure!" This was the first indication we had seen of any kind of intramural competition since our arrival two years earlier, and anything that might energize campus life was to be enthusiastically encouraged. Frank complimented the sports master on his imagination and initiative and proceeded to purchase a stunning array of trophies and prizes.

On the eve of the event, the deputy principal, who was of a very reserved nature, appeared at my home door with a message from the principal. The esteemed gentleman wanted me to know that it would be perfectly in order, and acceptable, for me to video- tape all the proceedings of the sports events, should I feel so inclined. In fact, the entire student body of one thousand students had been instructed to turn out for the event in full regalia, just in case. Africa had a fixation with uniforms. Everyone was decked out in one. The students at this college wore white shirts and sky-blue skirts and trousers.

I hadn't planned on filming anything, least of all a soccer match, but experience told me that this message was more than a gentle nudge. I had not been looking forward to sizzling in 35 degrees of heat under a scorching sun, either, but common sense also told me that I should at least make an appearance with the camera.

At 3:00 p.m., as I strolled over to the administration building to collect the storeroom keys, I was intercepted by a highly agitated principal heading my way.

"Mama Kaniah, (women were called by the name of their eldest child)" he wheezed, unaccustomed as he was to brisk movements. "You are already quite late. And where is your camera? We are all ready and waiting for you."

"Good Lord," I stuttered, suddenly all a-flutter, flustered, and confused. "I thought we were meeting at the soccer field at 3:30."

"Mama," he pressed on, as though talking to a particularly obtuse child, "The staff room is packed with tutors awaiting your arrival, with the camera. And the student body is gathered over by the incinerator awaiting the arrival of the dignitaries, and the camera."

"Jaysus," I thought. "What dignitaries?" I must have missed something big. I had thought we were going to a soccer match.

I sprinted off to the storeroom, cursing the sun and the heat, and limped back to the region of the incinerator, with the camera. I was mystified. A thousand voices were raised in song, all accompanied by the rhythmic clapping and stomping of feet.

As I made my way through the massed student body, I emerged on the front line to encounter a startled-looking Frank, flanked on all sides by the college principal, the deputy principal, the district commissioner, and various other prominent local personages. Green, white, and orange bunting flapped in the soft afternoon breeze.

The commissioner was already in full flight, singing the praises of the Irish people, St. Patrick, our Charge d'Affaires in Dar es Salaam, and our Korogwe project manager, the same Frank. The Charge d'Affaires would have been particularly surprised to learn that only the imminent state visit of President Mywini to Ireland had prevented *her* from officiating at this very important ceremony. The accolades had reached such a fever pitch that I half expected to see Frank seized at any moment, hoisted shoulder high and paraded around the cheering crowd.

A dainty white satin cloth, edged in green lace, covered one side of the incinerator. The commissioner impressed on us the fact that these two incinerators and four pit latrines exemplified the genuine affection that existed between the peoples of Ireland and Tanzania. I couldn't figure out what had happened to our mathematics project. It seemed to have got lost in all the excitement over incinerators. Then, with a dignified tug and amidst tumultuous applause, the gray, concrete incinerator was unveiled. Frank was now beaming as broadly as his overjoyed confederates.

As I had made a somewhat indecorous late entry to the festivities, the welcoming speech was happily repeated for the benefit of my camera. The bewildered guest of honor, the same Frank Gaynor, was then called upon to feel free to tell the whole story of the birth of the incinerator and pit latrines, the birth, life and death of St. Patrick, the birth of the Irish Nation, the birth of Irish/Tanzanian unity, as well as anything else he fancied himself. I thanked the Lord I was safely ensconced behind the camera.

At the conclusion of Frank's very illuminating and improvised talk, and to another tremendous burst of applause, the principal promised us that this would become an annual event. He hadn't told us yet what he planned to inaugurate the next year, but I had no doubt that St. Patrick was destined to become the patron saint of everything in Korogwe from pit latrines to college piggeries, if our crafty principal had his way.

At the conclusion of the official ceremonies, we all shuffled along, at a suitably slow and stately pace to the college soccer field, to continue the celebration. Without a shadow of doubt, our college principal was good! As the soccer match and netball games progressed, he made an impassioned pitch for sufficient material for new school uniforms - and a new car for himself. He also managed to toss in a request for a few more student fellowships to Ireland, as an afterthought. As I listened to his long list of needs, and as I nodded and commiserated with him for all his troubles, I remembered one of the first things he had said upon my arrival to this strange and misty land. It just about crystallized the inner workings of this man, and of Korogwe, and come to think of it, maybe even of Tanzania as a whole. It was a useful piece of native wisdom, and it went something like this:

"It is far better to have your enemy in your tent pissing out, than outside pissing in."

Printed in the United Kingdom
by Lightning Source UK Ltd.
107301UKS00001B/145-201